THE BLOODY

BIRTHRIGHT

**Different
Drummer
Press**

THE BLOODY

BIRTHRIGHT

A PINKY AND THE BEAR MYSTERY

BY

KEN DALTON

For further information concerning *The Bloody Birthright*, contact the author at ken@kendalton.com

Questions concerning publishing your novel through Different Drummer Press should be emailed to ken@kendalton.com.

ISBN 978-0-578-03444-7
1. Dark—Humor—Fiction. 2. Basque—Bartender—Fiction. 3. Devious—Lawyer—Fiction. 4. Loneliest—Road—Fiction. 5. Tuscany—Italy—Fiction.   I. Title

**Different
Drummer
Press**

ACKNOWLEDGEMENTS

A budding novel is like a child that requires a village to grow and develop into an adult.

As the parent of that child, I need to thank the following village members for assisting Pinky, Bear, and Flo through their initial murder investigation:

To my brother Richard, who advised me to stop talking about writing and write—thus pointing me in the right direction.

Joe Farmer, Dean Davis, and Sergeant Willie McFarlane, all retired, for their guidance through police and emergency 911 procedures.

Gary Passerino, the personification of an ethical attorney, for his assistance through the murky world of legal mumbo-jumbo.

Dr. Kirk Papas for his aid on medical questions.

Giovanni Giovannelli and Liana Pastacaldi for teaching me the true meaning of *la dolce far niente*.

My son, Hugh, for his astounding talent and endless patience.

Wendy Maxham for her self confessed, picky-picky editing style.

To Lorry Frost, Pat Means, Lorraine Foster, and Peg Boy, for their encouragement and support toward their slightly demented father, brother, and brother-in-law.

Finally, no successful writer works in a vacuum. I am blessed to have been a member of an excellent writer's group for the past ten years. We meet on a regular basis, encouraging, reviewing and critiquing each other's work. I should call this group the elders of the village—the wise ones who understand that without the fire of failure success will never be achieved.

The elders of my village are:

Editor-in-Chief Mary Madsen Hallock

Jon Gunner Howe

Norm Benson

Thea Howe

And last but not least, the divine Sarah Andrews.

This book, every word, comma, and quotation mark, is dedicated to Arlene—my best friend—lover—and wife of more than half a century.

Without her blue eyes, perfect smile, encouragement, and support, Pinky, Bear, and Flo would still be trapped inside my unhinged mind searching for an escape route.

THE BLOODY

BIRTHRIGHT

ONE

J. Pincus Delmont—Carson City, Nevada

"Pinky, scuttlebutt tells me that your client sitting in that room murdered his uncle. But the bastard didn't just kill him, he blew a big chunk of his head clean off."

Henry-the-guard backed away from the one-way glass window so I could take my first view of the accused.

However, before I could reach the vantage point, the guard's endless gibberish stopped me. "I never could figure out how you lawyers can stand talking to scum like that."

Henry had been escorting prisoners back and forth to their cells at the Carson City jail as long as I could remember—a career he was well suited for because the position required the ambition of a three-toed sloth combined with the IQ of a moose.

I said, "My good man, providing succor to the downtrodden is my calling."

Henry glanced at his watch, and said. "Right. Are you ready to go in?"

I hesitated. "Do not rush me, Henry. I see no reason to hurry the moment."

He shrugged, and I concentrated my focus on the potential client who waited on the other side of the glass. The young man's jeans were threadbare, and the wear went far beyond anything that could be deemed stylish, even by today's grungy youths. His tee shirt was stained and his hair was matted from what I assumed to be the lack of a daily shower, a decent shampoo, or both. Altogether he was a miserable specimen.

Henry said, "This one doesn't look like a big enough fish for you, counselor."

I said, "That's where you might be wrong." Henry was good at his job, but he was talking with the top defense attorney in northern Nevada! "Obviously you haven't reviewed his arrest report."

1

"Ah . . . . no . . . . what did it say?"

"The form included a most encouraging combination of letters and numbers—BMW 650i, to be exact. That young man, identified in the report as Richard Page, may seem a homeless waif to you, but if the vehicle he was driving is in top condition, Mr. Page will become my next golden opportunity."

"I get it now. No money, no Pinky Delmont. But that's a pretty cold way to deal with a guy who's facing a murder-one rap."

"My good man, in this life you get what you pay for."

Henry scratched his bulbous nose as his limited intelligence struggled to comprehend my last statement. "Are you telling me that if an attorney's not screwing his client, then his client's getting screwed?"

I was surprised at Henry's ability to grasp the reality of my profession. Crude though his wording might have been, I had to admit that the fellow had done an admirable job of defining the ideal attorney/client relationship.

"Henry, when circumstances, and my valuable time allow, I often cast my line into what you may perceive as an insignificant pond, but occasionally I will hook a big one lurking beneath the still water."

What I neglected to inform the guard was that prior to my discovery of the expensive BMW, I had been ready to turn Richard Page back to Judge Anderson, and to inform His Honor, with all deference and respect, that I had exceeded my pro bono quota for the month. However, the BMW had changed everything. It was possible that the miscreant I'd been about to discard could turn out to be the catch of the week.

With that postulate firmly in mind, I nodded to Henry. He unlocked the door and I strode into the interrogation room. "Good afternoon, Richard."

As I approached, Richard's overpowering body stench and the dark stubble of facial hair on his gaunt chin lowered the odds that he held clear title to his vehicle. But a simple question would clear up that matter, and the possibility that I might pick up a valuable new toy had to be worth an additional thirty seconds of my time.

"Richard, before I proceed any further, we need to discuss the vehicle you were driving the day you were arrested."

For the first time since I had scrutinized him through the glass, his blue eyes flashed some life. "I love my car."

"I'm sure you do. But who holds the title, you or the bank?"

He said, "I do. I paid cash less than a week ago. The receipt and pink slip are hidden inside an envelope taped to the roof of the glove compartment."

My gusto meter jumped one hundred percent. I said, "And what is the model?"

"It's a 650i convertible. Don't you think it's cool the way BMW puts that little i next to the model number?"

I paused for a moment to let his fetid breath dissipate, placed my hand on his shoulder, and gave it a calculated squeeze. "Congratulations, my boy, you've just retained J. Pincus Delmont as your attorney of record. Now, over the next few days we'll meet in this room several times so I can determine your optimum defense strategy."

"That sounds good to me, Mr. Delmont. It's about time that someone in this town finally wants to hear my side of the story. I didn't do anything!"

"My boy, your lack of guilt will have little bearing in the construction of your defense. By the way, from now on you should address me as Pinky. Now if you'll excuse me for a moment, as my British friends would say, I have to spend a penny."

I stood, slipped my notebook and recorder into my briefcase, and tapped on the door.

Henry opened it a crack. "Ready for me to take him back, Pinky?"

"Not yet. Just need to empty my bladder."

Twenty feet down the hall I ducked into the men's room and used the facility. After washing my hands, I combed my hair and smirked at my reflection. I was forty-eight, well dressed, not married at the moment, and very

3

pleased with my marital status.

According to each of my ex-wives, I was good looking. In fact, to quote two of them, their husband was a knockout. But I'm told that all humans have their negatives. In my case, one wife thought I was on the short side. Frankly, I don't consider five-foot-five and three-quarters-inches short, but that's one man's opinion. Short or tall, I remained the best damn attorney in northern Nevada, and I was Richard Page's only hope to escape execution.

Most of the lawyers in this town scratched out a living writing wills or handling divorce cases. Others spent their lives jockeying for a seat on the bench. In my case, I defended people accused of crime for two reasons—first, their constitutional rights guaranteed them a fair trial, and second, their hefty retainers kept me dressed in the best, custom-made Italian suits.

I adjusted my silk tie, and considered Richard Page's future. He would get his day in court, or at the very least the best plea arrangement I could broker, but there was no doubt in my mind that I was the right attorney for my new client.

When I rejoined the guard at the interrogation room door, I pulled out my wallet and extracted thirty dollars. "Henry, I have two requests. First, to cover my retainer, I will be transferring the ownership of Mr. Page's motor vehicle to me. Assuming that the vehicle is not a part of the Page murder investigation, I need to find out where the BMW is presently stored. Second, an attorney of my stature cannot afford to have a client looking and smelling like he just crawled out of a garbage container. Buy Richard a razor, soap, a toothbrush, some good shampoo, and keep the change for your efforts."

Henry grabbed the bills and opened the door. "Right, Pinky."

The moment I sat down, I jotted 'BMW 650i' on my note pad and reviewed the limited information I had concerning my newest client. Richard had been charged with the premeditated murder of his uncle outside the isolated, and rather unpleasant town of Eureka, Nevada. My initial

4

assessment of Richard's interrogation videotape had informed me that he suffered from total ignorance of his legal rights along with a near terminal case of naiveté. There was little doubt that this young man's very life perched precariously on the edge of an extremely slippery slope. Perhaps, as Carson City's only attorney with a perfect acquittal record concerning clients charged with murder, this would have been the prudent moment for me to bow out of the case. But the siren song of that free and clear BMW 650i forced me to consider all the legal avenues available for my client. At this juncture, the odds of taking Richard to trial, and maintaining my perfect record of acquittals looked astronomical. However, a plea arrangement to a lesser charge of manslaughter seemed to be a viable option that could save my client's life, along with my perfect courtroom record.

I said, "My boy, look at me."

He lifted his head and his eyes stared back at me with a sadness so heartrending he would have put a bloodhound to shame.

I said, "Richard, you don't have a clear understanding of your perilous situation. You've been arrested for murder. Once the authorities make an arrest, they usually cease searching for additional suspects. To get our relationship off to a good start, you need to comprehend that important fact."

"But, Pinky, I didn't kill my uncle. Can't you go file one of those habeas corpus things and get me out of here?"

"Richard, I am the lawyer here," I replied sternly. "Now let me go over this again. You are accused of murdering your uncle, William Page. The Nevada Highway Patrol arrested you because you were seen fleeing the scene of the crime. The District Attorney feels she has enough evidence to charge you with first-degree murder. From this moment on, no one, including myself, cares if you are innocent or guilty. As your attorney, I'm bound by law and my professional ethics to provide you with the best possible defense, and that may include negotiating with the DA to see if she will accept a manslaughter plea."

5

A look of puzzlement inched its way across my client's young face.

I hammered home my point. "You've been charged with the ultimate crime. In the eyes of the authorities, you drove seven hundred miles from Los Angeles to the eastern wasteland of Nevada with a single goal: to kill your uncle. The law-abiding citizens of this state take a dim view of murdering relatives. In fact, since 1905, Nevada has executed fifty-three convicted murderers in a state facility not far from this very room: ten were hanged, one was shot, thirty-two were gassed, and the last ten died by lethal injection. Now it's time you return to your cell and consider all your options. I'll be back tomorrow morning."

Richard's confused expression quickly shifted to total bewilderment, a look I had seen many times on the faces of clients when time and events had moved faster than his or her mind could process.

"But I don't understand, Pinky. Why do you think I should plead guilty to manslaughter when I didn't kill anyone?"

"My boy, we are talking about going to trial on a first degree murder charge. That means if the jury finds you guilty, you will be executed. As your attorney, my primary mission is to keep you alive. If your account of this squalid affair doesn't convince me that I can accomplish that singular task, then you will have two alternatives; accept a manslaughter plea, or inform me into which arm you want the executioner to insert the needle."

TWO

Bear—Carson City, Nevada

I grabbed a clean towel and wiped up the ice cubes and booze that Vern had just dumped all over the spotless mahogany bar.

God, I thought, the worst part of this job had to be cleaning up after a sloppy drunk.

I refilled his glass, and said, "Vern, you know the house rules here. Once you start dumping them over, it's time to go home."

"Come on, Bear, you're not my mother."

I threw the wet towel into the sink and glanced at the clock. I had to listen to that kind of crap for two more hours before Pete would drag his raggedy butt in here to relieve me.

"Right, Vern, I'm not your mother, but I'm big enough to kick your worthless butt all the way to Reno. Now drink up and clear out of here before I really get pissed."

While Vern's whisky-soaked brain struggled to come up with a clever answer, a phlegm-clogged voice came at me from the far end of the bar. "Bear, when you have a free moment, we'll require two more."

Now Senator Lard Ass wanted a piece of me—the crap I had to put up with in this dump was enough to make me puke!

"Bear, my new-found friend from the State Medical Association feels the need to spread a little more oil on the water to ah . . . . to continue constructing the walls of our budding companionship."

"Right, Senator." Having to deal with Vern wasn't enough. Now I had a politician jumping my ass. "Will that be two more of the same, straight up?"

I guess some bartenders would be proud to serve an elected official, but Lard Ass was only a state senator, and

7

to tell the truth, it didn't make any difference to me who I served as long as someone picked up the tab, and left me a good tip.

Lard Ass lifted his empty glass. His fat tongue jumped out and licked the last drop. "That is correct, my good man. Two Blue Labels, straight."

Johnnie Walker Blue Label was one of the most expensive whiskies we poured at the bar, but Lard Ass didn't care what it cost because he wasn't paying. I held off until I made eye contact with the lobbyist, and waved the Blue Label bottle, just to be sure he knew what he was buying.

He nodded. I could tell from the pissed-off look on his mug that he wasn't all that happy, but what was another thirty bucks to a lobbyist on an unlimited expense account?

I made two generous pours of the expensive stuff and carried the glasses down the bar to Mr. Expense Account and Senator Lard Ass.

Mr. Expense Account was decked out in an expensive dark suit, like most of his kind that lurked around the bars of Carson City. Blond hair covered his head, but his skin was paler than a loaf of bread before it was baked because he had spent almost all his life working dark alleys to swing a vote his way.

Senator Lard Ass was about seventy, and fatter than a champion hog at fair time. The joke around town was when he finally bought the farm the undertaker would be forced to bury him because the only crematorium oven in the county would be too small for his whale-like corpse.

The door opened and in walked J. Pincus Delmont, the man who had saved my sorry butt from ten years of hard time.

I reached for the gin. "The usual, Pinky?"

"That's correct, Bear. God, what a tough day."

About this time every evening, Pinky came in for his gin and tonic. He was a short bastard, but his shoes were always shined and he didn't have any gravy spots on his tie, so in this town he was considered a fancy dresser. He tried to con me into thinking that I was the best bartender in Carson City, but I knew that the only reason Pinky buttered me up was because I poured him a triple shot of gin and charged him for a single. Not because I liked the bastard, shit no. And it wasn't because he was a sharp dresser. It was because I owed Pinky big time.

A couple of years back I sort of caught my tit in the wringer. One night, a jerk tried to hit me. One thing led to another, and before I could stop myself, his head sort of got stuck between my fist and a brick wall. The next thing I knew, I was looking at a manslaughter charge. Now, anyone in Carson City, who was staring at heavy time, and who was born with at least the brains of a grasshopper, would hire Pinky Delmont for his attorney. Pinky was expensive, but he was my only hope to escape a bucket of years at the State slam. I pawned everything I owned, except my car, to cover most of his fee. Then I fibbed a little when I said I'd pay him the rest after the trial out of some money I got when my grandma died. I told Pinky the truth about my grandma being dead, but the money part was a stretch. When old grandma passed there wasn't enough money left to cover her bar tab.

To this day, I still don't understand what Pinky did during the trial, or how he did it, but when the verdict came in, the jury foreman said, "Not guilty."

I was a free man. I should have been happy. But I didn't have two nickels, and I knew I was up shit creek without a paddle because Pinky hated deadbeat clients. That's when I started to feel weird. The room sort of started to spin around. My knees got real shaky, and the next thing I knew, I was lying on the courtroom floor with Pinky staring down at me. I pulled myself up to one knee and confessed to Pinky that I had lied about grandma's money and I couldn't pay his fee. Pinky snarled, and for a second, I thought he was going to kick me or something. I grabbed his leg and promised I'd do anything to pay off what I owed him. Pinky flashed me that shit-eating grin of his, and told me that I owed him 1000 hours of work. I don't think so good when I'm on one knee, so I said, "Yes", in front of God, Judge Anderson, and the twelve patsies who had just decided I wasn't guilty.

Now you know why I don't like Pinky, but after listening to that lobbyist kiss up to Lard Ass all afternoon, I was happy to talk to anyone, even if it was my old lawyer.

I said, "Tough day?"

Pinky sighed, like he had just spent twelve hours hand-digging post holes in the hot sun. "Bear, I have a new client who's so wet behind the ears, I don't believe he's ever spent a night in jail."

Now that was something. "No shit."

"I'm not worried though. He'll come around by morning. I gave him the old needle line before Henry took him back to his cell."

"Jesus, Pinky, that needle bit's really cold."

Pinky took a bigger gulp than normal, like he hoped the gin might kick-start his engine. "Bear, you of all people should know that I occasionally have to hold a client's feet to the fire."

I knew better than to act friendly to the bastard, but bad days happen to shitty guys too, so I reached under the bar and pulled out the centerfold of last year's Miss August, my personal favorite. "Take a look at her, Pinky. Did you ever see a nicer pair than those?"

He pushed the centerfold away without taking a peek. "Bear, there is more to this world then a pair of well-formed mammary glands."

I checked out Miss August again. She was spectacular. "There is?"

"By the way, Bear, do you have any idea how much a near-new BMW 650i convertible is worth?"

"I don't know, but Beemer's are expensive cars. I'd bet more than forty, maybe even fifty."

Pinky nodded, sat back, and got that weird glow in his eye he gets when the gin finally cuts in. "Bear, didn't you once tell me that you were born in Elko?"

I grabbed the towel; scrubbed at the spot where Vern had dumped his glass over and tried to figure out what where I was born had to do with the price of a German car. Pinky's a sneaky bastard who's always about five jumps ahead of a dumb-shit bartender like me. I didn't know what was coming next so I wrapped the towel around my fist and backed away a little, just to be safe. "What's on your mind, Pinky?"

"My latest client was born in Los Angeles. Don't you ever feel stifled living in Carson City—a backwater burg where the endless wind picks up the sand and blows it all the way to Colorado—a town where the ratio of cowboy boots to Birkenstocks runs ten thousand to one? My God, man, do you plan on spending the rest of your life tending bar on the western edge of a rocky desert? Don't you have any ambition?"

Now I was sure he was trying to trick me into saying something stupid. "Are you talking about me?"

Pinky took a sip and nodded.

I said, "No, I don't feel stiff, or whatever that word was you said. Why?"

"I was just thinking. Compared to Los Angeles, Carson City is nothing more than a tiny road-side attraction."

"Huh?"

"You know, a wide spot in the road with a snake farm, or a phony museum. Why don't you make me another?"

"You got it."

Every night, when Pinky would ask me for his second G and T, I'd do my thing to get back at the man. He thought I was going to give him another triple, like the first drink. But I'd only pour a half-shot of booze, add ice, and top the glass with tonic. The funny thing was that after his first drink of almost pure gin, his brain was so fried that he never noticed the difference. Some nights, when I made his second and third drinks, I didn't give him any gin at all!

I pushed his fresh drink across the bar. "Pinky, to a kid who grew up in Elko, Carson City's a big town, and the state capitol of Nevada to boot."

Pinky took a big slug of his drink, and smiled.

"You've done it again, Bear. You make the best damn G and T in the state."

I forced out a fake grin. "Thanks. How about you, Pinky? I'll bet you could make a bigger wad of dough in LA."

11

"I'm not so sure." He took another big swig. "We both know Carson City is a dump, but at least we're surrounded with real people."

For a change, I agreed with the bastard. "Right! This town's loaded with patsies, but we've got a lot less than Reno, Vegas, or LA."

At the far end of the room, Lard Ass banged his ham-fist on the bar, like he'd just been told the funniest joke in the world.

Pinky waited until the pounding stopped. "As long as I continue to pursue the legal profession, I prefer to remain in Carson City, where I'm the Alpha male of the legal pack."

"Huh?"

"That's a euphemism, my good man. Another way of saying that I enjoy my reputation as the top defense attorney in Carson City."

"I knew that." Somehow the bastard always made me feel dumb. I glanced down and Miss August's round tits and taut nipples smiled back. I shoved the centerfold across the bar again. "Pinky, you've got to admit, she has a great pair of knockers."

Pinky finally gave in. He took a long look and Miss August worked her magic. He smiled. "Yes, and she's better to look at than my newest client, the young man who murdered his uncle. Bear, my good man, I believe I do have time for one more."

"You've got it."

THREE

Pinky—Carson City, Nevada

I wasn't surprised that after another night in jail, most of the life had drained from Richard's face. Twenty-four hours in a Carson City cell wasn't as bad as a day in a Soviet gulag, but it wasn't a week of vacation on the French Riviera either. I had counted on the mental picture of his pending death by lethal injection to assist his consideration of his two legal alternatives.

Although colorless and drawn, Richard's external form looked free from the dirt and impurities that had covered him yesterday. His brown hair actually sparkled. He wore a new yellow tee shirt, and the dark, hairy stubble that had covered his jaw had been scraped off.

"Richard, thanks to Henry's purchases, and your morning ablution, you look a new man. Now, before we start to determine your best defense options, we need to discuss my retainer."

Richard Page's eyes changed from tired to wary as the import of my statement sunk in. "But, Pinky, I thought you were free."

"No, my legal services are not free. In fact, you have retained the most expensive attorney in northern Nevada. Before we delve any further into my plans concerning your legal defense, my services will require a sizeable retainer. However, you don't have a thing to worry about as I'm sure the title to your BMW will cover my initial fee."

Richard jumped up and slammed his fist on the small table. "My car! Are you crazy? I paid over eighty thousand cash for that car."

"Richard, calm yourself. Sit down or I shall summon Henry and he will immediately return you to your cell. I've informed you what is financially required to retain me as your attorney. If you so desire, I can contact Judge Ander-

13

son and request he assign your defense to the Public Defender."

Richard's backbone compressed like a collapsed Slinky and he slowly dropped into his chair. "And how much will the Public Defender cost me?"

"The PD's free, and except for that nasty habit of picking his nose in court, he's a wonderful fellow. I'm sure you'll get along just fine. I've been told that he visits many of his former clients on a regular basis while they serve out their sentences in State Prison."

A frown crossed Richard's brow. "Hold on, Pinky, what do you mean, he visits his former clients in prison?"

"My boy, I believe the visits have something to do with you get what you pay for. Before you make your final decision, I should provide you with a few statistics. Over the last ten years, I've gone to trial with forty-seven clients accused of murder. All forty-seven were acquitted. Of course, as the mutual fund salesman always warns, a good past performance does not guarantee a good future. But forty-seven acquittals to zero convictions is a pretty good record don't you think?"

Richard leaned forward. "And how did the Public Defender do?"

I had to work to contain my joy when he asked the very question I had planned he would.

I said, "The poor chap ends up with so few murder clients. Let me see, fifteen of his clients were convicted, none acquitted, but he did have that one hung jury about three years ago. But don't take my word alone, I think you should seek another opinion."

I walked across the small conference room and opened the door. "Henry, would you be so kind as to step in for a moment?"

The guard walked in. "Is he giving you any trouble, Pinky?"

"No, my potential client has a question."

Richard shifted in his chair. "Pinky tells me he's the best attorney in town. Is that true?"

The guard nodded. "Kid, I've never been arrested, so

14

I'm not the best guy to ask for advice. But if I had a mur-der-one charge hanging over my head like you do, and if my choice came down to Pinky or the PD, I'd hire Pinky in a New York minute."

Richard's eyes shifted back and forth between Henry and me. "But Pinky wants the title to my new Beemer."

"It's your decision, kid, but I'd give him my car, my house and my first born son if that's what he asked for."

Henry turned and left the room while Richard squirmed with indecision, trying to decide what was more important, his BMW or his life. Then he said, "I give up. I'll write you a note turning over the title of the car."

"No need, my boy. Last night I took the liberty of drawing up a transfer of ownership document. All you have to do is sign your name and date where indicated."

Richard signed his name. I signed mine. Satisfied, I slipped the retainer into my briefcase.

"Now that the financial details are taken care of, I want you to tell me your side of what happened the day your uncle died."

Richard seemed a little bewildered by my statement, but I was positive he was ready to cooperate. Trading an expensive new car to escape a death sentence generally does get a client's attention.

I turned on my digital recorder and opened a new le-gal note pad. "Let's begin with your full name."

"Richard Milhous Nixon Page. As soon as I reached twenty-one, I considered going to court to legally change my name, but that would cost money, and . . ."

"Richard, spare me. When it comes to naming chil-dren, I know parents can do strange things. Take myself for example. You cannot imagine the grief I took as a child on the playground with the name of J. Pincus Delmont. And trust me, Pincus was better than what the J stood for. Now please continue, *Fugit inreparabile tempus.*"

A befuddled expression flooded Richard's face.

"Richard, that's a Latin phrase. Translated it means—time on earth is irretrievable. My boy, you're still young, but as you gain wisdom, you will learn that each precious second, once spent, is gone. I am a very busy man, and I'm due in court shortly. Please continue with your version of the events that led to your uncle's untimely death."

"Sorry. I live at 1268 Sunset Avenue, Arcata, California, 95518, in a house I share with two other guys and my girl friend, Julie Campbell . . . . Oh my God . . . . I haven't seen her for two days. What's happened to Julie."

I glanced at my watch. "Richard, we need to concentrate on the day your uncle was murdered."

"Pinky, I won't say another thing until I know that she's safe."

"Julie is presently residing at a motel near here. I'll be taking her statement in the next few days. Please continue."

The young man did not immediately respond, as if lost in the memory of a better time. I had to get him to open up, but feared that pushing too hard at this point could place our newly formed relationship at risk.

I said, "Richard, there comes a time where the client and his attorney reach a fork in the road concerning trust. You may think of me as a friend, or a mother, or your priest during confession. Frankly, I'm positive we'll never become friends, and God knows I'm not your mother. It's time for you to open up and tell me everything, as you would confess to your priest, or our legal relationship is doomed."

"I'm sorry, it's just that everything is happening so fast!"

"I understand. If beginning on the day of your uncle's death is too painful, start anywhere. What I am looking for is information that will help me to determine your state of mind."

"I don't understand what you mean?"

I had to learn the reason my client had driven seven hundred miles, and why his uncle was dead. Richard had to provide me something, anything, that I could use as a rational argument for why he was involved, but I could see that he still didn't trust me.

I said, "Go back a week or two and find a comfortable place to start."

16

"Okay. A week ago, I discovered that my father, a man I believed to be a paragon of religious virtue, was nothing more than a common criminal."

I pulled back my coat sleeve and I stared at my watch—holding that pose until Richard noticed that I remained concerned about the passage of time. "I trust your father's ethical dilemma had something to do with your uncle being murdered."

"It does, but I didn't find out about my father's crimes until after he died."

I said, "Hold on. You're confusing me. We both know your uncle's dead. Did your father also die?"

"Pinky, they're both dead. I told you that a lot happened to me in the last few days. First, my father died on a golf course."

"Did he have a heart attack?"

"No, he died when an old oak tree fell on him."

I considered the odds of his father standing on the exact spot so a falling tree would kill him and rapidly concluded that an accidental death was possible, but not an everyday occurrence. I jotted down a note to remind me to check into Richard's father's improbable death, just in case his defense went beyond a plea bargain.

I said, "Go on."

"After father died, I flew to LA. That's when I discovered he was nothing more than a common thief."

"Was your mother aware that your father was, to use your words, a thief?"

"Pinky, my mother's been dead for ten years."

I said, "Do you have any sisters or brothers?"

"No, I'm all alone." Richard started to cry and his shoulders slumped. It was as if, until that moment, he'd been unaware that he was an orphan.

I said, "I think I can relate to your situation. I was also an only child."

Richard sat up and smiled bravely. "Thank you, Pinky."

"So, as the last of your family, you had to arrange for your father's funeral?"

"Yes, and after the funeral I . . . ." Richard started to tear up again.

My client had the emotional stability of a sand castle. I decided to change the subject. "Richard, did you attend college?"

"Yes, Humboldt State."

"Did you graduate?"

"Yes. In fact, I was celebrating my pending graduation the night I heard about my father's accident."

"Did you say what your father did for a living?"

Richard frowned and straightened up, as if his backbone suddenly fused. "He was an ordained minister, but he didn't exactly have a church. He ran a non-profit foundation called Save One Sinner."

I said, "You'll have to excuse me, but I'm unfamiliar with that organization."

Richard snorted, "You and nearly every other American."

Again Richard fell silent, forcing me to grab the reins and forge ahead.

I said, "Am I correct in assuming that Humboldt State is part of the California State University system?"

"Yes. I majored in Forestry. I wanted to spend the rest of my life managing forest resources."

"Was there a reason you didn't follow in your father's footsteps?"

"Yes!" His positive response was cold, and bitter. "I hated him and his phony foundation!"

Richard's shoulders slumped, as if his angry outburst had used the last drop of gas in his tank. I considered asking him a few more questions, but decided it would be better to return him to his cell—to stew in his juices one more night.

I said, "I'm sorry to cut this short, but I'm due in court. Tomorrow morning we'll pick up where we left off."

I left the jail and strolled about two blocks toward the complex of government buildings in the late afternoon heat. I reached the DA's office where my favorite ex-wife, Willow Stone, held the title of Chief Deputy of the Criminal Division. I sprinted up the stairs to her office, waved a greeting to her secretary, and walked into Willow's private office.

In the past, Willow had been a formidable legal opponent, but our matrimonial relationship required that we not spar in the courtroom anymore. She was stretched out on a leather couch opposite her desk, and I salivated at the thought of being close to her again. A black sleep mask covered her eyes.

I whispered, "Willow."

"Stop whispering, Pinky, I'm not asleep. I'm going over my closing argument for the Ekberg trial."

Willow was the Deputy DA responsible for the prosecution of all crimes committed in Carson City. Her next step up professionally would be the elected position of District Attorney. The present DA was a man in his early seventies, respected by the voters, and to Willow's probable dismay, he showed no inclination toward retirement.

While she waited for her boss to ride off into the sunset, Willow cherry-picked cases that would keep her name in the public's mind. With the Ekberg trial, she'd hit the proverbial publicity jackpot! The case included murder, rape, incest, and the ironic fact that the accused killer was the respected president of a local bank. The seamy details of the crime were so sensational that Reno, Vegas, and Court TV were covering the daily proceedings.

I said, "How's it look for the money lender?"

"If I could get someone to kidnap juror number three, the prison tailor would be fitting Ekberg for a new set of togs the day after tomorrow."

Willow removed the sleep mask from her face and stood. My ex-wife wore a tailored linen suit and the natural beige material was perfectly complimented by a sea foam green scarf that echoed the color of her beautiful eyes. In my humble opinion, Willow Stone was the only other attorney in Carson City, beside myself, who possessed proper sartorial judgment.

She said, "Actually my case looks good. I'm sure that number three will come around after my closing."

She flashed her haunting eyes at me. That nether re-

19

gion below my belt tingled and I almost forgot why I had stopped by her office.

"Pinky, stop looking at me that way. Those urges are nothing more than lust and pent up sperm looking for an egg."

She was correct about being pent up. God knows I wanted to ravish her on the couch, but she was wrong about my yearnings. They were much more than simple lust. Willow meant more to me than that.

I said, "I don't agree. Unlike the rest of my ex-wives, you hold a special place in my heart."

"Damn, you really know how to sweet talk a girl. Now go away. I really do have a lot of work to do."

Once again, I had tried to profess my true longing for Willow, but for some reason the skill to impart my feelings had eluded me.

In truth, my ability to communicate with Willow had failed from the start. For example, she'd been a young, and vibrant thirty-six when we had walked down the aisle. She'd wanted to have a child but her window of opportunity was slipping by, and she knew a pregnancy had to happen soon. However, before we married, it had never occurred to me to ask if she wanted to become a mother.

Prior to the wedding I was forty-three. As far as children were concerned, I was ambivalent. In all my previous marriages, I had never fathered a child after God knows how many attempts. To me, getting a woman pregnant was like shooting craps. You either conceived a baby or you didn't—you either rolled a seven or you didn't. Willow and I tried for two years with no success. Eventually, she convinced me to go to a fertility clinic. I discovered that my sperm were hard to find, and the pathetic little buggers had poor motility. The test proved I was the problem. The fertility doctor suggested that Willow was a perfect candidate for the clinic's sperm donor program. She loved the idea. I hated it. One thing led to another and within a few months we filed for divorce. But our disagreement over procreation didn't change my feelings for her. After multiple failed marriages on my part, Willow was the only wife whom I truly loved.

But that was yesterday. Today Willow had replaced a desire for children with her goal to become Carson City's first female District Attorney.

I smiled. "I have a suggestion. As soon as you complete the Ekberg trial, we should drive to one of our condos in Tahoe for a couple of days of mad, unbridled sex."

She laughed. God, she was beautiful. Her green eyes, coal black hair, and high cheekbones came from her father who was one-quarter Cherokee. Her milk-white skin, freckles, and the red undertones of her hair came from her one hundred percent Scottish mother. "Pinky, you are incorrigible, now clear out of my office. I have work to do."

"Not until I get an answer from you concerning the Page murder."

Willow's smile faded a touch too quickly. "What's the question?"

"I appreciate the photos of the body, and the video tape of Richard Page's interrogation with your stellar police detectives, but for some reason, your office neglected to turn over any information concerning the murder weapon. Remember, William Page died from one or more gunshots. Half of the man's skull ended up on the carpet. So where's the gun?"

She tried hard to maintain her stony expression, but I had shared a bed with her for three years and didn't miss the tiny, nearly imperceptible narrowing of her green eyes. She had just informed me that the police didn't have the weapon in their possession. I could tell that she was upset that her clever ex-husband had trapped her. Willow was a proud woman and she didn't like being placed in that position.

I smiled. "I know we each have a job to do, but other than the fact that my client drove from LA to the middle of Nevada, you seem a bit short of evidence to prove premeditation. Perhaps, to save valuable time for the both of us, I wouldn't be averse to a plea arrangement. For example, my client would consider involuntary manslaughter. That way you office could—"

"Pinky!" Her tone lost all of its friendly banter and took a cold business turn. "In the future, please direct any questions or deal proposals concerning the Page murder to the assigned deputy . . ." She flipped through her stack of files, as if to make me think that she didn't remember the name of the minion she had assigned to the case. "Aha yes, it's Miguel Vaca. Now if you'll excuse me, I have to work on my closing argument."

"I'd much rather spend the rest of the day with you, but if that's the way you feel we should handle the Page case, so be it"

Before she could back away, I gave her a loving peck on the forehead and walked out of her office.

As I headed toward the Old Globe, my mind concentrated on that flash of angst I had picked up in her eyes. Something about the Page murder investigation bothered her—and I would be willing to bet my newly acquired 650i that the source of her anxiety had to do with the missing weapon.

FOUR

Bear—Carson City, Nevada

Damn! Last month the boss came up with another of his loony ideas. The casinos in town give away booze, as long as you lose more money than you win. But most of the local drunks know that they have to make up for the free drinks in lost bets, so most of the resident drinkers spend their hard earned cash at local bars like the Old Globe. But the boss wanted to suck up every buck in town, so he came up with this stupid happy hour idea.

One night a week, every Tuesday to be exact, the well drinks were cut to seventy-five cents and beer was a half a buck. At that price, every drunk within fifty miles showed up. Each Tuesday, between the hours of five and seven, I'd work my ass off pouring booze for the cheap crowd, while I tried to figure why a happy hour lasted twice as long as a regular hour.

Most of the time the boss was a pain in the ass, but he was the boss, and when the boss told me to shovel shit, I knew enough to ask him how high he wanted it stacked, or I'd be looking for a new job.

By five after seven, my ass was dragging. The place was nearly empty when the door opened and in walked Pinky.

"Bear, my daily, please."

"How's it hanging, Pinky?"

"I managed to make it through another day of legal madness. How about you?"

"Same as ever. I pour booze into a glass. The customers empty the glass. How's that new client of yours doing?"

"You mean the young man who's accused of murdering his uncle? He's fine."

"He murdered his uncle? I don't remember hearing that anyone around here got bumped off. Did you say who

23

he killed?"

"Bear, my client's innocent until proven guilty. You of all people should know that."

That was total bullshit, and we both knew it, but I said, "Right."

The mayor and a member of the city council staggered in and waved at me to say they wanted their usual.

"Pinky, I'll be right back after I pour a couple of Wild Turkeys on the rocks."

Pinky took a big gulp and dropped the level of his G and T two inches.

"I'll be here when you return."

After a minute, I got back to him. "Okay, so your client didn't do it, but who didn't he kill?"

"A gentleman named William Page."

I said, "That name doesn't ring a bell."

"I'm not surprised. The unfortunate man lived and died on a ranch two hundred miles east of here. In that vast Nevada wasteland surrounding the town of Eureka."

"Pinky, I'm dumb, but not that dumb. Your client shouldn't be sitting in a Carson City jail if he murdered some poor bastard two hundred miles east of here."

"Bear, remember, my client is innocent. But you are correct on the jurisdiction point. He shouldn't be incarcerated in the Carson City jail. A few days ago, he languished in Eureka, but the man he was accused of killing was a well-known figure, which isn't hard in a County that has a population of less than 2000 people. A local judge decided that a change of venue would be a prudent move."

"Is that like one of those fair trial things?"

"Correct. Now I could use another."

After I set down his new drink, I said, "Pinky, how did you end up with the case?"

Pinky took a sip, smiled, and said, "I guess you could say that old Judge Anderson owed me a favor."

"You think he did you a favor by handing you a client who killed his uncle? Damn, I'd puke my guts out if I ever found myself in a courtroom again."

"Ah, but there's the difference between being the de-

24

fendant, and the defendant's attorney. For a professional like myself, a juicy murder trial offers an opportunity to gain fame, and bank a sizeable fee. It's a little like watching a circus, with clowns driving around in little cars and a trapeze artist swinging high above the ground. The clowns supply the laughter, and the guy hanging sixty feet off the ground provides the suspense."

"I guess you're right."

But I knew Pinky wasn't right 'cause I'd been there—staring at ten years of hard time—and it wasn't funny to me.

FIVE

Pinky—Carson City, Nevada

First thing the next morning, I stopped by my office.

My secretary Mabel said, "Henry called. Your BMW 650i is parked in the impound lot next to the City Center Motel. I didn't know you were looking for a new car. Was something wrong with the old one?"

Mabel Sullivan, a woman who had been with me for ten years, was my only employee. Don't ask me how she did it, but by using her untold powers, she managed to keep my legal practice running smoother than an expensive Swiss watch. She unlocked and locked up the office each day; kept my desk clean and polished, and parceled out each minute of my valuable time with the precision of a top brain surgeon. Mabel took a sip of coffee and handed me the daily printout that contained my court and office appointments.

I glanced at the list of meetings and said, "No, nothing wrong with my old Jag. I just couldn't pass up the opportunity to pick up a nearly new convertible. According to today's schedule, I should return around four-thirty. See you then."

On the way to the lot, I stopped by the Sheriff's Office and presented the ownership transfer papers to the Sergeant responsible for inmates' property. He pulled out Richard's package and handed over the keys to his car. Five minutes later I stood next to a dark blue convertible that set my macho heart aflutter. I had been a Jaguar man all my life, but one glance at that stylish mass of blue steel instantly converted me into a BMW devotee.

Pleased with my exchange of legal advice for the sleek mode of transportation, I left my old Jag in the adjacent parking slot, put the top down, and cruised around town before my third meeting with Richard Page. The question of the missing weapon nagged at me, but I was sure that by

26

the end of this session, I would have a track on the weapon. It still looked to me that Richard's best bet was to spend the next five to ten years as a guest of the State of Nevada. I knew he wouldn't be happy with a manslaughter plea, but he would remain alive and he'd be back on the streets before he reached thirty.

By the time I arrived at the interrogation room, Henry had Richard ready and waiting for my arrival.

I thanked Henry for locating the car, and then turned my full attention towards my client.

"Good morning, Richard. I trust a good night's rest provided us both with renewed energy. Last evening, I reviewed my notes, and rather than have you pick up where we left off yesterday, I'd like you to begin when you arrived at your uncle's place, the site of the murder."

Richard said, "But Pinky, I have to go back to where we left off yesterday, or what happened at my uncle's place won't make any sense."

"Fine, tell me more about your father. Exactly what terrible thing did he do?"

"I discovered that he was stealing money that belonged to someone else."

"Do you mean he was embezzling from his foundation?"

"It's possible he was doing that too, but no, this was something else. A day before the funeral, I opened a piece of mail that was addressed to my grandfather."

That was strange. Yesterday Richard had stated that after his father died, he was alone in the world, but before I could challenge this obvious discrepancy, he continued. "Inside the envelope was a check made out to my grandfather, Theodore Roosevelt Page, for $501,212."

The skin beneath my eyebrows started to itch as I considered that my client had just informed me he was a member of a family with real money. That information placed me at an interesting tipping point. It was possible that if I brought Richard's wealthy grandfather into the financial picture, my client could afford a real defense— something much more complex than a simple plea arrangement—a defense that would require an investigator—a defense that would cost him a lot more than a near-new BMW 650i.

"Richard, I'm truly pleased to learn that you have a very rich grandfather. Now—"

"You don't understand, Pinky. My grandfather died seven years ago."

The momentary vision of the wealthy grandfather faded.

"Are you sure?"

Richard's thin frame gave off an involuntary shudder. "Yes. I attended his funeral and saw his body in the casket."

I sat back and pondered the situation. The grandfather was long dead, but his son had received a hefty check made out to the grandfather's name. Obviously, some brilliant skullduggery had been going on in the Page family, and Richard acted as if he knew nothing. Could he actually be as ignorant as he seemed?

I said, "Tell me more about your grandfather."

"He never missed sending me a present on my birthday and for Christmas."

"Richard, what else do you remember about your grandfather? Did he drive a big car, or wear fancy clothes?"

"You know, when I saw the size of that check, I wondered the same thing, but I don't know. My presents came in the mail. I only remember seeing him on a couple occasions because he and my father didn't get along."

"How old was your grandfather when he died?"

Richard thought for a second. "I don't know. Somewhere in his eighties I think."

I recalled my own grandparents and realized how little I knew about them as people. They were both old. Grandma kissed me too much. Grandpa never hugged me. Grandma handed me an envelope each birthday and Christmas with a ten-dollar bill inside. Ten bucks was a real thrill when I was seven, but by the time I had reached eighteen, that niggling amount didn't pack the same punch.

I said, "What did your grandfather do for a living?"

Again, Richard pondered the question. "For some reason I think he worked in the oil business, but I'm not even sure about that."

"Let's move on. After you opened the envelope with the check, then what did you do?"

"I called Julie and told her I was in over my head."

"Was she still at your house near the college?"

"Pinky, I don't want to bring Julie into this mess."

Richard Page was an interesting study. He still thought he was running this show. However, regardless of his admonition to ignore his girl friend, my job was to defend him against a murder charge. For all I knew, Julie was the one who pulled the trigger.

I said, "And what did you and Julie talk about?"

Richard jumped up. "Pinky, I meant what I said. Julie had nothing to do with Uncle Bill's death."

"My boy, you have to trust my discretion concerning your female friend. Now sit down and answer my question."

He hesitated, then the weight of his predicament pressed him back into the chair. "The minute I saw the check, I knew that I should call the police, but as much as I disliked my father, I didn't want to see his memory dragged through the mud."

Understandable when you consider they both carried the same last name, and Richard was the only male member of the Page family left alive.

I said, "Go on."

"First I have to explain something. I really didn't know much about what my father did concerning his SOS foundation. Each year he'd go to Italy for half the year to expand the foundation. Then he'd spend six months in Los Angeles. A couple of years after Grandpa passed, my mother died from pancreatic cancer. Then I left for college. Twice a year, Father would send me a measly five hundred bucks. The rest of the expenses were my problem."

I said, "Richard, I'm sure your father's parsimony is very important to you, but you've been accused of first degree murder. What happened to the check that was made out to your grandfather?"

"I stuck it in my wallet. The next envelope I opened

29

was the bill for my father's funeral. It came to a little more than seven thousand bucks. Pinky, I had about seventy-five cents in my pocket, no job, and no prospects. That's when I decided to violate my father's rule and break into his office."

"Where was his office located?"

"In our house."

"Richard, how long did you live in that house?"

"All my life."

I said, "Do you mean to tell me that your father had an office in your house that you had never entered?"

"That's right. Father kept the office door locked 24/7."

Richard must be a saint, I thought. How could a child live in a house for eighteen years and never try to sneak into his father's office. Was it possible this saint was innocent of his uncle's murder?

A touch shaken by my last thought, I said, "Go on."

"I found the office key hidden in Father's bedroom, unlocked the door, and turned on the light. Pinky, what I saw blew me away. The walls, unlike the rest of the house, were paneled with a dark, expensive looking wood. The floor was carpeted. On a huge desk sat an expensive laptop computer. But seeing a half filled whiskey bottle on the desk, that was the biggest shock."

"Richard, I take it your father did not drink."

"That's an understatement. The SOS foundation was set up to rescue those unfortunate souls who abused alcohol. To the best of my recollection, I never saw my father drink anything stronger than tea. I sat down behind the desk and that's when I noticed the answering machine. A flashing light indicated there were seven messages that hadn't been answered. I rewound the tape and hit the play button. The first message was from my Uncle Bill."

"Richard, for my notes, what was your Uncle Bill's full name?"

"William Howard Taft Page."

"And I don't have your father's name."

"Herbert Clark Hoover Page. But he was known as Clark Page."

"I find that interesting. Apparently, every male in

your family was named for an elected Republican president. Are you aware of a family story concerning the unusual naming scheme?"

"I heard that my great-grandfather, a staunch Republican, started it. He felt, according to my father, that a strong Republican name would help a man succeed in life."

Now I understood why Richard wanted to change his name. His father ignored the Herbert Hoover part of his given name and called himself Clark Page—he wanted to escape being thought of as the man who drove the country into the Great Depression. But Richard was stuck with Milhous Nixon, and it would take many future generations before America could forget the disaster created by Richard Milhous Nixon.

I said, "Go on, what was the message from your uncle?"

"He was upset about not receiving his share. He actually threatened to fly to LA to get what he claimed was rightfully his."

"Did you know what share he was talking about?"

"Not at that point, no."

"And the other messages?"

"Uncle Bill had left four. Two came on the very day my father was killed. All of his messages said about the same thing. The rest were from a woman. She didn't speak English. It sounded like Italian."

"Did you erase any of the messages?"

"Well, yes—I erased all of Uncle Bill's messages, but I left the ones from the Italian woman."

Damn! I thought. That's another reason I need to press Willow for a plea arrangement. Richard erasing those tapes would be hard to explain to a jury.

"Any reason why you erased the messages from your uncle?"

For some reason Richard seemed to struggle with his answer. "I'm not sure. He was very upset and on the last message, he actually threatened me."

"Can you recall what he said?"

"It was something like, Richard, just because your fa-

31

ther is dead, don't think you can keep all the money. I have to have my share now. Don't make me come to LA and take it from you.'"

Now I understood Richard's concern about the erasures. I would have done the same thing if they were my uncle's messages.

I said, "Did your uncle attend your father's funeral?"

"Yes, and he wanted to talk with me, but every time he tried, somebody, or something would interrupt. After the funeral, some friends, including my uncle, stopped by the house. I saw Uncle Bill try to get into father's office, but the door was locked. The next thing I knew, he had left the house without saying goodbye."

Curious. Uncle Bill had been agitated enough to leave a lot of messages, and fly to LA, but whatever his problem was, he didn't want to discuss it in front of a crowd.

"After you listened to all the messages, did you leave the office?"

Richard sighed. "No. While sitting at my father's desk, I looked through all the drawers. The only thing inside was a metal box. I opened the box."

Richard glanced around and lowered his voice, as if there were a dozen people sitting nearby. "Pinky, the box was filled with cash."

My ears perked up like a Dalmatian's when a fire alarm bell rang. "Richard, you need to understand that I represent you concerning your uncle's murder. What you did or didn't do with that money could fall outside of our privileged, attorney/client relationship."

"Pinky, are you saying that I shouldn't tell you?"

"I just want you to consider your words very carefully. How much was in the box?"

"Over two hundred thousand. I knew the money didn't belong to me, but I had father's funeral bill to pay. Before I did anything, the phone rang. It was Uncle Bill."

"What kind of work did your uncle do?"

"Uncle Bill is a . . . . excuse me, he was a CPA. He lived on a ranch outside of Eureka, Nevada. I think he did some accounting in the area."

"I know the area well. Five years ago I did some work for a woman who had to run a gold mine after her husband was killed in a mine accident. As I know from personal experience, there's a good reason that section of Highway Fifty is called the loneliest road in the world. Never had I felt more isolated from civilization. But I digress, what did your uncle tell you?"

"He asked me if I had received a very large check made out to my grandfather. I told him yes. He said that before my father's accident, every six months my father would receive a check, deposit it into the SOS account, and then write Uncle Bill an SOS check for half of the total. Uncle Bill told me that since my father was dead, I had to get Grandfather's check to him at once. He would deposit the check into one of his accounts and mail me half. Just before he hung up, he begged me to hurry because getting that money was a matter of life or death."

Each year the two brothers would divvy up a million in cold, hard cash. Now I understood why Uncle Bill felt the need for some private time with his nephew.

I said, "So your uncle was in partnership with your father."

"That's what it looked like to me. Anyway, I told Uncle Bill I'd leave at once and meet him at his ranch sometime the following afternoon. I called Julie and told her that I would FedEx her some money for an airline ticket. Pinky, by now I'm sure you've figured out that I took . . ."

I had already determined that any legal fees beyond my initial retainer might come from that box, so I didn't want to know too much about its origin. As long as I remained in the dark, I could continue as if he hadn't told me a thing. Most people forget that the police are paid from the bottomless purse called local taxes. The DA's investigative team's funds come from the same source. But a top-notch defense for one of my clients is totally dependent on his financial resources. My client now had enough money, and if I added the missing murder weapon to the recording of Uncle Bill telling Richard he was concerned for his personal safety, I had more than enough reason for a full defense.

33

"Richard, do not discuss what you did or didn't do with the money in the box. We have a murder charge to work on."

His shoulders lifted, as if a large bird sitting there had suddenly taken wing. "Man, that's a relief. An hour later I stopped by the local BMW dealer and bought my 650i."

Richard was not shy when it came to using other people's money.

I said, "And that was the vehicle you were driving when the Highway Patrol pulled you over near Fallon?"

He nodded and a tiny smile tugged at the corners of his lips. "Pinky, that 650i can scream. I did a hundred and twenty on the straight, and there's a ton of straight around Eureka, Nevada."

"I'm sure there is. Now, Richard, I want you to take a look at a couple of photos." I wasn't sure what he would do or say, but I was interested in his reaction to the shots of his uncle.

"Pinky, thanks for all your help."

"You're welcome."

After observing Richard's first and only upbeat remark in three days, I decided this moment was not the time to inform him that my initial retainer would only cover a manslaughter plea—that going to court would require further legal time and investigation, and that those expenses would require a substantial increase of fees.

I reached into my briefcase and pulled out three graphic photos of Richard's deceased uncle given to me by the DA's office. The first one showed Uncle Bill, dressed in jeans and a flannel shirt. He had been shot behind his left ear, and where the bullet entered the area didn't look too bad. The second photo showed where the bullet had exited through a gaping hole that used to be his forehead and an eye socket. The last photo was a close up of what looked to be about a half-pound hunk of ground beef lying on the shag carpet, but upon closer inspection, turned out to be a healthy section of Uncle Bill's gray matter.

I placed them on the table in front of my client.

Richard glanced at the photo that showed the large

glob of his uncle's brains spread over what once had been a beautiful carpet. He made a retching sound and then lunged toward the metal trashcan. Leaning over the opening, Richard managed to deposit most of his breakfast into the container. The rest splattered across the floor and onto the baseboard.

To me, the result of regurgitation is a vile amalgamation of undigested food and should remain out of a civilized man's sight and smell. I grabbed my handkerchief, covered my nose and mouth, and sprinted for the door.

As I ran past Henry, I took a quick gulp of the fresh, sweet hallway air and said, "Sorry, old friend, but I'm due in court."

That wasn't true, I didn't have a date in court, but poor old Henry didn't need to know that. As I moved from the acrid, nearly visible stench, Henry, still blissfully ignorant of his impending doom, flashed me a friendly smile.

SIX

Bear—Carson City, Nevada

The afternoon crowd had left, and except for Vern, the Old Globe was empty.

Vern fumbled through his wallet and pulled out a pair of single bills that looked damn near as old as the white hair that circled his bald dome. "Bear, I believe I have just enough for one more."

"Okay, but that will be the last one you get from me tonight."

I poured his whisky over the rocks and rang up his two bucks.

I hated busting my ass when the bar was full, but empty, tending bar at the Old Globe was even worse. Talking with Vern was limited to one subject, gambling. The old fart thought he still had a chance to hit the big one, so Vern swept the floors every day at the big hotel casino. He collected a small salary, and would occasionally come across a stray chip lying on the floor.

Every Wednesday, the poor bastard would take his weekly check, pay his room rent, and then lose most of what he had left at the crap table.

Once in a while he'd win a couple of bucks, but usually, Vern would struggle through the wait 'til the next payday by working me for a free drink at the Old Globe.

As Vern lifted his glass, the door opened and in walked Pinky. As I reached for the gin, my stomach turned to ice water. Pinky was whistling, and when Pinky whistled, he was about to do something bad to someone, and that someone was usually me. I poured his gin and tonic and wondered if I'd get fired if I ran out and hid in the alley.

"How's it hanging, Pinky?"

"My friend, I had a very productive day."

Oh-oh, Pinky just called me his friend. That was never

good. I stood back and tried to act nice. "How's it going with the new guy?"

"Bear, the lad is as ignorant as a newly hatched duckling. I asked him if he understood that once he was arrested, he didn't have to talk with anyone but his lawyer?"

"What did he do?"

"Just about the worst thing he could—he agreed to a taped interview with two of Carson City's finest . . ." Pinky grabbed his glass and downed his gin and tonic like it was the first liquid he'd had after three days on the desert without a drop of water. "Would you be so kind as to make me another?"

"You got it."

While I made his next drink, Pinky kept talking, sort of like he was talking to himself. "Bear, I watched the video of that interrogation. Did you ever know Detective Jeff Shea?"

"Yeah, he used to work with a gorilla called Ice O'Conner."

Pinky took a big slug of his drink. "They still work as a team. O'Conner plays the bad cop, and Shea's highly skilled at pulling off the Stockholm syndrome scam, you know, where the person they're interrogating begins to think Detective Shea's his number-one buddy."

I wiped the bar and tried to keep up with what Pinky was trying to explain to me. "I've had dealings with Ice. He's bad news. Don't know much about Shea except he always seemed nice enough."

Pinky slapped his hand on the bar and the loud noise scared Vern so much that he damn near spilled his last whisky of the night. "You're supposed to think O'Conner is bad news, and Shea's your friend. Then you'll confess all your crimes to the good cop, and spend the next twenty years doing laundry in the nearest state facility."

"Oh."

"Exactly, and that's why I told my client to shut up. He's not sitting in the Carson City jail to expand his circle of friends.

Pinky sat back, drained the last of his drink and said,

"I'll have one more and then we need to discuss a little business."

I knew what Pinky meant when he said a little business. The last time he told me that, I spent a week scrounging through every back alley in Vegas looking for a deadbeat client that tried to stiff him. I finally found the poor bastard, and had to tie him up, and throw him in the trunk for the return trip to Carson City. The work wasn't hard, but every time I left the Old Globe, my boss, John, told me it might be the last time.

I growled, "I'll fix your drink, but this had better be a local deal, something I can do and still cover my shift here at the bar. I hate being a bartender, but it's the only job I've got."

SEVEN

Pinky—Carson City, Nevada

I stared at Bear, hoping against hope that I had chosen the right man for this task. He was a large sized, muscularly built Basque, who answered to the name of Benate Zabarte. Translated into English, Benate meant Bear, and the frightening power of a Grizzly flowed from his every pore. There was no doubt that Bear was a tough guy and trustworthy enough to accomplish the job in southern California.

Bear frowned at me. "Pinky, when you walked in tonight you were whistling, and you scare me when you whistle."

"It's been a long day. As soon as I take a sip, we'll discuss your next investigative assignment."

Bear placed his elbows on the bar, leaned forward, and pleaded. "I know I owe you, Pinky, but John told me that the next time I had to leave town on one of your bullshit jobs, he'd—"

"Calm down. Your boss owes me a few favors. John fully understands our arrangement. Don't worry, your job will be waiting for you when you return."

According to my accounting, Bear still owed me 686.5 hours. Someone had to go to Los Angeles to pick up that cash and look into the questions that had piled up. As much as I would have enjoyed a few days of relaxing under the southern California sun, my daily calendar was filled. So my Basque friend was about to learn that he had volunteered for the LA duty.

As I sipped my drink, Bear scowled and grunted, but eventually, his expression told me that he had become resigned to his fate. "All right," he said. "What do I have to do this time?"

Before I arrived, I had summarized the items that required further investigation. I placed my summary on the bar, and said, "At the top of this paper is the Los Angeles address for the home of a client. Inside the house is an office with a desk. Inside the middle desk drawer is a metal box. You need to retrieve that box and deliver it, unopened mind you, to my office in Carson City. Bear, I will tell you this much. There's a very large sum of cash inside the box. However, I know to the penny how much money the box contains. I'll add two hours of work for every dollar that doesn't complete the journey north to Carson City. Now nod your head so I'll know you understand."

The Bear growled, but nodded.

"Good. Once you have the box, find out everything you can about a non-profit organization called SOS, that's short for Save-One-Sinner. According to my client, the office was the headquarters of the SOS Foundation. I have to learn the size of the foundation—annual income— bank accounts and balances—branch offices—number of employees."

"But, Pinky, I—"

"Once you complete your investigation at the SOS office, learn what you can concerning the accidental death of a man named Herbert Page. Find out if his death really was an accident. Then you'll head north to Bakersfield to get background on a dead man named Theodore Page—his source of wealth, spending habits, did he die rich or poor? He may have been involved in the oil business."

"Damn it, Pinky, shut up for a second and listen to me. I can't go to LA 'cause I'm broke."

"I'll give you seven hundred to cover your expenses. You should make it, as long as you stay at cheap motels, average about twenty miles per gallon, and eat all your meals at McDonalds. Any questions?"

I looked at Bear's dazed expression and took pity. "Don't worry, Bear, I have all the details written for you on this paper."

I pulled out my wallet, removed a dollar for the gin and tonic, and followed the single with seven crisp, new Ben Franklins.

Bear's nose flared. His hand gripped a shot glass so

hard I thought he'd crush it back into silica. Then, slowly, he calmed down; as if he finally understood that the time for discussion had passed.

Bear said, "All right, how should I contact you?"

"Write up each day's activity and Fax it to my office at five. Wait thirty minutes, and then call me. If I'm there, we'll discuss your Fax. If I'm not, leave a message and we'll talk the next day."

"Sorry, Pinky, I can't do the job. I lost my cell phone because the chicken-shit phone company didn't believe that I had mailed them a check."

My past experience with Bear told me that he considered anyone who paid his bills to be less than a man, but I didn't have time to argue with him. I reached into my jacket pocket. "Here, you can use my cell phone."

The moment he took control of the cell phone, Bear attempted to take command of the situation. "This investigation will cost you at least 240 hours off my account."

I admired his courage, but all the admiration in the world didn't trump reality. "Bear, I alone will decide how many hours to deduct after you've successfully completed the job and returned the box to my office. Don't forget, everything you accomplish has to meet with my complete approval or you'll still owe me 686.5 hours. It's nearly eight. If you leave at once, you'll arrive in time for breakfast at one of LA's finest McDonalds."

"But I can't just walk out and leave the Old Globe untended."

At that precise moment, John, Bear's boss walked through the front door.

I said, "Bear, I took the liberty of informing John that you would be leaving before your shift ended. Now, don't forget, I'll expect the first report on my Fax by five tomorrow evening."

Bear took off his apron and tossed it at John. "Pinky, I know you have me by the balls, but I'm not going anywhere until you tell me exactly how many hours I'm working off."

I was proud of Bear. There had been times when his bravado had grated, but this time he was correct. I pulled

41

out a calculator, and pretended to run some numbers. "You were very close. Once you complete this task, you will see a reduction of 202.5 hours, leaving you with a balance of—"

"Damn it, I can do the math," growled the angry Bear.

EIGHT

Bear—On the road to Southern California

Damn him! Every guy in the Carson Valley, even those poor old bastards walking around without their marbles, knew that Pinky had kept my sorry ass out of jail, but everyday he looked for a new way to bust my chops. I knew that he was a kick-ass attorney, but that son-of-a-bitch never missed a chance to rub my face in my little manslaughter mistake. And then he gives me a measly seven hundred for ten days. Was the bastard kidding? How was I going to eat, sleep, and buy gas for ten days in La-La land on a lousy seven hundred bucks?

But the master had spoken—the time for argument was over. By nine-fifteen, I had reached Gardnerville, twenty miles south of Carson City. A mile south of the city limits, I picked up a kid hitchhiker who told me he was heading to Barstow. He was nineteen, and anyone that young was a kid in my book. He was an out-of-uniform Marine heading back to base after a fourteen-day furlough. I figured we'd keep each other awake and that part worked. Seven hours later, I dropped the kid off at the Highway 395 and 14 junction, and continued south to Mojave. On the southern edge of town, I stopped at McDonald's and dropped six bucks for breakfast. After I plunked down $42.00 to fill my gas tank, I spotted a Motel Six sign that advertised a single room for $48.00. That's when I knew my seven hundred was going to come up way short.

The rest of the drive, I cursed Pinky, his murdering client, my fifth grade teacher who I still hated, and every bastard that got in my way as I pushed my car through LA's crazy morning traffic. It took me nine hours to drive six hundred miles and two hours more to fight my way across the giant parking lot called Los Angeles.

Finally, I arrived at the address and parked the car on

the street. The house in question looked like shit, but the joint fit right in with the rest of the neighborhood. All the buildings were beat-up frame houses, or boarded up store-fronts, with peeling paint. Sidewalks were cracked and buckled by crazed tree roots. Metal bars covered all the windows, like anyone in their right mind would want to steal the worthless crap stored behind the smog-stained walls.

My watch showed 9:30. I grabbed my duffle and walked up to the front door. I knocked and glanced around. Nobody stuck a head out of a neighbor's window, or seemed to care that I was standing on the front porch, so I popped the front door lock using an old credit card.

I ducked into a dark room and closed the door behind me.

I couldn't remember if Pinky had said if anyone lived in the house so I stood and listened for a few seconds.

I called, "Hello, anybody here?"

No answer.

Along the far wall stood a couch and chair covered with clear plastic. The carpet looked and smelled worse than the men's can at the Old Globe saloon, and the walls were at least fifteen years past their painting due-date. Down the hall I found the bathroom and let go of the Mojave coffee I'd been carrying around through all the traffic-choked freeways.

Next to the bathroom, I spotted a small bedroom with a single bed. I tossed my duffle onto the floor and lay down. For a second I thought about checking out the office, but I had driven all night, and my eyelids had other ideas. Just before I fell asleep, I smiled for the first time since Pinky had handed me the seven hundred. "Guess what, you cheap, bastard, lawyer, I just checked into the poor man's Motel Six!"

NINE

Bear—Los Angeles, California

Buzz.

I lifted my head and opened one eye.

Buzzzzzz.

There it was again. I sat up, feeling like shit. I couldn't figure out what that noise was. Then it hit me. Someone was at the front door, and they were leaning on the doorbell. I jumped up. My right foot clipped my duffle and the next thing I knew my elbow hit the floor.

Buzzzzzzzz. Buzzzzzzzzzz. Buzzzzzzzzzzzz.

Jesus Christ, get your thumb off the buzzer. I'm moving as fast as I can. I limped into the living room, rubbing my right elbow. I peered around the edge of the front window. A woman stood there with her finger poised over the door buzzer, but this wasn't just any female, she was a real woman. My eyes settled on her chest and that's when I forgot all about my elbow. The broad had the best set of knockers this side of my favorite Playmate, Miss August. My mouth dropped open. She was, without a doubt, a woman who'd been born for a single reason, to comfort a man. And as I gave her a second going over, the rest of her wasn't all that bad.

Buzzzzzzzzzzzzzzzzzzzzzzzzz.

I ran a hand through my hair and opened the door.

"Hi, I'm the next door neighbor. I just got back from the store and didn't recognize the car parked out front, but then I noticed that the car had a Nevada license plate, so I figured you must know Clark's brother, Bill. Am I right? Tell me I'm right because I'd feel pretty stupid standing here talking with a stranger if I was wrong. Are you a friend of Bill's?

The bright sun behind her head made my eyes all squinty. I didn't have a clue what the hell she was going on

45

about, but I nodded anyway.

"Good, I thought so. Do you have any idea what's happened to Clark's son, Richard? That boy left here a couple of days ago in a fancy, brand new car. God knows where he got the money for a car like that. Anyway, he drove away, and I haven't seen hide nor hair of him since. I warned Clark that he was spoiling that boy, paying his way for college and all. Tell me, would you ever send an ungrateful child to college?"

The words flew out of her mouth faster than I could walk them into my ears. While I shook my head, the woman pushed past me into the living room and plopped her cushy, well-formed butt onto the plastic-covered couch.

"See, I thought so. Kids nowadays are never satisfied. Wasn't it terrible, Clark dying that way? I mean an oak tree! But you never know. My mother always told me to wear clean underwear every day because you never know when something bad is going to happen to you. Can you imagine, me lying on a gurney in an emergency room with soiled underwear? That's the reason I won't wear a pair of nylons with a run. But I wasn't worried about Clark. His underwear was in great shape. Ever since Clark's wife died, I've helped him out with things around the house. The poor man always had so much to do, and so little time. That's exactly what he used to say to me. Flo—actually my full name is Florence, but Clark called me Flo—he'd say, Flo, in this life you'll always have too much to do and not enough time to do it. That's pretty profound, considering what happened when that oak tree fell on him, don't you think? By the way, my name is Flo. What's yours?"

I closed the front door and sat down on the chair next to her. We were around the same age, and I was sure that she was making a move on me. My Johnson twitched, and that was hard to believe because this broad, great tits and all, had one of the worst cases of mouth diarrhea on record.

"Name's Bear."

She sat up straight. "Bear, what kind of a name is that?"

"My mom and pop named me Benate. In the Basque

language, Benate means Bear."

"Basque? What's that?" She frowned, "You're not some kind of an Arab are you?"

What a dip. I shook my head. "My pop, Gotzon Zabarte, was born in the mountains between France and Spain. Somehow he ended up in Nevada. Like a lot of the Basque men, he became a sheepherder. Then he met my mom, Alona. She was the head cook at The Star Hotel in Elko. They got married and here I am."

Flo patted the couch, like she was asking me to sit by her. "That's a good story, Bear. Now, what are you doing in LA, and how long will you be here? If it's a lengthy stay, I'd be happy to do your laundry."

I'll bet she'd do more than my laundry, I thought, if I gave her half a chance.

At least now I knew the name of the man who owned this house, and that he was dead. And the dead guy had a son named Richard. And Richard drove off in a sports car and never came back. And the dead guy had a brother who lived somewhere in Nevada. And the brother's name was Bill. I'd bet fifty bucks that the somewhere in Nevada was Eureka, and the murdered guy was Bill, and Richard was Pinky's new client. Not bad for keeping your mouth shut and nodding your head. I wondered what else she could help me with. "Flo, I'm here to . . . . sort of . . . . like clean up a few business problems concerning your friend Clark's death. I'd like to hear your side of the story."

She jumped up and headed down the hall. "Come with me. I'll fix us a cup of coffee, and then tell you everything I know."

I watched her walk away, concentrating on the cheeks of her ass as they jumped around like a gunnysack full of baby panthers. If Flo knew her way to the kitchen, she'd know her way to the bedroom.

I checked my watch. It was two thirty. I still had three hours before I had to send my first Fax to Pinky. Hell, there was no doubt. This broad was hot and ready to trot. I might pick up more information, and get lucky too. I licked my lips. "Flo, that's the best offer I've had this afternoon."

47

TEN

Pinky—Carson City, Nevada

George Sterling's trembling hand grabbed my arm. "Pinky, do I have a prayer of beating this rap?"

I glanced at my watch and saw that there was no way I could make it back to the office in time to catch Bear's phone call. I shook my head. "It doesn't look good."

George was my one and only genuine pro bono client, and as such, he was worth his weight in gold. I looked into his wasted eyes. The whites were murky and dotted with tiny yellow globs of scrambled egg. His blowzy nose was pocked and littered with scaly skin. George's right hand slipped off my arm and clutched the front of his sweater in a futile attempt to dampen the tremble.

"George, this was not your first DUI. So far you've been lucky. You haven't hit, hurt, or killed anyone, but I'm afraid that your days of driving a car are over until you kick the booze. I'm going to ask the judge to suspend your driver's license, and turn it over to me. I'll put the document in my office safe, and return your license, if and when the judge decides you're ready to drive again. In the future, when you feel the urge to drink yourself to death, call a cab. They'll happily drop off a couple of cases of Vodka and you can complete the task inside the safety of your apartment."

George started to blubber softly. I had known him before he began his precipitous slide to an alcoholic oblivion. At one time, George Sterling had been a respected pit boss at the Nugget. He lost that job after he had been caught running a scam with a blonde Blackjack dealer. Then George turned into a full-blown alcoholic who was going to kill himself or someone else with his drinking. I shuddered at the thought of how many times he'd recklessly driven his old Buick through the streets of Carson City.

"George, we have a court date tomorrow morning. At

48

that time I'll inform the judge that you are willing to give up your right to drive. I'm sure he'll take that as an act of contrition and show you some leniency."

I was confident that as long as the court held me responsible for George's drivers license, I could claim him as an active pro bono client. Why did I need at least one pro bono client? Because pro bono work perpetuated the myth that attorneys are true humanitarians.

But my solitary pro bono client didn't look very healthy. I knew that once he passed on to that big distillery in the sky, I would have to discover a new George—a pro bono client who would take no more than a few minutes of my time each month. Trust me, clients like that are hard to find.

I left the jail and I walked back to my office. It was nearly six by the time I unlocked the door. The first thing I noticed was that Mabel's chair was empty, and a note had been placed in the exact center of her desk requesting that I call her as soon as I came in.

Mabel was in her mid-fifties—never married and seemed firmly determined to remain that way. She guarded my gate as fiercely as a fire-breathing dragon. Her devotion and diligence allowed me to come and go at will. She was usually sitting behind her desk when I arrived in the morning, and was still there when I left for a libation at the Old Globe each evening.

I walked past Mabel's desk into my office, sat down, and dialed her home number. Mabel must have been hovering over the phone because she answered on the first ring.

"Pinky, I have to take three weeks of vacation. I'm sorry about the short notice, but I catch a plane at the Reno Airport tomorrow morning at seven."

Her statement stunned me. Last year, I damn near had to force Mabel to use up her three weeks of vacation a day at a time. To the best of my recollection, she had never been out of the office for more than two days at a stretch.

"Mabel, what's going on?"

"Nothing, really. A distant relative is undergoing major surgery and I told her I'd come to help her recuperate.

She lives in Montana, that's why I need the three weeks."

Over the past ten years, Mabel had never once mentioned any family. Not a brother, or sister, or anyone. Now she was going to fly off to Montana for three weeks to help a distant relative? I didn't want to make her feel uncomfortable, but there had to be more to this story. "Montana? Where in Montana? Billings, Helena, Great Falls, Butte?"

She hesitated. "I'm not sure. I know this all happened very fast, but my airline ticket is to Helena. My relative said she'd meet me at the airport. I'll send you a note from my new place so you can mail me my check."

"You don't know where you're going, but you're willing to spend three weeks there? Mabel, that doesn't make any sense to me."

Her voice sounded tight. "That's right . . . . Three weeks . . . . I'll drop you a note."

Something was wrong here. Mabel was the least adventuresome person I knew. To her, an evening of madness was renewing her year's subscription to TV Guide.

"Mabel, level with me. Did I do, or say something that upset you?"

She paused. "No, Pinky, you didn't do anything wrong. I just think that this vacation is in my best interests."

I tried to think of something I could say that would bring some reason into this conversation. If Mabel had left me, who'd open the office each day? Answer the phones? Make my . . . . then her last statement sunk in. "What do you mean, in your best interests? You don't even know where you're going. How could that be?"

"I've already said more that I should. Good bye."

What the hell was going on? I walked back to Mabel's workstation, sat down and looked over her desk. As usual, the wood was spotless and smelled of the lemon polish she used each afternoon before she closed up the office. Her wastebasket was empty. The area was not only clean, but also as sterile as if she had never worked here. That was when I realized that the picture of her cat was missing from the prime position of honor behind her phone. At least once each week she would bore me with the latest adventures of

50

the feline, a furry ball of white with the name of Fluffy or Puffy, or something like that.

I didn't then, and still don't own a cat, so I found it hard to comprehend Mabel's devotion toward that animal, but love it she did. If her stories were to be believed, the vet bills for that white ball of fluff exceeded the medical expenses of a family of four.

But why would Mabel take the picture if she were only going to be gone three weeks? And where would Fluffy or Puffy live while she nursed someone back to health in Montana? I considered calling her back to ask those questions, but her final words, "I've already said more that I should", stopped me.

Wake up and smell the coffee, Pinky. Mabel's a grown woman. Perhaps she's found her knight-in-shining armor, or needs a change of scenery. Or maybe she has decided I'm not paying her enough. Who knows these days?

I returned to my office and saw a single sheet waiting for me in the incoming bin of the Fax terminal. At least I could count on the Bear.

Pinky:
Arrived in LA this morning. Crapped out after driving all night till nearly five. Haven't checked out the office yet. Will get on it first thing tomorrow morning. Motels are more expensive than you thought. Had extra expenses getting this typed up and Faxed. I'll need more money by Bakersfield. My guess is it will cost you an extra five hundred. I'll let you know where to send the cash when I get to Bakersfield.
Bear

ELEVEN

Bear—Los Angeles, California

The kick-ass smell of bacon frying in the kitchen woke me up. I rolled over and the other side of the bed was empty. I got up and yelled down the hall, "Flo, are you fixing breakfast?"

"Bacon, eggs, toast, and coffee. Everything a strong man like you needs to keep his energy up."

I grinned. After a full yesterday afternoon, and never-ending last night, my energy wasn't the only thing I was worried about keeping up. I threw on some shorts and followed my nose to the kitchen. Flo looked damn good standing at the stove in that old blue robe. I reached around, gave her big boobs a squeeze, and kissed her neck; she smelled good, almost as good as the bacon.

She pulled away and said, "Sit down, or your breakfast will get cold."

I felt like taking her robe off and doing it right there, next to the hot stove, but my plate of bacon and eggs looked like a billboard picture for a Denny's Grand Slam Breakfast. I gave her giant mam's a final tweak and sat down. Damn, this woman could cook. While I tossed down breakfast, I reminded myself that this broad did laundry, was great in bed, and cooked. What more could a real man ask for?

"Bear, when we finish breakfast, I'm going to the store and pick up a few things. While you were sleeping I went through your suitcase. You are in desperate need of new underwear and socks. I noticed that some of your socks have small holes in the toes, and the condition of your underwear is deplorable. Is there anything you can think of besides underwear and socks? I know you didn't ask me to do this for you, but experience has taught me that most men need a woman to look after them. I can guarantee that if taking care of you was my full time job, you would never find another hole in your socks or wear shabby shorts again—like that threadbare pair you're wearing now."

Did she just say that she went through my suitcase while I was sleeping? Jesus Christ, this broad was ready to take over my life!

I threw my fork down. "Flo, we have to talk. Baby, you're great in bed. And you cook a cool breakfast. But you've got to learn to leave my stuff alone. And stop telling me what to do, like buying new socks. What makes you think I don't like socks with holes in the toe! God damn it, woman, I live the way I do 'cause I like it that way."

I took two pieces of bacon and stuffed them into my mouth as Flo's face got all scrunched. Her eyes sort of clouded up, and she started to cry. "I'm sorry, Bear. I was only trying to help."

Damn, I hated to see a woman cry, and I sure as hell didn't want to kill off the golden goose before I got my hands on all the eggs. I jumped up, wrapped my arms around her, and kissed that soft, nice smelling part of her neck underneath her ear.

I said, "Hey, I'm sorry. After you get to know me, you'll know that I'm a grouchy bastard 'til I down my second cup of coffee. I know you're just trying to help!"

Flo's water works dried up faster than the Truckee River that disappeared into the desert sink east of Reno.

She said, "Good. You finish your coffee. I'm going shopping. Later, after you let me see you in your new underwear, we might find the time to engage in a little afternoon delight."

She kissed my forehead and left the house.

There was no doubt in my mind that Flo was a woman to be reckoned with. She knew what I liked. She had a bucket-full of good things going for her, but that motor mouth and her need to dig through my stuff was a big problem.

She left to shop, while I finished my second cup of coffee. Then I started to nose around the house. As Pinky had told me, the office door was locked, and it took ten seconds longer to break into the office than the front door. Stepping into the office was like going from mom and pop's old black-and-white to a color TV. I stopped for a second and scoped the place. A really cool desk sat across the room, but what really caught my eye was the nearly full bottle of whiskey sitting on a shelf behind the desk. I headed to the booze and found out it was a Glenmorangie 18, one of the world's kick-ass whiskeys.

At the Old Globe, the boss had a bottle of Glenmo-rangie 18 on the back shelf for the giant-pain-in-the-ass leader of the State Senate. The stuff cost ninety bucks a bottle wholesale, and our distributor had to ship the damn thing all the way from England. One day, when the bar was empty and the boss was away, I took a sip and let me tell you, that shit was something special.

Now I sat in an empty office, in the middle of a crappy old house, surrounded by a run-down neighborhood. I held a bottle of the world's best whiskey, and it was all mine. God damn, this was a funny world! On a hunch, I opened the cabinet door below the bottle and damn near passed out. There was a whole case of Glenmorangie 18 lying on its side—with one empty slot, and eleven unopened bottles of the world's best just waiting for the Bear. I sat down and poured myself a glass. I took a gulp, and opened the middle drawer of the desk. In the drawer sat the box that Pinky told me to carry unopened, to his office in Carson City. I took a second gulp and opened the box. Holy shit! Out popped a huge pile of Franklins! I emptied the glass and counted the cash. The total came to $121,900. Jesus, I was in deep shit. I was pretty sure that Pinky didn't know how much was there. He was just jerking my chain and I could pocket half the wad. Or I could close the damn box and de-liver it, with all the cash inside, to Pinky's office. Or I could take the cash, and Flo, and run to Mexico. The only thing I was completely sure of was that I didn't have to decide right now. I carried the cash, along with the case of Glenmo-rangie 18, to my car trunk and covered everything with a blanket.

TWELVE

Pinky—Carson City, Nevada

Eventually it sunk in that Mabel leaving suddenly wasn't my only problem. I have a busy law practice to run, and I needed someone to cover my office while I was gone, which was most of the time.

The first thing the next morning, I called a local temp agency and explained that I needed a quick replacement.

A man's voice responded, "I'll have someone at your office by ten, Mr. Delmont."

"Look, you'll have to do better than that. I'm due in court in forty-five minutes."

"Let me see. Oh, I see your office is just around the corner. I'll send you someone immediately. She'll be there in thirty minutes, or our name isn't Rapid Replacement."

I checked my voice mail and was jotting down a few notes when I suddenly remembered that Mabel had a voice mailbox. I called the number, and when the recorded voice asked me for Mabel's pin number, I punched in the name of her cat, Fluffy. That didn't work so I tried Puffy and got through. Mabel had no voice messages.

I walked to Mabel's desk and opened the drawers. All empty. Even her can of Lemon Pledge was gone. That, plus the missing picture of Fluffy or Puffy clinched it. For some inexplicable reason Mabel had left, and it looked to me like she wasn't coming back.

A general feeling of unease settled on me. Was it possible that something, or someone had frightened Mabel? I had practiced law in Carson City for fifteen years. During that time, I had received numerous threats from those clients who felt that I had failed them, but until today, no employee had ever left without any notice.

Pinky, I thought to myself, stop being such an egotistical bastard. You've jumped to the conclusion that the only

55

reason Mabel would disappear would have to do with you and your legal practice. Could it be possible that my portly, fifty-plus, cat-loving secretary lived a secret life outside the walls of my office? Perhaps Mabel was a closet, black latex-clad dominatrix.

A glance at the clock forced me to switch my attention from Mabel's possible activities to the lack of my daily appointment schedule—an easily understood piece of paper that she handed me each morning. Over the past seven years, through some sort of computer printer alchemy, Mabel had created my schedule, and without that piece of paper, I was as lost as a blind man in the Antarctic.

I turned Mabel's computer on and spent a few fruitless minutes trying to decipher where I was supposed to go after my court date with George Sterling. I was lost in my thoughts when the front door opened and in walked a young female with orange spiky hair and a diamond stud gracing the side of her right nostril. I groaned inwardly and wondered how many tattoos lay hidden beneath her bright orange blouse.

She nodded. "Good morning, Mr. Delmont. My name is Loretta Evans. You can call me Lottie. I'm your temporary. I get a twenty minute break each morning and afternoon, and an hour off for lunch. You don't pay me directly. Each day you'll sign my time sheet and Rapid Replacement will bill you at the end of each week."

Before I could open my mouth, Lottie walked around the desk, looked over my shoulder, and said, "Could you use some assistance with your daily calendar program?"

I controlled my initial impulse to plant a kiss on the tip of her diamond-studded nose and said, "Yes. I require a printout of my appointments for the day. I'm due in court in a few minutes, and I needed my schedule five minutes ago."

"No problem."

She hit a couple of keys and the printer started to push out a piece of paper. I grabbed it. Like magic, this weirdly dressed female had produced my schedule for the day—so much for first impressions. I scanned my day and said, "Perfect."

As I stepped toward the door, I absently went through my usual last minute routine. I checked to be sure my wallet was tucked in my right rear pocket. My car keys were in my left pocket, my cell phone was in my jacket pocket . . . . wait, it's not there. Damn, last night I gave the instrument to Bear. "Lottie, somewhere around here, I don't know exactly where, Mabel hid two extra cell phones. All I know is that they're plugged into a charger because I forget to charge my phone at the end of each day."

She spun her chair around, and opened the cabinet door behind Mabel's desk. "I found them, Mr. Delmont."

She handed me one as I headed to the door.

I said, "Lottie, you're wonderful. I'll return around—"

She glanced at her computer monitor. "According to the screen, you'll be back around four. Have a good day, Mr. Delmont."

As I walked toward the courtroom, I looked skyward to acknowledged a fortunate streak of outstanding luck.

THIRTEEN

Bear—Los Angeles, California

With the whiskey safely tucked away in my car trunk, I walked back to the office, sat down at the desk, and pulled out Pinky's list.

1. Investigate a non-profit organization called SOS, or Save-One-Sinner.
2. The size of the foundation.
3. Annual income.
4. Bank accounts and balances.
5. Branch offices.
6. Number of employees.
7. Check phone recorder messages.

Jesus, where was I going to come up with all that crap? I opened the top drawer, and except for the missing moneybox, it was empty. The drawer on my right was filled with personal bank statements for a guy named Herbert Clark Hoover Page. Jesus Christ, that moniker made Benate Zabarte sound damn good. Weird name and all, the poor bastard didn't have a pot to piss in. His statements showed a deposit each month of fifteen hundred bucks, and by the end of every month, his balance was near zip.

I took a sip of the booze, and opened the left drawer. Son-of-a-bitch! There were five years of Save-One-Sinner Foundation bank statements neatly filed by year. I laid out the last three years of statements.

While I nipped at the good shit, I noticed that each January, a check for $450,000 plus was written to the S-O-S Italian branch. Each month the foundation sent a check to Herbert Clark Hoover Page for fifteen hundred along with an occasional thousand dollar check made out to Herbert Clark Hoover Page for petty cash.

The real kicker came toward the end of each year. The October statement showed a deposit of $500,000 followed in

58

few days with a check drawn for $250,000 and sent to William Howard Taft Page.

Each year the pattern was the same. Twice a year, the foundation would receive a deposit for around a half a million. A few days after the big deposit, a check for half that amount would go to William Howard Taft Page. Every February, a check was sent to Italy for most of the balance and the rest of the account was emptied through "petty cash" or monthly checks to Herbert Clark Hoover Page. As far as I could see, the work of S-O-S Foundation consisted of no more than a way to move money from one pocket to another and with a shit-pot of bucks ending up in Italy.

I heard the key slip into the front door lock. The door opened and Flo yelled, "I'm home. Where are you? Just wait 'til you see your new socks."

I jumped up, downed the rest of my drink, and closed the office door just before Flo rounded the hall corner.

She smiled. "There you are. Come into the bedroom. After you model your new underwear, who knows what might happen."

An hour later, with both of us sweating like pigs, I rolled off her and stared at the ceiling. "Flo, you have more moves than Elvis in his prime."

"Thanks, you're pretty good yourself. I'd better get up and start dinner."

"Slow down and talk to me for a minute. Tell me a little about Clark. Was his full name actually Herbert Clark Hoover Page?"

Flo lay back. Her massive boobs flattened out and sort of slid down her sides. "Yes, that was his full name, but I never heard anyone call him Herbert. He was always Clark to me. Why?"

"And what about his brother, Bill? Was his full name William Howard Taft Page?"

"I don't know." She pulled away. "Why are you asking me these questions? I thought you said you were Bill's friend from Nevada, and you were in LA to clear up some business concerning Clark's death?"

"I'll confess that I'm not a friend of Bill's. In fact I

never met the bastard. But I was telling you the truth about the business concerning Clark's death. I'm just trying to understand why he didn't use his first name, that's all."

She snorted. "And these questions comes from a man who answers to the name of Bear?"

I could tell that I was losing ground fast. I needed what Flo knew about this operation almost as much as I wanted to bury my head between her tits. I kissed her gently. "Flo, I'm sorry about the little misunderstanding concerning Bill. What do you say we take a shower and then we'll go out to dinner? My treat. Any place you want to go."

Her face lit up and she jumped out of bed. "You're a devil. The shower's a great idea, but if we're going to make dinner, you better not try to play drop the soap."

After a very long shower, we sat down at a small table toward the back of Flo's favorite steak joint. A blonde broad with a big ass took our steak order. Flo told me they had a great house red so I asked for a liter. The wine turned out to be some real crap that tasted like grape Kool-Aid laced with Everclear. Flo touched my glass and we sort of romantically sipped the wine. Actually, I sipped; Flo slugged down two full glasses before I finished a half of one. I had hardly buttered my bread when the waitress delivered our first course—a salad with rusty edged lettuce and a tiny sliver of an almost-ripe tomato. The greens were buried under a thick glob that looked, and tasted like wallpaper paste.

All my friends knew I could tell good food from bad. When I grew up, my Mom ran the kitchen at the White Star Hotel in Elko. Later, after I left home, most of the jerks I hung with bitched that they missed their mom's cooking. In my case, that was a real gripe. Every day my mother would feed me fresh, well-prepared food. She taught me what was good wine. Yeah, I've heard all that bullshit that kids shouldn't drink wine, and that's what it is, pure bullshit. I know that I'm not what Pinky would call a gourmet, but I sure-as-hell knew the difference between good and bad restaurant food.

I almost picked up the gooey salad and threw it at the big-assed blond, but I was afraid that would piss-off Flo.

60

Keeping her happy was why I was eating in this dive, so I pushed my fork around the salad plate.

Flo, who was sucking up her fourth glass of wine, said, "I never called Clark anything but Clark, but there was something about that man, like he was a big jigsaw puzzle with a couple of pieces missing. I know his wife died, and he had a whiny prick of a son, but Clark always seemed to be holding something back, like he was better than me. You know what I mean?"

I grabbed the wine carafe. Flo set her glass on the table for a refill. I filled her glass and handed the empty carafe to the waitress. She nodded. I didn't want to make Flo drunk, but I didn't want to run out of the lubricant before she spilled her guts concerning her old neighborhood lover.

I smiled at Flo. "Yeah, I know what you mean." I really didn't know what she meant, but Flo's train was finally rolling down the track, and my only job was to keep the damn wheels greased.

"Bear, that's the difference between you and Clark. You've been completely honest with me."

Jesus, I thought. What a dip! "Flo, give me an example of a time Clark was dishonest."

"Each year, Clark would go to Italy. He'd be gone five to six months. When he'd come home, I'd ask him what he did there. He'd feed me some bull shit about expanding his foundation. I mean what did he have to expand? As far as I could see, the whole foundation thing was nothing more than a tax scam. Tell me, did you ever hear of SOS?"

I shook my head as the waitress delivered a full carafe and our steaks.

Flo slammed her glass on the table. As I filled it she said, "See, that's what I mean about you, Bear. You're an honest man. You didn't try and bullshit me. Anyway, you've seen how Clark lived. There isn't anything in that whole house worth more than a hundred bucks."

She took a big swig.

I took a bite of my plate-sized T-bone. Jesus, the steak had been tenderized to death. The surface was mushy, and the interior was as tough as an old tennis shoe. I glanced at

61

Flo and guessed that she had better slow down on the vino and eat something or I'd be carrying her back to the car.

I said, "Flo, you're right, this place does a great job with a steak. Mine is juicy and tender. Just as good as my mother served at her hotel. How's yours? Is it as tender as mine?"

Flo set her glass down and poked her fork at her steak. After a couple of seconds, she took another gulp of wine. "And that son-of-a-bitch never asked me to go with him to Italy. And when he came back, Clark was tanned, well fed, and happy. We both know that a real man can't go more than a few days without sex and look happy. So you can understand why I was sure he was holding something important back."

I nodded. "What about Bill, Clark's brother?"

She drained her glass and shoved it toward me. I filled it and pushed the breadbasket in her direction while I tried cutting a different corner of my pound slab of leather.

Flo ignored the bread and concentrated on her wine. "Bill? I only met him twice. The first time was at Norma's funeral. Norma was Clark's wife. Bill seemed like a nice guy. He was a few years younger than Clark. About the same build, but Clark was better looking. Bill told me that he used to live in California, but he moved to Nevada, near a town called Eureka. I told him that living in Nevada sounded very glamorous. He laughed and told me that Eureka was an old mining town, and far from glamorous. The only other time we met was the day of Clark's funeral. That time Bill looked bad, but I didn't think his poor condition was because of sympathy for his dead brother. No, he didn't look sad, he looked scared. Once, at the cemetery, he nearly jumped out of his shoes when someone slammed a car door. What's your interest in Bill? Are you from his town?"

I laughed. "No, Eureka's too small for me."

"So where do you live? Reno? Las Vegas?"

"Neither. I come from Carson City. We have a few casinos in town, but the main business is government business. Carson City is the capital of Nevada."

"Are you sure about that? I'm pretty sure that Vegas is the capital of Nevada." She waved her glass around in the air. "Do you like this place? I know the owner. Well I knew the owner, before he got married. What do you think about the house wine?"

I hesitated, and that was enough to tell Flo my opinion.

"So, the big Bear is a wine snob. Frankly, I don't give a shit what you think. I like their house red." Flo stuck her tongue out at me—then her eyes closed, and all the air went out of her balloon. Her head drooped and then started toward the table.

I grabbed her chin just before her nose hit her steak. I waved at the waitress. "The check please, and a doggy bag for the lady's meat."

Jesus, what a dip!

FOURTEEN

Pinky—Carson City, Nevada

"Pinky, the judge just took my license away and I don't think he's going to give it back." George turned his head toward me, his eyes tightened to a narrow squint. "Don't he understand? I can't drive my car without a driver's license."

Poor old George had destroyed so many brain cells that he didn't remember what we had discussed yesterday. "George, we've gone over this scenario more than once. You had two choices; give up your driver's license or go to jail."

George shook his head so hard that a couple of drops of drool flew from his slack jaw and landed on my briefcase. "No jail, Pinky. I'd die in there."

I pulled a fresh handkerchief from my breast pocket and wiped the offensive matter from my hand-tooled brief-case. "And that's why you surrendered your driver's license."

"Oh!"

Before I closed my briefcase, I glanced at my schedule and saw that I was to meet with Julie Campbell in fifteen minutes. "Here's ten dollars so you can take a cab home. Sell your car, and don't, and I mean don't ever climb behind the wheel again."

I gave an appreciative nod to the judge and walked out of the courtroom. I had seen a snippet of Julie Campbell on the videotape when she talked with Richard, and from that fleeting view of her on the small screen, I decided that she was a comely lass.

Ten minutes later I knocked on her motel room door. The moment it opened I knew I had been correct in my brief assessment—Julie was a very attractive female.

"I'm J. Pincus Delmont, Richard's attorney. May I come in?"

"Please do, Mr. Delmont." She stood aside and gestured toward a small table with two chairs by the window. "The room is small, but I guess all motel rooms are small. Now, what did you want to talk to me about?"

I sat down, opened my briefcase, and pulled out my notes from Richard's interview. "Miss Campbell, please call me Pinky."

"I will if you'll call me Julie." She smiled.

Besides her pretty face, the young woman had a shapely body, but she concealed most of her curves beneath a long paisley skirt and a coarsely knit rust colored sweater. Her hair was brown and braided in a hippie style that became passé thirty years ago.

I said, "Julie, I've talked at length with Richard about your visit to his uncle's ranch. I'd like to hear your version of the story."

"Pinky, before I say anything, you need to know that the moment you entered the room I felt the universe come together. I understand you're here to discuss a death, the death of Richard's uncle, but your vibes and the strong aura emanating from you informs me I can trust you."

Often my name brought a chuckle, but never before had I been complimented concerning my ability to unify the universe, or the glowing aura that leaked from every pore. I was rapidly adjusting my take on Richard's girl friend— nice body, but perhaps too many puffs of the wild weed of Humboldt County. I turned on my recorder. "Thank you, Julie. Now tell me about your trip to the ranch."

She sat down. For a moment Julie stared blankly out the window at the near-empty parking lot below.

I cleared my throat.

She jumped slightly, as if she was surprised to find me sitting across from her.

She smiled and played with the end of one of her braids. Then her right hand edged toward a large bag at her feet, but she stopped and moved her hand to her lap.

Julie said, "It's been a weird few days. I grew up in Arcata, California, no more than a couple of blocks from the little house Richard and I live in. My dad works at Humboldt State, my mom at the Co-op. I still work with my mom

65

part time. So when Richard wired me the money to fly from Humboldt County to the San Francisco Airport, I was excited, but to tell the truth, I was scared. To me, downtown Arcata is a big city, so going to San Francisco was something else. I told Richard when and where I would be, and he picked me up in a really cool Beemer. He wouldn't tell me where he got the car, but I knew something had to be wrong, because in the two years we've lived together, I don't think Richard ever had more than five hundred dollars in the bank. Some months, if I hadn't liberated some food from the Co-op, we would have gone hungry."

She started to reach for the bag at her feet a second time, and stopped again.

Julie said, "Can I fix you a cup of coffee? The motel provides a coffee pot and the all makings."

I shook my head. "No thanks."

"It's okay, the maid will give me more coffee if I need it."

"No thanks."

Julie sat back and started to make little drumbeats on the table using her fingernails, as if she could hear some music playing in the otherwise silent room. She was nervous. She wanted something in her bag. But she didn't want me to know what was going on.

Julie said, "Anyway, we left the Airport sometime after I landed, which was around eleven, and drove straight through the night heading for his uncle's ranch. We got to this little town in Nevada around seven, stopped for breakfast, and then drove to the ranch. That's about the whole story."

There's got to be more to it than that, I thought. She jumped up and started to pace. Upon closer inspection, Julie's skirt looked threadbare, as if she had bought it twenty years ago, and had worn it every day. She threw her arms in the air and stretched. Her sweater was a bulky, loose knit cotton, and for a fraction of a second, I caught the outline of Julie's young, perky breasts. Come on, Pinky. Focus on the task!

I said, "What happened after you arrived at the

66

ranch?"

She considered the question, then grabbed her bag, rummaged through it, and pulled out a hand rolled cigarette. "Do you mind?"

I did mind, but I needed to hear her side of the story, so I said, "No, go ahead."

She lit up, and the pungent aroma that filled her room told me, and anyone walking on the balcony outside her window, that some powerful marijuana was being put away in room 23A.

Why did I care if Julie smoked pot? She was a virtual stranger to me, but she and her habit reminded me of my third wife. Beth was smart, beautiful and perfect in every way but for one tiny flaw. She smoked grass, lots of it. First, she'd only do one or two at night with me while I drank my gin and tonic before dinner. She told me that I had my form of escape, and she had hers. But within six months of our nuptials, she quit her high paying job to become an oil painter. She converted the spare bedroom into a studio and spent every day painting, but as far as I could tell, she never completed a canvas. Later I learned that all she did every day was smoke grass. When we agreed to dissolve our marriage, I stayed in Carson City while Beth decided to move to Alaska. A week after she left, I called her to wish her good luck in her new location, and Beth's response was a velvet slur. A few months after she moved north, Beth froze to death during the winter because she hadn't paid her utility bills. She had more than enough money in the bank; I think it was just too much trouble to write out a check.

That's why Julie's pot-centered life style bothered me. She took a second drag, exhaled and her agitation toward my question ceased, "What happened after we got to the ranch? Not much. Richard told me to wait. I waited. He came back in a couple of minutes and we drove back to the little town."

"Exactly how long are a couple of minutes?"

"One, no, two cuts from the Motley Crue CD, <u>Too Fast For Love</u>."

Julie took a drag, closed her blue eyes, and started to sing, if you called the noise she made singing, "Take me to the top and throw me off." She opened her eyes and smiled, "Don't you just love Nikki Sixx and Mick Mars?"

I feigned interest. "Yes, they're great. So you think you were alone in the car for about five minutes?"

Julie gazed at the parking lot again. "I guess so. Why? Is the amount of time I was in the car important?"

If she sat in a closed car, listening to a heavy metal CD, Richard could have exploded a stick of dynamite inside that house and she wouldn't have heard a damn thing.

I said, "It could be. After Richard returned to the car, what happened?"

She leaned back, and again a flash of Julie's soft skin peeked through the large gaps in her sweater. Even in her half-drugged state, she was quite delectable. I forced my gaze and my concentration back to my note pad.

She said, "He started the engine and we drove down the highway."

"Julie, how did Richard look to you when he returned to the car?"

"Fine, I guess." She leaned forward, took a final drag, and said, "What do you mean, how did he look?"

I shrugged. "Was he happy or grim? Was he agitated or calm? In other words, was he the same Richard you knew before he went into the ranch house or was he different?"

She looked perplexed, as if my explanation had created more mental confusion. I was afraid I was losing her to the weed when she perked up and said, "I guess he was the same. You need to know that Richard is a very quiet person. The whole time he drove from the airport to the ranch I listened to Motley Crue CD's. That sums up our relationship. Life was the same at our place in Arcata. Richard would read. I'd listen to CD's. Richard would meditate. I'd watch General Hospital on TV. Richard would study. I'd do a little pot. Can you get him out of jail soon? I want to go back home where I feel comfortable."

So Julie felt that Richard acted the same when he returned to the car. That didn't match my take on the man. If he had just shot his uncle, the Richard I knew would have displayed his nefarious deed on every pore of his face.

I said, "I'll do all I can, but murder is a capital crime. I'm afraid that without some new evidence, he'll remain locked up in jail. Now, let's get back to you and Richard. He told me he just graduated. How about you, Julie, what is your major at Humboldt State?"

"I don't have a major. I dropped out. As I said before, I work part time at the Co-op. It's a really big store in Arcata. Organic rice, grains, all the good stuff you should eat."

So Richard's Julie had youth, a pretty face, and an outstanding body underneath all that clothing, but she seemed lost in a seventies time warp. I hoped she could discover something she wanted to do with her life before the pot mellowed her brain into oblivion. "One final question. Did Richard stop for any reason before the police arrested him?"

"No, he didn't . . . Wait, we did stop after we left the ranch. Richard told me he had to pee. The only other time we stopped was when the cops pulled us over."

Aha! If I were going to ditch a murder weapon, the wasteland known as northeastern Nevada would be the perfect spot. Now we were getting somewhere.

"Julie, did you tell the police about the time you pulled over. Where Richard had to pee?"

"Yes."

So Willow either had the weapon and was keeping that information from me, or Julie's description was so vague that the police weren't looking in the right place.

"If we drove that road today could you find that exact spot again?"

She shook her head. "Don't think so. All the rocks look the same to me around here."

I sat back and stared out the window. She was right. That section of Nevada was so desolate that even the locals got lost now and then. Then I recalled Julie's unique way of measuring time during Richard's absence at the ranch. "Do you remember what song Motley Crue was playing when Richard stopped to pee?"

She flashed a child-like grin. "Yeah, it was the last cut, <u>Stick To Your Guns</u>." She started to sing again, "Take a look at yourself or your dreams—you're losing sight—it ain't right—it ain't right."

I said, "Julie, one last question. How fast do you think Richard drove his car?"

"That's easy. He told me a car that cool needed to go fast, so he'd always set the cruise control on eighty."

She started to sing again.

I blocked the musical drivel out of my mind and thought, Pinky, you could drive Julie to the ranch, set her CD on the correct song, and then drive eighty miles per hour until you reach the last cut. But that begs the obvious question—if you find the murder weapon, what will you do then?

FIFTEEN

Bear—Los Angeles, California

Flo was totally zonked. In fact, after I dumped her gorgeous body onto the bed, her snorts and grunts echoed down the hall to the office. I figured she would sleep it off while I finished Pinky's list. After I was done, I'd crawl in next to her, catch a couple of winks, have breakfast, kiss my sexy laundry-woman goodbye, and get my ass over the Grapevine to Bakersfield.

First I had to hope that Pinky wasn't out-of-his-mind pissed off at me for missing my Fax and telephone call deadline. It was nearly seven-thirty by the time I finished writing out my findings. This time I used the Fax in the office and made the phone call. With any luck he would be gone for the day, and I smiled when his voice mail answered. "Pinky, sorry I'm late, but you know how it goes; been working like a one-armed paper hanger since I got here. As you can see on my Fax, the SOS foundation has more holes than a piece of Swiss cheese. It's a tax scam if I ever saw one. As far as I can tell, the whole operation is a Herbert Clark Hoover Page one-man band. Can't find anything that showed how many sinners were saved, but each year around a million bucks ended up in various pockets. It turns out that one of those pockets belongs to a guy who lives in Nevada, outside of Eureka. He went by the name of William Howard Taft Page. My guess is that the Nevada connection is why you and I are involved. I have a couple of things to finish up here and then I head north to Bakersfield. I'll call you from the motel and give you the address so you can wire me five hundred more. Sorry about the high cost of living in California, but I don't set the prices. Call you tomorrow at five-thirty."

I sat back, poured myself a glass of the whiskey, and then hit the playback on the phone recorder. The first mes-

71

sage was a female voice, but I couldn't understand a word she said because she talked a weird language. The second message was the same broad. No English again, but this time I picked out what sounded like a first name, Maria. The last message was from the same broad. Whatever she said, I could tell that she was pissed off. I took the message tape out of the recorder and figured that I'd let Pinky figure out the damn thing. Shit, he's a college guy; let him translate that broad's . . .

"What the hell is this place?"

Flo's voice startled me and I damn near dropped my glass. "Jesus, Flo, you scared me half to death."

Flo walked into the office. From the confused look on her face, it was obvious that she had never been inside before. "Bear, just look at this place. The rest of the house is a pile of shit, but this room is—"

I set the glass down, walked toward Flo, and wrapped my arms around her. Her hair was all squished down on one side, but other than that, she seemed to be okay. Damn, she could throw down a bucket of wine and come back ticking, just like a Timex watch.

I said, "Hey Babe, nothing like a little snooze to perk you up."

"See, this is what I meant about that bastard Clark. Two months before that oak tree killed him, the son-of-a-bitch borrowed five hundred bucks off of me."

"Yeah, he was a dishonest bastard, all right. The son-of-a-bitch had lots of money. Look at these old checking accounts . . ."

Whoops! I slammed my trap shut, but it was too late. Pinky had told me that I was a dumb shit, and this was one of those times that he was right.

Flo pushed her soft body into me, but she wasn't trying to act sexy, this time she was pissed. "What do you mean, Clark had money?" She grabbed at the bank statement I held out of her reach. "Just how much money are you talking about?"

"Slow down, Flo. I'm working on undercover shit here. I can't let anyone outside my organization—not even you—

see these statements. They're confidential records."

She eased off an inch or two and snorted, "Under-cover? Undercover for who?"

"I can't tell you, but trust me, it's important."

She backed away.

I couldn't believe it. Flo fell for that line of bullshit. She thinks I work for the CIA, or the FBI. Big boobs and all, this broad was too gullible for her own good.

She pounded her fist on the fancy desk, and damn it, there came those tears again. "Clark owed me money, lots of it."

I considered her situation. Flo lived in a shitty neigh-borhood. She didn't seem to have a job, so a lot of money to her could mean anything from five bucks to five thousand. I said, "Did you give him money more than once?"

"You didn't listen to me, damn it. I didn't GIVE Clark money, I LOANED IT TO HIM." She turned toward the of-fice door. "You wait right here. I'll go home and get you the signed notes to prove it."

I listened to her footsteps fade away and the front door slam loudly.

By the time I'd finished the last of the Scotch, Flo had returned. She spread out a dozen pieces of paper on the desk. I looked at the top few and they all said the same thing:

'I owe Florence Sonderlund five hundred dollars.'

They were all signed and dated by Herbert Clark Hoo-ver Page. The latest one was dated three months ago. I counted the IOU's that scumbag signed and the total came to $11,500 spread out over a ten-year period. I didn't know what to do or say next. I could tell that she was about to blubber again. I was afraid that if I told her that all her money was gone, the dam would break.

I said, "Hey, your life's not in the crapper. I know an attorney. I'll see him in a couple of days and ask him what your rights are with these notes. It seems to me that you could have some kind of hold on Clark's estate."

Her crinkly look got better. "Clark had an estate? Are we both talking about the same Herbert Clark Hoover

Page? How much of an estate are you talking about? Do you think your attorney friend can really help me?"

"Hold on, I didn't say that attorney was a friend. In fact, I don't like the son-of-a-bitch, but he owes me a couple of favors."

I was really slinging the shit now, but once in a while, when a big glob of it hit the fan, even a Bear comes out clean. I looked at Flo. Her hair was still smashed against the side of her head. She had little wrinkles next to her eyes, and just a tiny bump of a second chin, but for some reason, in that light, she looked fine.

I said, "Do you think you can get away for a few days?"

Flo blinked. Her face was wet, red, and puffy. She nodded slowly.

I smiled. "Babe, we both know that I'm not the best catch in the ocean, but if you're willing, go home, pack your bag, and those IOU's. Tomorrow morning, after one of your kick-ass breakfasts, we're driving north to Bakersfield."

Flo took my hand and pulled me toward the bedroom. "Bear, I love you."

The next morning, after Flo cooked up another kick-ass breakfast, we left the land of smog and drove to Bakersfield.

SIXTEEN

Bear—Bakersfield, California

As I watched Traffic City fade in my rear view mirror, Flo bounced around the front seat like a kid on Christmas Eve. She giggled and punched my arm as the car rolled along Highway 5 through the brown hills of southern California.

When I pulled the car into the motel parking lot of The Oil Patch Inn, Flo planted a big, wet kiss on my cheek and said, "Bear, this is a pretty fancy place. Can you afford it?"

Flo had a great body, and she was good to be around most of the time, but she could be had for less than a Carson City politician.

I said, "We can do better than this dump, but when I saw that pool, I was pretty sure you'd like it. Remember I'm undercover, so I might register under any name. Don't say a thing when I check in."

She nodded and we walked into the lobby. The first thing I noticed was a pile of religious papers on the counter advertising a revival meeting down by the Kern River that evening. The guy behind the counter, a round, fat bastard, saw me staring at the ads and said, "Are you and your lovely wife part of that wonderful revival group?"

I didn't say anything, but I guess I nodded a little.

He pounded the counter. "Hallelujah brother, your organization is the best thing that's happen to this God forsaken town in ten years. I can only imagine how difficult it is to get people to accept salvation. Sir, I hope you will allow me to provide your room at no charge—a humble gift—my way of saying thank you Lord, and many thanks to you and your lovely wife."

So I signed in as Mr. and Mrs. Benate Zabarte.

When we returned to my car, Flo said, "It looked like you registered us as husband and wife."

"Remember? I'm undercover."

"Oh."

We walked into our motel room, and before a minute had passed, Flo took over my suitcase. While I tried to figure out where ESPN was on the TV, she had dumped all my clothes into drawers and spread out my toothbrush and all that other shit onto a shelf in the bathroom. This woman was a living, breathing nest builder!

Flo disappeared into the bathroom while I checked out the phone book for a listing on Theodore Roosevelt Page. Pinky had told me he was dead, but you never knew. Nothing! Then I recalled Pinky said this Page guy might be involved with oil. That made sense. Bakersfield was big in oil, but where do I start looking for a dead guy?

"What do you think, Bear? Do you like my new bathing suit?"

I looked up and Flo stood framed by the door. She had changed into a white bathing suit sort-of-thing, and her best parts nearly popped around the little hunks of cloth. I took a deep breath and a lot more than swimming jumped into my head.

I said, "You're a knockout, Flo. You go ahead. I have to finish some work first. Then I'll join you at the pool."

"Come on, Bear." She rubbed her giant boobs against my arm. "All work and no play makes for a very dull boy."

Boy? Did she just call me a boy? Jesus, this broad had a million ways to burn my ass. "Damn it, woman, I told you I'd be along in a minute. Don't look to piss me off!"

"All right, you go do your CIA, or FBI undercover work. I'll see if there is a good looking guy at the pool whose workday has ended."

She stomped out the door, and the room got quieter than a graveyard at midnight.

I opened the yellow pages to see how many oil companies there were in town. Shit, there were hundreds. Then I saw a paper sitting next to the phone. It advertised a new exhibit at the Kern County Museum.

Black Gold: The Oil Experience, A Permanent $4 Million

Damn. Flo could be a giant pain in the ass, but ever since she knocked on that front door, she'd been like my lucky charm. I read the flyer, and it said that the museum closed in thirty minutes. I ran down the stairs to the pool. Flo was lying in the sun, on her stomach. She had untied her bathing suit straps so she could tan her back. I yelled, "Flo, I'm going out. Be back before dinner."

Flo lifted her head, and scrunched her nose, like she had just caught a whiff of a ripe, refried bean fart.

She said, "Whatever."

I could tell that Flo was pissed, but I didn't care because I had to get to that museum pronto. Fifteen minutes later I walked into the Museum building and spotted a lady with a pile of gray hair, a wrinkly face, and a neck with more ridges than a pair of corduroy pants.

I said, "I wonder if you can help me track down a man who worked in the oil business, fifty, sixty years ago."

The prune looked at me. Her face was old, but her eyes had the shine of a young woman. "What's the name?"

"Theodore Roosevelt Page."

The woman sat back and grabbed a note pad. "That name doesn't ring a bell to me, but you need to ask the men who live at the Black Gold Home." She scribbled something on a paper, and said, "The house is a board and care facility where six old roustabouts live. We used a lot of their expertise to set up the exhibit here at the museum. One of those guys might help you."

I glanced at the note where she had written an address, thanked her, and turned to leave.

The wrinkled one said, "If it were me, I'd wait till morning. That's when their brains will be fresh."

"How old are they?"

"Late seventies to early nineties."

I nodded and headed back to the motel. Once I reached my room, I grabbed a piece of motel stationery, wrote out my report to Pinky, and closed with a desperate plea for the extra five hundred. Then I went to the front desk where a pretty clerk with small, but perky, young tits Faxed my note to Pinky.

My work done for the day, I returned to the room, put on my trunks, and joined my grouchy female friend by the pool.

SEVENTEEN

Pinky—Carson City, Nevada

After a nutritious breakfast of oatmeal and bran muffins, I called the court clerk's office on my cell phone. "Alex, this is Pinky. I need a favor."

"Hell, I owe you a bunch of them. What can I do?"

"I'm scheduled to appear at two preliminary hearings tomorrow morning and I'm afraid I'm going to come down with the stomach flu. Can you work out a continuance?"

"For you, Pinky, no problem. Will you recover from this pending attack the day after tomorrow, or do you foresee that your illness will linger longer?"

"No, the malady will be the twenty-four hour variety."

"Good, I'll call your office and give Mabel your new court date and time."

"Mabel's not with me anymore. My new girl is named Lottie."

"Sorry to hear that, I liked Mabel."

I did too, I thought. But Lottie had stepped in, vigorously picked up the slack, and now Mabel was but a distant memory. "Yes, she was a good employee, and I was sorry to see her go. Thank you, Alex."

A half-mile from my office, I called the motel. "Julie Campbell's room, please."

After two rings a female voice said, "Hello."

Julie's voice sounded soft, just like Beth after what she called a full night of super mellow. "Good morning , Julie, this is Pinky Delmont. You and I need to go to the scene of the crime. I'll stop by to pick you up at eight in the morning. Bring your walkman and your Motley Crue CD."

The morning fog that had covered Julie's vocal cords faded and her tone sounded anxious. "Are you talking about driving all the way to the ranch?"

"That is correct, so plan on a full day. It will take us

approximately three hours each way and we need to add a few hours so I have enough time to look around the ranch."

"Pinky, do you really need me? I don't like that place. There's no trees. It's nothing but brown dirt, sand and rocks out there."

I shuddered as I realized I'd be trapped in a car with her for a full day. She and her boy friend Richard had to be two of the whiniest clients I have dealt with in years.

Bringing my angst under control, I said, "Yes, Julie, you are a required participant on this trip so I can construct a proper defense for Richard. Or would you rather sit outside the execution chamber and watch the state pump him full of poison?"

"Huh? What do you mean, poison? I . . . Oh shit, I understand now. Okay, I'll see you around eight."

Damn, this woman was getting on my nerves. "No, Julie, not 'around' eight, but eight o'clock on the dot. That means that you'll have to get up early, like seven, so you'll have time to eat breakfast, brush your teeth, comb your hair, and be waiting for me in the parking lot when I pull in."

She hesitated. I almost wished she would tell me to go pound salt, or drop dead, or anything that would indicate to me that she wanted more out of life than sitting in a dingy Arcata house all day, watching TV and smoking pot.

But the reincarnation of my ex-wife didn't, or couldn't, muster up the courage to fight back. "Okay, Pinky, you win. I'll be standing in front of the motel office at eight."

I slipped the cell phone into my jacket pocket as I rolled the BMW 650i into my parking lot. When I strode through my office door, Lottie looked up and said, "Pinky, you just missed a phone call from a guy who wouldn't leave his number. He did leave you a verbal message. He told me to tell you that he thought you were smarter. I told him I didn't understand what he meant, and asked him to explain. He said Pinky should ask Mabel and hung up."

My brand new day was sliding down the hill. I'd spent the last twenty minutes arguing with a pot smoker, and now I was supposed to call Mabel? I did not even know where she was.

Frustrated, I said, "Lottie, tomorrow I'll spend all day driving to Eureka, to the scene of the murder at the Page ranch. Alex, the court clerk will call you with my new appointments."

She said, "What do you want me to do if something comes up here? Do you want me to try and reach you?"

"That's an excellent plan. I'll have my cell phone with me."

EIGHTEEN

Bear—Bakersfield, California

A few seconds after I stretched out next to Flo on the warm pool deck, she patted my butt. "Sorry I was a grouch earlier. I don't know what comes over me at times."

That made two of us!

Suddenly she propped herself on her elbows and flashed me a little peep show.

She said, "Did you finish all your undercover work?"

"No, we'll need to spend at least one more day. Why?"

"That's good. I've decided that I was born for the life of the rich and famous." She rolled from one side to the other, and kind of covered herself with the towel, but somehow Flo's boobs jumped through the folds. "Now I know how a famous movie star feels, lying by her pool all day, surrounded by her admirers."

Loose screws and all, this broad had a great body. The longer I stared at Flo, the harder Mr. Johnson got.

I glanced around the pool. There were a couple of kids playing in the water, a woman I'd bet a buck was their mom, and three guys laying near Flo, hoping she'd stand up before she covered up.

I said, "Let's head back to the room. It's getting crowded around here."

Flo wrapped a towel around her, got up, and flashed me a wicked grin. "You devil."

As we walked away, I saw the three horny bastards, the ones that had been near Flo, get up and move closer to the pool.

The next morning, after breakfast in the coffee shop, Flo headed back to her favorite spot and I drove to the address of the Black Gold Home. The building was a nice place on a hillside overlooking the town of Bakersfield. I rang the doorbell and an old man opened the door. "Mornin' young fella, what can I do for you?"

The old guy was bald, tall and as skinny as a fence post. The backs of his hands were covered with those dark purple spots that old people get from bumping into stuff.

I said, "I'm looking for some information on a man who worked in the oil business in Kern County back in the thirties and forties."

The old coot's eyes lit up. "You've come to the right place. My name's Harold Zeiss, and if I don't know the answer, then you can check with one of the other geezers. Let's grab us a cup of coffee in the kitchen."

He left the front door open and I followed him down the hall. "Thanks, Harold, I could use a cup."

Old Harold looked pretty spry to me for a guy that needed a good night's sleep to polish up his brain.

After I took a few steps, I passed a room with a big-screen TV, where five old farts were sitting around watching a football game. One of the guys had a Niner cap on; the other wore a Seahawk cap. The two wearing caps were arguing over something. The TV screen showed a zebra with his head lost in that damn replay-viewing thing. An old guy without a cap poked his bony elbow into my leg. "Young fella, tell me what you think about this instant replay invention."

"I hate it." I sat down next to the old coot. "And I don't know why the NFL decided to give it a try. As far as I'm concerned, pro football is a man's game, right?"

The old guy nodded.

I said, "We all know that a guy makes mistakes once in awhile, so if a referee screws up, just get over it. And to call that crappy idea instant replay is stupid. How long has that referee—"

Harold stuck his head around the corner. "Young fella, would you rather watch the game or get a cup of coffee?"

"Harold, this looks like a good game. What's the score?"

"If I remember correctly, twenty-eight to twenty-eight. In about ten minutes, the Niner's will win the game, thirty-one to twenty-eight when their kicker hits a fifty-yard field goal—"

"Hey," It hit me, "this is Monday morning. There's no live NFL game on TV now."

"You're right. This is a replay of yesterday's game. We have Tivo. We record each game and—"

"But, Harold, if the game's recorded, what are those two guys arguing about?"

"'Fraid they don't remember anything as recent as yesterday's football game. Now if you were to ask Paul, he's the one wearing the Niner's cap, where he worked in 1930, he'd tell you that he was part of the crew that drilled the deepest well in the world to that date." Harold squinted his eyes and said, "And if I remember correctly, that was the Standard Mascot #1. Damned impressive if I do say so. Paul punched a rotary bit 9,629 feet deep into the Midway-Sunset field."

I flashed Paul the thumbs up sign and said, "Way to go, Paul."

Paul stopped yelling for a minute, looked in my direction, nodded, and then started to argue again.

I said, "Harold, where's the coffee?"

We walked into the kitchen and there was a Latina woman standing at the stove. Harold nodded in her direction. "Maria, meet Mr—"

"Zabarte, but you can call me Bear."

Maria looked up from a bubbling pot that was cooking what looked to be about a twenty-pound hunk of beef or pork.

She said, "Buenos dias, señor."

Harold sat down and motioned toward a chair opposite him. He said, "Bear, that's an interesting name. But you wanted to know about a man who worked in Bakersfield sixty, seventy years ago. What's his name?"

"Theodore Roosevelt Page."

The wrinkles around Harold's eyes jumped like he'd been shocked by a car battery. "God damn, you're asking about the old Rough Rider. I hadn't thought about that old bastard for decades. Yes, I knew him. In fact, I worked for him in the forties and into the fifties. God damn it, they

84

don't make men like Page anymore. Of course, that might be a blessing, because if he was still alive, he'd own most of the land between LA and Fresno."

I said, "So Page was well off?"

"Well off? Are you kidding me? The old bastard was a multi-millionaire, and that was back in the days when being a millionaire meant something. Page was a magician at discovering the next field before the big guys got there. For example, he locked up a big hunk of land about a year before one of them college boys found the Ten Section field using some new fangled thing called seismic analysis. And when Standard moved into the Paloma and Coles Levee anticlines, Page was already there. They did all the drilling, but the Rough Rider took home the big bundle from that find."

Harold took a swig of his coffee and tilted his head toward the TV room. "Paul doesn't like me to bring this up, but in '43, I was part of the crew that took away Paul's record. We got down to 16,246 feet with the Standard 20-13 on the South Coles Levee. I'm proud to say that record stood 'til '53."

Harold knew some interesting shit, but I wished the old coot would stick to my question. "Did you know Page's family?"

"A little. I know he was married and had two kids, both boys. I remember that after the boys grew up the Rough Rider got pissed off at them for one reason or another. One son became some kind of a preacher. I don't know what happened to the other one, but I remember that Page didn't like it. Sometime in the sixties Page sold everything, and became a kind of hermit, sort of a Kern County Howard Hughes if you know what I mean. Some years ago I saw a notice in the paper that he died. I heard that he set up a trust so he could control what happened to his estate from the grave. Good for him! If I had big pile of money, and didn't get along with my sons, I'd do the same."

I had learned all I needed to know, so I pushed away from the table. "Harold, thanks for the coffee and the information, but I've got to move along."

"Hey, stick around for lunch. We don't get many visitors, and Maria makes the best beef enchiladas in the county."

I was tempted, but I had work to do, and an afternoon with Flo sounded even better than a plate of good Mexican food.

"No thanks."

I walked past the five men who were still watching yesterday's football game. The score was 28 to 28, and I considered picking up a quick ten bucks by betting Paul that his team would win the game on a field goal, but my heart wasn't in it.

I returned to my car, and before I turned the key, my skin crawled at the thought of those old farts sitting around the TV room. God damn it, I thought, I hope I don't live so long that I lose my marbles like those poor bastards.

I drove around Bakersfield until I found the county government buildings. I parked by the Records Office and walked in. The babe behind the counter was just that, an absolute, knockout babe. She was about five six, a hundred and ten pounds, and a giant pair of knockers almost as good as Flo's.

I smiled. "Hi, beautiful. Has anyone ever told you that a body like yours belongs in a Playboy magazine?"

Her frown told me that she wasn't exactly thrilled at my attempt to be friendly. "Sir, you have ten seconds to state your business, or I'm calling a security guard."

I sighed. It was downright weird how some women don't know how to take a compliment.

I said, "I'm looking for a death certificate for a guy named Theodore Roosevelt Page."

"Do you know the year?"

"No, but I'll make one up if it means that we'll keep talking."

She grabbed the phone.

"I'm sorry. I won't make any more jokes. I really don't know the year he died."

She frowned again, but typed the name into her computer. A moment later I heard a printer make some noise.

She bent down. I leaned forward and took a peek down her blouse. The view of the deep canyon was worth the risk.

"That will be five dollars for the copy."

I paid her and said, "If you're ever in Carson City, stop by the Old Globe Saloon. I own the place, and sweetheart, your drinks will be on the house as long as you want to sit there and drink."

She turned and walked away. Yeah, I know I don't own the bar, but she didn't know that. Besides, I could tell from the start that she wasn't going to come to Carson City anyway.

I glanced at the death certificate for Theodore Roosevelt Page. With his date of death in hand, I drove to the office of the Bakersfield Californian, the local scandal sheet. A pimply-faced kid stood behind the counter.

I said, "I want to find the obit for a guy who died a few years ago."

The kid pointed to a computer terminal sitting on the counter. I don't know shit about computers, but this was my last job, and a full afternoon with Flo was waiting, so I gave it a try. I hit a few keys. The screen kind of jumped around and then showed a list of newspaper sections along the left side. I found obituaries, clicked, and up popped a box that asked for a name and the date of death. I typed in both, and bingo, there was Page's obit.

Theodore Roosevelt Page

Kern County oil legend Theodore Roosevelt Page died last Sunday after a short illness. He was 88. Page, who had lived in the Bakersfield area since the early thirties, made his fortune in the development of the Ten Section, Paloma, and Coles Levee oil fields.

He is survived by his two sons, Herbert Clark Hoover Page and William Howard Taft Page.

At his request, no formal services were held.

For a big time oil millionaire, the obit seemed damn

short, but by the time he died, his sons probably didn't give a shit what the newspaper printed about their father. I loved my Mom and Pop, and made damn sure that the Elko Times said nice things about them when they passed on. But I'm just a dumb shit Basque bartender from Carson City.

I printed out the obituary and made a beeline back to the motel. Waiting at the front desk was a money order for five hundred bucks. As I walked to the room, I passed the pool and Flo was lying on her towel.

I was damn sure that if I asked Flo if she was happy with me, she'd say, "Bear, you're great."

I watched her snooze in the sun and couldn't wipe the stupid grin off my face. I had finished everything on Pinky's list—still had a little more than a thousand cash in my wallet—nearly two thousand bucks worth of Glenmorangie 18 in my car trunk, and an afternoon of sexual madness sleeping by the pool. Turns out that working for Pinky has a few perks.

NINETEEN

Pinky—Eureka, Nevada

Occasionally, my initial judgment of a person would turn out to be incorrect. However, please recall that the definition of occasionally does not mean regularly or frequently. You can imagine my surprise the next morning, when I drove into the motel parking lot at precisely 7:59, and saw Julie Campbell standing outside the motel office.

The moment she entered my Jaguar—I had decided that trying to explain my recent acquisition of Richard's BMW would have been too much for Julie to comprehend this early in the morning—I noticed that Julie's once-stringy hair was clean and the pungent aroma of a motel-supplied shampoo filled my nostrils.

I said, "Good morning. We have a long drive ahead. Did you have something to eat?"

She nodded, and gave me a tiny smile. "As instructed, I ate breakfast, brought my Walkman, and the Motley Crue CD."

Her voice was clear and bright, as if she had been awake for at least an hour. And, my God, the woman had put on makeup.

As I drove toward the east side of town, I surreptitiously glanced at my passenger. She wore a pair of jeans—in place of that threadbare, mother-earth skirt—topped off with a western style, red and white checked cotton shirt. The transformation was astonishing. Overnight, Julie Campbell had gone from a Humboldt County hippy to a Carson City cowgirl.

She said, "Will we be back in time so I can visi Richard?"

I said, "I believe so. Of course, it all depends on how much time we spend at the ranch."

We reached Highway 50, turned left, and inside a

minute, we had left civilization behind us. I had expected Julie would slip on her earphones and disappear into her musical world. But for the second time that morning, she caught me off guard by voluntarily starting the conversation.

"Pinky, yesterday, when you called me at the motel, I'm afraid I was a little wasted. I recall you told me that we were going to Eureka, but that's crazy. Eureka's a couple of hundred miles north of San Francisco. It's ten miles from where Richard goes to school, and where we live."

"My dear, you're thinking about Eureka, California. There are cities and towns called Eureka all over America. In Arkansas, Montana, Missouri, California and Nevada according to the latest reference book I read. The California Eureka, the Eureka you live near, is a thriving city located on the coast, next to the Pacific Ocean. That city has a population of nearly thirty thousand people, giant redwood trees, massive lumber mills, fisheries, and lots of tourists. The tiny town of Eureka, Nevada, is located more than seven hundred miles from the Pacific Ocean in the middle of a vast wasteland known as northeastern Nevada. Instead of redwood trees there's sagebrush, desert and rocks, millions and millions of rocks. Except for a played out gold mine, the Eureka we are heading for has no industry, and I'm afraid to say, fewer tourists. Our destination today is a minuscule island of nothing in the middle of nowhere where a few hundred rugged souls struggle to scratch out a living."

Julie smiled. "Thanks, Pinky. If Humboldt State had a professor who explained things as well as you do, I might still be in school. If nothing else happens today, I've learned that there's more than one town called Eureka in this world."

She turned and stared out the window at the morning sun reflecting off the hills. The colors flowed between red, orange, yellow, rust, and at least ten shades of brown.

"Pinky, it looks like someone came out here last night with cans of house paint and decorated the landscape. When Richard and I came through here the other day, it was in the afternoon, and I was tired. I don't remember the

90

hills looking this pretty."

I glanced at the surroundings. "Even the loneliest road in America has a haunting beauty."

Julie stared at the emptiness for a moment. "Why did you just call this the loneliest road in America?"

"Twenty-five years ago, Life Magazine ran a very negative article about Central Nevada titled, The Loneliest Road. In the article, a spokesman from the Automobile Association described Highway 50 as totally empty with no points of interest. Needless to say, AAA didn't recommend using Highway 50. In fact, they warned against using the highway unless the drivers were confident of their survival skills."

"Gosh, it doesn't look that bad."

I chuckled. "Don't worry, Nevada won in the end. The Chamber of Commerce in Ely suggested the state officially give Highway 50 the title of the "Loneliest Road in America," and the Nevada State Tourism Commission agreed. Now tourists travel thousand of miles to drive this 250-mile, two-lane lonely route to nowhere."

Julie nodded and returned her attention to the window. "Come to think of it, I haven't seen a car or ranch house for fifteen minutes. I don't think that's lonely. I find it peaceful."

We drove the rest of the way in Julie's definition of peace until we reached Eureka. I stopped at the County Courthouse to pay my respects to Sheriff Durham. His full name was Robert Warren Durham, but I soon learned that he answered to the obvious nickname of Bull.

Prior to our trip, I had called Willow to ask for her assistance. "Sweetheart, I'm going to Eureka tomorrow—to walk through the murder site, and I'd appreciate a call from you to the local Sheriff, to grease my visit, so to speak."

"Damn it, Pinky, stop calling me sweetheart. You're talking to the Chief Deputy District Attorney of the Criminal Division of Carson City. Besides, I know Sheriff Durham, met him at a conference in Reno last . . . hold on a minute. Did you run this request past Miguel Vaca? I've told you more than once. Vaca's the deputy I assigned to the

91

Page murder. Vaca is the man that should be talking to Sheriff Durham about your—"

"I tried, but Vaca was out of his office. I heard he was in court and that the rumor floating around town that Miguel was spotted playing golf at Eagle Valley North has little or no credence."

I heard Willow suck in a gulp of air. "Damn it, are you telling me that someone saw Vaca playing golf during office hours again?"

"Please don't let it get around that you heard it from me. I'm sure it's all just a case of mistaken identity. Now would you make that call for me? I'd hate to drive all that way and not have a law enforcement officer waiting to let me into the ranch house."

Obviously Willow had put in a good word for me, because when Sheriff Durham walked out of his office, he flashed me a big smile and thrust a giant paw in my direction. The man fit the movie image of a western lawman. He was big, not fat big, but strong big. As my hand disappeared into his, Durham's voice boomed, "Mr. Delmont, Carson City District Attorney Willow Stone called me yesterday to inform me that you'd be stopping by today. What do you need from my department?"

I extracted my hand before the bones were crushed beyond repair and forced a smile. "Sheriff, I represent Richard Page. I am here to gain access to the murder site at the ranch of the deceased, William Page."

He frowned. "You plan on going all the way out to Bill's place? Do you realize that's more than sixty miles from my office?" He sighed, as if I'd had the temerity to ask for the key to the magnificent city of Eureka. "You see, we have only one deputy covering the area that includes Bill's ranch, so I can't guarantee immediate access. We're talking about a section of ground out there that's nearly half the size of Rhode Island. I'll ask my clerk to contact the deputy, and while we wait, we'll head down the block to The Owl for a cup of coffee."

"A cup of coffee sounds wonderful, Sheriff, but we need to stop by my car on the way. I have a passenger and—"

"No problem, bring him along."

The moment Julie stepped out of my car, the Sheriff's reaction informed me that he immediately recognized his grievous error of gender. Bull removed his hat with such a flourish that I thought we had gone back in time, perhaps to the era of the Three Musketeers.

Sheriff Durham dipped his head. "Howdy, Ma'am. My name is Bob Durham, but I hope you'll call me Bull, cuz that's what all my friends call me, and I'm sure that from this moment on, you'll be my friend."

He tucked his thumb behind his badge. "I'm the Sheriff of this county." He stepped closer to Julie. "What brings a lovely lady such as yourself to my friendly community?"

Julie blinked her eyes rapidly, like some females do when confronted with overt male fawning—then I noticed that it was the bright sun hitting her face that caused her reaction, and not the Sheriff's testosterone charged advance. That's when it hit me; Julie was one of those rare females who didn't realize, or comprehend their effect on the male species. Back at the motel, Julie's sensual movements and momentary flashes of skin had not been staged for effect. That was just the way she dressed and acted.

Now I wasn't surprised that she responded to the Sheriff's move on her with the same nonchalant ignorance that she had used toward me in her motel room. It was as if she were oblivious to the flood of male hormones that flowed from Sheriff Bull's pores.

She said, "No big reason, Sheriff, I just came along for the ride."

Bull's face wore his bewilderment poorly. My guess was that the majority of the good ladies of Eureka seldom ignored a compliment from him. But he did his best to cover the moment of awkwardness. "Of course you did, little lady. I'd be tickled pink if you'd join us. We're heading to The Owl for coffee, and in honor of your visit, I'm buying."

I spent the next half hour nursing one of the worst cups of coffee I had ever been served, while Julie continued to ignore the Sheriff's accelerating advances. I had no doubt that Sheriff Durham thought Julie was a keeper, but I decided that the entire female population of Eureka must offer the town's males slim pickings based on Bull's desperate attempt to win her over.

The Sheriff's cell phone beeped. He answered and grumbled, "Okay, that'll work."

Bull dropped the phone into his pocket. "Mr. Delmont, if you leave in a few minutes, Deputy Appleby will arrive at Bill's ranch around the same time you get there."

Then, finger-by-finger, like a spider stalking a fly caught in its web, the Sheriff walked his giant hand across the table toward Julie. "Ma'am, are you going with Mr. Delmont, or would you rather stay here with me so I can give you a—shall we call it a personalized tour of my fair city?"

I felt that Sheriff Durham had gone a touch too far when he called Eureka a fair city, and I was positive that his personalized tours of ten to twelve run down structures would take no more than five minutes. Julie seemed confused by his offer, rather than pleased, or pissed off, or any other normal female reaction to the Sheriff's obvious proposition. In fact, she appeared totally mystified. I was now sure that I understood Richard's girlfriend.

I pushed away my cup of black tar and shook my head. "Sorry to ruin your day Sheriff, but Miss Campbell will exit this wonderful town with the same man she came with."

It took a moment for my sarcastic remark to seep through the thick bone that surrounded the law man's miniscule brain, but then, like the big bad wolf from the fairy tale, Bull huffed and puffed, and for a moment, I thought he might blow me away. I made a mental note to guard my words carefully because it seemed that I was dealing with a man with a volatile temper, and that explosive anger lay dangerously close to the surface.

The flash of Bull's rage faded as quickly as a Nevada rainstorm sinks into the sand. He tipped his broad Stetson in Julie's direction. "Ma'am, I know you'll come back someday and my offer of a personalized tour will be good anytime."

Bull turned to face me, and moved so close that I

couldn't avoid the sour tang of the bacon he had eaten for breakfast. "Mr. Delmont, take Highway 278 north for a touch more than sixty miles. On the right you'll see a couple of rock pillars about six feet tall and a wrought iron sign over the top that says, Page Ranch."

He leaned closer and whispered so my right ear was the only recipient of his final words of wisdom. "Bill Page was my friend, and we both know that your piss-ant client murdered him. One final word of caution, Mr. Delmont. Discover everything you need during your first visit, because I don't want to see your runt of the litter body, or your fancy big-city car, in my county again. I assume you're smart enough to catch my drift, so get your worthless ass out of my town."

Oh yes, I thought, I'm smart enough to catch your drift, and I'm also smart enough to keep my mouth shut, at least for the moment. There was definitely a dark side to the man who hid behind his shiny badge, a holstered colt 45, and a phony smile.

The three of us casually strolled to my car, and while Julie buckled her seat belt, I opened the door. "Sheriff, thank you for the coffee. I'll be sure to tell District Attorney Stone about your hospitality."

I got in, started the engine and then rolled down the window. "By the way, as an officer of the court, I feel I need to remind you about that silly constitutional concept concerning presumed innocence. I truly understand the problems that view creates for a professional lawman like you— heavens to Betsy, your department might have to discover some actual evidence. Furthermore, I realize how often that presumed innocence crap gets in the way of your desire to hang someone you don't like from the nearest tree, but occasionally, one of your arrests might actually make it to a trial. Don't fret, Sheriff, we'll see each other again. But the next time we'll be in my neighborhood. You'll be sitting in a Carson City court of law, answering my questions concerning your inept band of Keystone cops. And don't forget, you'll be under oath!"

I gunned the engine and pulled away from he curb before the Sheriff could drag me through the window, and beat me to death. While the Jag cruised down the two-lane blacktop toward the ranch, Julie stared at the empty land-scape that makes up most of Nevada's interior. "Pinky, was that guy hitting on me?"

Ah, there was hope for the next generation! "Yes, my dear, that's exactly what he was doing."

"That's why I feel comfortable around you. I don't have to be constantly on guard for subtle remarks. You're a gentleman, Pinky, and a friend, or like my brother."

Humph! I hate being told that. I hadn't planned on taking advantage of Julie, but I like to think that she'd at least expect me to try.

A silence settled between us. At mile sixty-two, I turned onto the entrance road to the ranch and watched the plumes of dust boil up in the rear view mirror. I had just made a mental note to take the Jag in for a major wash job when the ranch house and the deputy's car popped into view. A young, uniformed officer stepped out of his car as I pulled up in front of the house.

He tipped his hat. "Mr. Delmont, I'm Deputy Appleby. Bull told me you'd be stopping by to check out the scene of the murder. If you're ready, we can go in now."

Before I got out of the car, I watched Julie put on her Walkman earphones. "Julie, can you hear me?"

She nodded.

"Are you going to wait out here?"

She nodded.

"I could be inside the house for an hour, maybe more."

She shrugged, flipped a switch on her Walkman, set-tled back and closed her eyes.

I exited the Jag and shut the car door. "Let's go, dep-uty."

The deputy tore away the plastic tape that criss-crossed the doorframe, and cut the seal on the front door. The air inside was cool with just a touch of a musty, anti-septic smell. The deputy led the way across the entry hall and stopped above a large, western style, sunken living room. I recognized the general area from the photos of the body.

He pointed down to the dark tile floor. "You're standing near the exact spot where we found Bill's body."

I crouched down. "Did you know Bill Page?"

The deputy was dressed like a picture-perfect model taken off the cover of a law enforcement recruitment pamphlet. "Oh, yeah. There's a lot of land out here, but very few people. I'd say that I personally know everyone living in my area of responsibility."

"Were you the first officer to arrive on the scene?"

"Yeah. I got here first. Then I called Bull and told him we had a real mess out here."

"Deputy, as you said, your area of responsibility covers an extremely large area. What caused you to come to the ranch the day Bill Page was murdered?"

"It's funny you should ask that because, to tell the truth, it seemed kind of strange to me at the time. Gert got a phone call. The caller told her someone had been shot at the Page ranch, they needed help, and to send a deputy, pronto."

If the caller had actually used the word 'pronto', I thought, that alone would eliminate Richard, along with the majority of the people who speak proper English.

"Deputy, who's Gert?"

"She was the dispatcher on duty when the call came in."

"Was the caller polite enough to leave a name?"

"'Fraid not, and before you ask, the voice sounded like a male, according to Gert."

I considered not asking the next question. A wise attorney never asks anything unless he has a damn good idea of what the answer is going to be, but this might be my only shot at Deputy Appleby outside of court. "Deputy, do the phone calls that come to your dispatcher indicate the telephone number and address of the caller?"

"Yes."

I hesitated, and waited for him to finish his answer. But that was it, a simple yes. If I wanted more information, he was going to make me dig for it. For a moment, I considered two possibilities—Deputy Appleby was smart enough to hold back information or he was so dumb that he not understand the importance of my questions. The man looked sharp enough, but there was something about his manner that told me the Deputy, like a large percentage of the world's workforce, had reached his level of incompetence.

I said, "Deputy, did the phone call come from this ranch?"

"No. A telephone number didn't appear on Gert's screen. Later, Bull told me that happens when a call comes from a cell phone."

"Did you or anyone check the phone at the ranch the day of the murder to see if it was working?'

"Ah . . . . no, I didn't. I don't think—"

"Why don't you check for dial tone?"

He walked down two stairs to the lower living area, and picked up the phone. A big smile crossed his handsome, but vacant face. "That was a great idea, Mr. Delmont. I'll call Gert and let her know we're here."

While the whiz kid talked with his office, I knelt down and noticed a trail of ants marching between the wall and the tile floor. The column went down the carpeted stairs toward the living area. I followed the moving line and found it ended at a half-inch hunk of Uncle Bill's skull that was lodged in the thick carpet at the foot of the first step. The tiled landing, a step above where the body had been found, was spotless. I guessed that Sheriff Bull's crack forensic team, assuming they had such a thing out here in the middle of nowhere, had just missed the chunk of Uncle Bill. After the deputy hung up the phone I said, "Your guys missed a good sized piece of the murder victim's skull, but don't fret, in a few more days the ants will complete the job."

Deputy Appleby's face turned the color of a rusty pipe. He grabbed the phone and dialed his office again. While he waited to talk with his boss, I turned and walked down the hall. I peeked into a bedroom, a second bedroom, and finally an office. I entered the office and left the door open. I didn't want Deputy Appleby to think I was trying to hide anything from him.

I looked about the room and muttered, "Okay, Bill, where did you hide the safe?"

I checked the drawers and looked under the desk. Nothing but some paper clips, pens and a pad of Post It notes.

I lifted the two pictures that hung on the wall, but found only painted stucco.

The floor was covered wall-to-wall with a dark blue carpet. I went to each corner and kicked at the carpet with my heel. On the third try, the rug popped back to reveal an **AMSEC** B3800 floor safe. I was impressed. That was the exact model of floor safe I had in my office. It seemed that Uncle Bill and I'd had identical taste when it came to protecting documents from the casual visitor.

Far down the hall I heard the deputy call my name. "Mr. Delmont."

Then I heard his boots hit the tile floor as he ran down the hall toward the office. "Mr. Delmont, Bull told me I shouldn't let you out of my sight. Mr. Delmont, where did you go? I could get into real trouble."

I dropped the carpet, tucked the corner into place with the toe of my shoe, and met him at the office door. "Nothing to worry about Deputy, I was just looking for the bathroom."

He escorted me out of the office to a bathroom and stood guard outside while I peed. I called through the closed door, "Deputy, I've seen enough. I'll be ready to leave as soon as I wash my hands."

A moment later, Deputy Appleby plastered new tape across the opening, and resealed the front door. When I returned to my Jag, Julie was still there, scrunched down, eyes closed while her fingers drummed a beat on the Walkman case. I climbed in. She didn't move. I started the car and the vibration of the engine caused her to open her eyes.

"Pinky, are you finished here?"

"Yes. Now set up your Walkman to the exact spot where you and Richard started back to Eureka."

While she pushed a few buttons, I beckoned to the

Deputy. He strolled over to my car, leaned over, and touched the brim of his hat to acknowledge the passenger sitting at my side.

He said, "What do you need, Mr. Delmont?"

I smiled. "Appleby, did you pass the suspect's car on Highway 278 when you drove to the ranch the day of the murder, or did you come from the north?"

"No, I came from the south, and yes, I remember passing him because he was driving one of them fancy German cars, a Beemer I think it's called."

"When the Highway Patrol pulled over that car outside of Fallon, did they find either a cell phone or the murder weapon?"

"Uh . . . no. When they brought those two back to Eureka for booking, all the HP turned over was the suspect and his girlfriend."

"Do you think you'd recognize the suspect's companion if and when you saw her again?"

"Yup, I'm sure I would."

I waited for a moment, to give him the opportunity to tell me that she was sitting next to me on the front seat of my car. Then I shrugged my shoulders, and waved goodbye to the man. He wore the uniform of a Deputy Sheriff of Eureka County, but it turned out he was a clone of Barney Fife.

As I backed up, I said, "We'll give the deputy a few minutes to get out of sight. When I give you the sign, you start the music. I'll accelerate to eighty and hold our speed there."

TWENTY

Bear—On the road to Nevada

Flo was a real find, but as I have said before, when the masons slapped her wall together, they must have mislaid a couple of her sophistication bricks.

Ten miles outside of Bakersfield, she confessed to me that she had never been north of Fresno. In my opinion, Fresno is the armpit of California, so if Flo had lived this long, and she'd never been north of Fresno, she made a nun's life look exciting.

I said, "Let's play a game. You told me that you watch Jeopardy on TV. Flo, I'm going to give you the chance to become a contestant. This is the final Jeopardy question. Eighty-five thousand bucks hang on your answer. You ready?"

Flo's eyes were lit up like a Christmas tree. "Yes, ask me the question."

"If Fresno is the armpit of the golden state, what other section of the human body would you use to define Sacramento?"

"Bear, Alex Trebek is a gentleman," she snapped. "He'd never ask a nasty question like that."

"Sorry, Flo, your thirty seconds are up. If you wrote down, what is where the sun don't shine, you are today's Jeopardy champion."

Flo glared at me and said, "That wasn't very nice. I don't like you making fun of Alex Trebek."

Shit, I thought I was pretty funny. I was only trying to make a joke, but Flo didn't have a sense of humor when it came to Alex Trebek. She gave me the frosty treatment until we reached Sacramento.

Like a horse heading back to the barn, I punched the gas a little harder when I turned east onto Highway 50.

I glanced at Flo. Her head was back on the seat. Her

101

eyes were closed. The shoulder part of her seat belt crossed between her tits, making them sort of stick out more than usual, like those babies needed any help. As I stared at her boobs, one of California's dumber drivers damn near clipped my left fender so he wouldn't miss his off-ramp. I swerved hard right to avoid hitting the bastard and Flo woke up with a startled snort.

She yawned and stretched.

I said, "So what do you think about California north of Fresno?"

"Flat and boring. Can we stop soon? I need to pee."

I pulled off the highway at Placerville, and we stopped at a giant, multi-island gas station. While I filled the tank, Flo emptied hers. Before I paid for the gas, I grabbed a couple cups of coffee that, according to the sign, claimed to be a gourmet blend of Moka-Java, Columbian, French roast, with a hint of Hazelnut. Shit, gourmet coffee at a truck stop. California is a crazy place.

Flo smiled as she sipped her coffee. "This is good, and the scenery has improved now that you've found me some hills and trees. How much farther is it to Carson City?"

"About seventy-five miles."

"Good. We have time to talk. Tell me, when you were little, were you a good boy, or did you give your parents a lot of trouble? Did you get along with them? Where did you grow—"

"Damn it, Flo, I don't want you asking me that kind of shit."

"Why not?" she snapped back. "Are you trying to hide something from me?"

If she only knew! "Me, have something to hide? Okay, I give up. What did you ask me?"

"Were you a good little boy?"

"Not really, but what little boy is? But I guess things were a little different because my Pop was a sheepherder."

Flo sat up and stared at me, like I had just told her Pop was an alien from outer space.

She said, "No way."

"It's true. I lived with Mom in a back room at The Star

Hotel in Elko. She was the head cook. Today you'd call her a chef, but back in those days, she was happy to be a cook."

"How did your father get home every night if he was out herding sheep?"

The sad memory of those long gaps of time between seeing my Pop came back.

"He didn't."

"So your mother had to raise you all by herself. That's tough. Do you hate your father for that?"

Shit, there she did it again. "God damn it, Flo, you have a way of saying things that piss me off. No, I didn't hate Pop then, and I don't hate him now. My Pop did what he had to do to make money for our family. And every night he was gone, Mom would tell me a different story about Pop, or about her growing up in the Pyrenees, that's a bunch of mountains between Spain and France."

"Sounds nice. I wish my Mom had done that. Do you remember any of the stories?"

I did, but that was kid's stuff. "Nope, not a single one."

"Bull shit! I'll bet you do." Flo put her hand on my knee and started to move her fingers toward my crotch. "Come on. I'll tickle you if you don't tell me one."

She had found out that I was ticklish the first time we did it. Actually, it's kind of fun when you're naked, but not when you're in a car that's shooting down a highway doing seventy-five.

"Okay, I give." I pushed her hand away. "I'll tell you the story about the day that Pop was almost eaten alive by Basa Faun."

She chuckled, "What the hell is a Basa Faun?"

"According to Pop, Basa Faun was a gigantic, hairy ogre who lived in the back country of Nevada, and his favorite food was Basque sheepherders."

Flo shivered. "That's creepy. Is this really a story your mother told you, or are you making this up as you go along?"

"Flo, I'm hurt that you'd think I'd ever lie to you."

"I'm sorry. Please go on."

"Okay. It seemed that all the cool shepherds kept

103

some salt in their pocket to protect them from Basa Faun. If he came by, all they would have to do was throw some salt in his direction, and he'd run away."

Flo arched her right brow. "Salt? Just salt? Doesn't seem to me that he was a very tough ogre."

"Shit, Flo, he was tough enough to wolf down a whole human in one meal, but salt was this weakness. Just like Kryptonite knocks Superman on his ass. Salt was like Kryptonite to Basa Faun."

After I waited for a second, so Flo had enough time to figure out all that stuff about Kryptonite and Superman, I said, "One day, Basa Faun jumped out from behind a big rock and surprised Pop. Then and there, Pop dropped to his knees and begged for his life."

Flo's eyes got real big. "I'd do the same."

"Lucky for Pop, and me too, because I would have never seen my Pop again, Basa Faun decided to give him a sporting chance to live. He told Pop that he wouldn't eat him if he could tell him three truthful statements.

"Pop scratched his head for a moment, and then he said, 'Some say that when the moon is full, the night is as clear as day. But you and I know that the night is never as clear as the day.'

"Basa Faun told my Pop that was one."

Flo smiled. "Your Pop was quick on his feet. Bear, you're just a chip off the old block."

I frowned because I didn't know what she meant about that chip part.

She said, "Hey, that's a compliment. Say thank you, and finish your story."

"It's not my story, it's Pop's. Anyway, then Pop told Basa Faun, 'Some men say that corn bread is as good as wheat bread. But you and I know that corn bread is inferior to wheat bread.'"

Flo said, "I like corn bread better than wheat bread."

"Damn it, Flo."

"Go on, Bear, finish the story. I'll keep my trap shut."

I said, "Basa Faun nodded. 'Go on, human, you must come up with one more truthful statement or I will start a fire, cook you and eat you for my dinner.'"

Flo shuddered again.

"Pop looked that ogre straight in the eye and said, 'Had I known that you were going to be hiding behind that rock today, I would have stayed home in Elko. And we both know that is a true fact.'

Basa Faun laughed and spared my Pop, but from that day on, Pop always carried some salt in his pocket, just in case they met again."

"I'm glad your father escaped, but I can't help wondering what Basa Faun ate for lunch."

"Flo, it's a story."

She tugged at her seat belt. "I knew that."

Sure she did!

She smiled. "I was only kidding. Now, did you tell me that you grew up in Elko?"

"Yes I did, but what about you, Flo, were you born in LA?"

"Yes, about a mile from the home I lived in when we met. Nothing as glamorous as Elko. My parents were both working stiffs. My father died first, and then my mother passed and left me the house. I've been married twice. The guys were nice enough, but they both turned out to be drunks. Of course I met both of them in a bar, so what should I expect. Since then, I've stayed away from men who hang around bars. Bear, meeting you made me happy I made that decision. What about you? Have you ever been married?"

Oh shit, wait till she finds out what I really do for a living. Of course, I stand on the business side of the bar while the boozers sit on their fat asses on the other side.

"Bear, did you hear me? I asked you if you have ever been married."

"No, but a couple of times I came close to—"

Pinky's cell phone chirped. Jesus, I hadn't thought about his cell phone, or used the damn thing since I had conned it off him back in Carson City. I pulled it out of my pocket.

"Hello."

A female voice said, "Pinky, is that you?"

"No, and this ain't Pinky. This is Bear. You don't sound like Mabel. Who the hell are you?"

At that moment, Highway 50, the divided, four-lane highway I had been cruising on at more than seventy, suddenly narrowed and the cars and trucks on the highway looked like a herd of cattle being forced into a squeeze chute. A semi on my right, his lane disappearing, shoved his big-rig left into my lane. I had to do something fast. I dropped the cell phone, closed my eyes and slammed on the brakes. Through the cry of screeching tires, I heard Flo say, "Bear, I think it's against the law to drive and talk on a cell phone in California."

Between Flo's bitching, fighting to keep the car on the road, and the unknown voice squawking at me on the cell phone, there was a second where I thought I was going to lose it.

I yelled, "Everybody shut up!"

The smoke of burning rubber and glazed brake pads filled our car. I don't know how I missed hitting the semi, but once the haze cleared, the big-rig was settled in front of us.

I grabbed the cell phone off my lap. "God damn it, who is this?"

"What happened? I heard a squealing sound."

"Jesus Christ, answer me. Who am I talking to?"

"My name is Lottie. I'm Mr. Delmont's secretary, and—"

"Lady, that's bullshit. Pinky's secretary's name is Mabel."

"Mabel had to leave suddenly and I'm a temp covering for her while she's gone."

I glanced at Flo. She had scooted as far away as she could and had pasted on her pouty expression. "Flo, I'm sorry I had to yell like that, but—"

She shook her head. I could tell that I wasn't going to get anywhere with her, so I went back to the cell phone. "All right, whatever your name is, why are you calling me?"

"Look dipshit, I didn't call you. I dialed Mr. Delmont's

cell phone number and you answered. His ex-wife called me with an emergency. She wanted Mr. Delmont to meet her at—"

"Willow's in trouble? No shit. What's the emergency?"

"You know Mr. Delmont's ex-wife?"

"Babe, Willow Stone's the top female DA in the state of Nevada. Everybody who's anybody knows her."

"What did you say your name was?"

"Bear Zabarte. I'm Pinky Delmont's chief investigator. He gave me his cell phone so I could use it during my investigative trip to LA. Now stop screwing around and level with me. What's Willow's problem?"

"I could lose my job telling you this, but Mr. Delmont's ex-wife was extremely upset when she called me. She wanted Mr. Delmont to meet her at their Lake Tahoe Condo above Zephyr Cove. The local fire department called and told her that there was a small fire in the middle of the living room. After the firemen put the fire out, they found a note pinned to the fireplace mantle. They're looking for Mr. or Mrs. Delmont to gain permission to open the note."

TWENTY-ONE

Pinky—On Highway 278 north of Eureka, Nevada

I had waited a full five minutes after Deputy Appleby left before I said, "Okay, turn on the CD player and give me a nod when it's time to start."

I started the engine and watched her face. She seemed lost in the music.

"Julie, have we reached that spot on your CD yet?"

She shook her head.

Suddenly, she nodded and I hit the accelerator pedal.

I said, "Between the Ranch road and the highway, it's a little more than sixty miles to Eureka. If we've timed everything correctly, in fifteen minutes we'll go about twenty miles. As soon as we stop, we'll get out and look around. I'm hoping you'll recognize something about the area. A tree, a dry creek bed, anything."

Julie had parceled out one ear to me and the other one to the Walkman earpiece. "Pinky, what exactly are we looking for out there? All Richard did was take a piss. What's out there to see?"

I sat back and considered her question. This wasn't the first time that Julie hadn't seemed to comprehend her boyfriend's grave situation. Either she was a great actress, or she really didn't understand what was going on.

I decided it was time to invite her to the party. "Why do you think the police stopped you and Richard outside of Fallon?"

"I heard them say something about Richard's uncle, like he was hurt, or maybe they said he was dead. I don't remember which, why?"

"Do you understand that Richard has been arrested for his uncle's murder?"

She sat back and worked my question through some sort of mental labyrinth. "Yes, I guess on some level I knew that, but I also know Richard didn't do anything. Besides, he's not capable of harming another human. I'm positive that the police will figure that out soon and let him go."

She suddenly bolted up and her eyes asked me the question before her mouth did. "They will find the real killer and let Richard go won't they?"

Now, at last we were reading off the same page. The only problem was that I wasn't as positive as she was concerning her boyfriend's innocence. As far as the police were concerned, around the time of Uncle Bill's death, Richard was inside the ranch house. Continuing the police thought process, Richard or Julie were the only people who could have shot Bill Page. It wasn't like Uncle Bill lived in an apartment at the corner of Fifth and Main, where at least five hundred people could have easily dropped in, pumped a couple of bullets into his brain, and then retired to the corner bar for a drink. From Sheriff Bull Durham's viewpoint, who else but Richard Page could have pulled that trigger?

And where was the murder weapon? And what was Richard's motive?

"Julie, that's why we have come here today. I did come up with something I can use. Deputy Appleby told me he passed your Beemer on his way to the ranch. His office received a call, and that call did not come from the ranch . . . by the way, does Richard have a cell phone back home in Arcata?"

"No. We wanted to get one, but they were too expensive. Why?"

"According to Deputy Barney Fife . . ."

"I thought you said his name was Appleby."

"You're right, and Julie, that was my first and last attempt at humor. Now, according to Deputy Appleby, this county is set up to show the telephone number and address of all calls coming into the Sheriff's office."

I could tell from her expression that I hadn't completely broken through her wall of music.

She said, "But what does that have to do with Richard?"

"The day of the murder, a call came into the Sheriff's

office, and there was no display. That meant someone had used a cell phone for the call, and you and Richard don't own a cell phone."

A big smile worked its way across Julie's pretty face. "So now they'll let him go?"

"Not likely, but at least I have something I can use during the trial, to start dragging the jury somewhere past the line of reasonable doubt."

Suddenly Julie pounded on my highly polished walnut dashboard.

"Pinky, stop the car. This is the song, and I remember, Richard stood over by that big red rock."

I skidded to a stop and steered the Jag onto a narrow shoulder. I got out and scanned the horizon. Deputy Appleby's car was long gone and as far as I could see, this car and its two occupants were the only people left on the face of the earth.

As I closed my door, Julie jumped out to join me. Was it possible that an understanding of Richard's danger was finally sinking in?

She looked at the red rock. "Why are we here? Pinky. And what are we looking for?"

Up to that point I had wanted, in fact, I had needed Julie's involvement, but she had asked me the one question I had hoped she would not ask.

I said, "Do you recall the murder weapon and the cell phone?"

Julie edged away, as if I had just come down with an infectious disease. "Oh my God, you think that Richard threw them here, while he was turned away from me?"

Before I could answer, she faced me and I watched tears roll down her cheeks. She said, "Pinky, just come out and say it. You think Richard killed his uncle."

"Listen to me, Julie. I'm an attorney. My job is to defend people accused of a crime. Some of my clients are guilty, and others are not. As their attorney, it makes little difference to me."

Julie's anger changed to anguish, and her wet tears fell onto the dry, red soil. "Pinky, I love the guy, so it makes

110

a huge difference to me."

She turned, ran back to the car, and slammed the door while I walked toward the red rock that loomed fifty feet away. I searched the area very carefully, and to my surprise, I didn't find either the murder weapon or a cell phone.

TWENTY-TWO

Bear—Zephyr Cove, Nevada

Before I turned off the cell phone, I repeated the condo address to Flo, who, after a long frosty glare, dragged her attention away from the view long enough to write down: 35A Boulder Way, Zephyr Cove. After that, I had to listen to her ooh and ah all the way around the south shore of Lake Tahoe.

"God, Bear, I've never seen anything so beautiful as the water in this lake . . . Look there, that ski lift comes right down to the road . . . Just look at all those fancy hotels. Sweetheart, I'd love to spend the night at one of those someday . . . Wow, look at the snow. I can't believe there's still snow on the tops of some of those mountains."

And on, and on, and on. "Flo, I hate to interrupt you, but there's a Lake Tahoe map in my glove compartment. I know how to get to Zephyr Cove, but I need to find Boulder Way."

She opened the glove compartment and screamed when my weapon fell out onto her lap. "Oh my God, I hate guns! You didn't tell me you had one of those in there."

Jesus, sometimes explaining things to her is like talking to a twelve-year-old. "Look, I need to find Boulder Way now. We're a half-mile from Zephyr Cove. After you've done that for me, pick up the gun and put it away. It won't bite you."

She glared at me for a while and then opened the map.

Lucky for me, she found the street as we passed The Zephyr Cove Inn.

"Turn right at the next street and then take the first left. That's Boulder Way according to your map. And the next time you ask me to do you a favor, don't talk to me like that. I know guns don't bite."

If I hadn't had both of my hands busy holding the

wheel, I would have stuffed the damned map into Flo's flapping mouth, but I knew that would have screwed up what otherwise seemed like a perfect relationship.

A few seconds later I cranked a right off Highway 50, and one street later, turned left onto Boulder Way. We had no trouble finding 35A, because all I could see was water hoses, fire trucks and cop cars.

I parked as close as I could get, and as we walked toward the row of condos, I spotted Willow talking to a cop.

I waved. She turned and ran toward me. Then she stopped. From the look on her mug I could tell that she was surprised to see me. "Bear Zabarte? What are you doing up here? I thought you were tending bar at The Old Globe!"

Flo grabbed my arm and snapped, "What did she say about you tending bar?"

I did my best to ignore her, and trust me, that's not an easy job. "Willow, I got a call from some broad in Pinky's office and she told me you needed help."

Willow suddenly forgot all about the fact that she was talking to the man she once tried for manslaughter. She burst into tears and grabbed my arm. "The note said that if Pinky doesn't turn the Richard Page case over to the Public Defender's office, they'll barbecue him over a fire until he's as crispy as a rotisserie chicken. There's a five foot hole burned in the middle of the living room floor to prove they can do it." Willow sniffed and wiped her nose on my shirt-sleeve. "Bear, on top of the arson, extortion, and threatening bodily harm, the bastard that did this didn't know that the condo isn't Pinky's anymore. The property belongs to me as part of our divorce settlement."

I pulled my arm away and looked at the slimy smear on my shirt. Willow is one beautiful broad but trust me, snot is snot. While I rubbed my sleeve against a boulder, I tried to figure out what was her biggest problem; the threat to Pinky's life, or that the hole burned in the living room floor happened in her condo, not Pinky's.

Flo stuck an elbow into my ribs. "I'm waiting for an explanation who this woman is, and why you let her wipe her nose on your arm?"

Damn! I wished Flo would shut up. I stepped back from Willow. "Flo, meet Deputy District Attorney Willow Stone. She's the reason the streets of Carson City are safe for people like you and me."

Willow thrust her hand in Flo's direction. "Bear's correct. My department handles all the crime. Another group takes care of civil matters. Frankly, I find the civil side of law very dull. I'm sorry, with all the commotion around here, I didn't catch your name."

"Flo Sunderland. I'm a friend of Bear's."

Willow looked at me and I think that she was having a hard time to keep from laughing. "I'm sure you are, Flo. Now, Mr. Zabarte, as I asked you once before, what are you doing in Zephyr Cove?"

I wasn't sure how much I should tell Willow, with her and Pinky working two different sides of the fence. "I went to LA for . . . . it was sort of an investigation job . . . . for Pinky . . . . and me and Flo were driving back to Carson City when Pinky's cell . . . ."

Willow cut me off with a wave of her hand. It was creepy, like she was in court, addressing a jury. "I know. You told me about that call before. Let me guess. I'll bet your visit south concerned a man named Page who was murdered, right?"

I nodded, and smiled at Flo. "See, I told you she was the best DA in . . . ."

Willow flashed me her stare of doom, the one she uses only during important trial summations. "Bear, once we track down the murder weapon, the evidence we have against Richard Page is as solid as your head. In fact, I'm so confident of a conviction that I assigned the case to Miguel Vaca."

"No shit! Miguel Vaca? Does Pinky know that?"

"Yes, as a matter of fact, he does. He and I were discussing Vaca yesterday, and that boss of yours lied to me. He told me that my man was playing golf instead of doing his job in Superior Court. This morning I talked with the judge and the bailiff of that court. They both told me that Vaca was in court all afternoon. I know Pinky does improper things—damn, how I know that man—but he thinks he can do or say anything he wants to help a client. Bear, this time Pinky's shenanigans have gone too far. If you run into him before I do, you tell that scheming shyster that I'm going to file a formal complaint with the Ethics Committee of the Nevada Bar Association."

A fireman rushed up and said, "Mrs. Stone, we discovered a can of accelerant near the car port. The captain wants a word with you."

Willow arched one of her beautiful brows at me, sighed, and left with the fireman.

Flo pulled my arm. "What's an accelerant?"

"Anyone who isn't an arson investigator would have called it a can of gas."

She nodded and then said, "I don't understand something here. Did she say that Clark was murdered? That's ridiculous; an oak branch fell on him. If that dippy broad thinks that's murder, and you agree with her, I'm afraid your carnal desires have shorted out your brain."

My carnal desires, what the hell did that mean? I shook my head. "Babe, you're confused. Willow was talking about Bill Page. He was Clark's brother. He was the one who was snuffed."

Flo took my arm and wrapped it around her back. She pushed her pelvis into mine, like she wanted to do it right there while we standing on a fire hose. "I'm sorry I doubted you, Bear, you were telling me the truth. You are a big-time investigator."

Had we been alone, and I was a little loose from half a bottle of Scotch for courage, that might have been a good time to tell Flo the truth. But we weren't alone, so I gave her a big squeeze and said, "I've got to find Willow. I need a copy of that note so I can give Pinky a look as soon as I get back to town."

"Bear, is this guy Pinky—the man that you and Willow keep talking about—is he an attorney?"

I nodded.

"And is he the attorney that you think can help me get my money back from Clark's estate?"

115

I nodded again, but this time I hoped that Flo didn't notice that my heart wasn't in the nod.

"For my sake, I hope you're right about him. I don't know the man, but Pinky doesn't sound like a proper name for a big time attorney. With a silly name like that he could be—no—he should be a teenager flipping hamburgers at McDonald's."

TWENTY-THREE

Pinky—Carson City, Nevada

By the time Julie and I reached the outskirts of Carson City, the sun had dropped behind the wall of the Sierra.

When I turned into the County Jail parking lot, Julie woke and looked out the window. "Did we get here in time?"

I checked my watch. "Yes, you have fifteen minutes before the scheduled time to close. If you want to stay longer, and get any guff from the jailer, tell him that you were with Pinky, and it was my fault you were late. I'm sure he'll cut you some slack."

Julie scooted across the car seat, brushed her lips against my cheek, and said, "Thanks, Pinky. This is the first time since the cops arrested Richard that I've felt comfortable."

I wished I felt the same. "Good. Tell Richard we'll talk again tomorrow after I make a few required appearances in court."

When I returned to my office, I was quite surprised to walk in the door and find Lottie sitting at her desk reading a book.

"Mr. Delmont, don't worry, I'm not expecting to get paid while I sit here and read. I've stayed on my own time."

"I'm not worried. What are you reading?"

She flushed. "It's Tom Sawyer."

"One of my favorite books by one of my favorite authors. I've read Tom Sawyer a dozen times and never failed to gain some insight that I had missed before. Clemens really knew how to identify the foibles of the common man."

Lottie smiled. "Mr. Delmont, I stayed because I knew you needed to get this message."

She handed me a note: There's been a fire at the Zephyr Cove Condo. Come at once. Willow.

I glanced at the time received, and it had come in three hours earlier. "Thank you for staying. I might have missed this without your being here."

"Mr. Delmont," Lottie was starting to tear up. "I really stayed because you might want to fire me. I read that message to an obnoxious man who answered your cell phone. Now I realize that I overstepped my authority when I gave out information that I shouldn't."

"Do you mean Bear? Did you give this message to Bear?"

Lottie's shoulders were quivering, and it looked to me that she was near a complete breakdown. "Yes, and I'll understand if you—"

I leaned over and stared into her tear filled eyes. "Lottie, when you walked in this office, I knew immediately that you were an exceptional woman. I'm glad you took the initiative and gave the message to Bear. I understand he's an obnoxious bastard, but at the moment that obnoxious bastard works for me, and he would be the perfect man to send to Tahoe in my place. Now, Lottie, think a moment before you answer this." I hesitated for a moment while she wiped her eyes. "If I were to offer you a full time secretarial position, with a twenty-five percent increase over what you are making today, would you say yes?"

"But Mr. Delmont, I made a terrible mistake. This morning, when I handed you your cell phone, I didn't know that you owned two. So this afternoon, when I tried to call you, I dialed the wrong cell phone number."

"I understand that. You were also sitting at your desk waiting for me, an hour and a half after you should have gone home. Everyone—well almost everyone—can make a mistake, but to discover an employee, like yourself, with a vein of loyalty as wide as the Comstock silver discovery, is a rare occurrence indeed."

Lottie sat back for a moment, and then she nodded. "Yes, Mr. Delmont, I'd love to fill your vacant secretarial position."

"Excellent. Now that you're an employee, stop calling me Mr. Delmont. I'm Pinky!"

She wiped her tears. "I'll try to do that, Mr. Delmont."

"Lottie, I'll leave some written and recorded notes concerning my trip to the Page Ranch ready for you in the morning. First thing tomorrow, type them up. Make two copies. Place one on my desk and drop the other copy into the Page file."

"I'll do that first thing in the morning. Now it's time for me to say good night, Mr. Delmont . . . ah . . . Pinky."

TWENTY-FOUR

Bear—Carson City, Nevada

The car almost drove itself down Highway 50 to Carson City. Inside ten minutes I stopped outside Pinky's office. The lights were still on. "Flo, let's head in. It looks like he's still there."

"I'm hurrying, but not because I want to meet this guy. I have to pee, and I mean soon."

Here was Flo's chance to shake the hand of the best criminal defense attorney in Northern Nevada, and all she could think about was taking a piss. Hadn't she just peed a couple of hours ago? "I'm sure that Pinky will let you use the bathroom in his office."

I opened the office door and there he was, standing by Mabel's desk, except that the woman sitting behind the desk wasn't Mabel.

I said, "Pinky, here's the note that was left for you in the condo. Willow sends her love, and wants me to tell you that she's turning you in to the Bar Association for some scam you pulled on her."

I nodded to the woman sitting in Mabel's chair. "Excuse me, but Flo has to pee, real bad. Can you take her to the bathroom?"

The woman said, "Of course, and Flo, if I recognize the look on your face, you need to get there quickly."

She jumped up and the two of them ran down the hall.

Pinky said, "Glad you're back, Bear. I picked up a few interesting items during my trip to Eureka. How was your visit to LA?"

I handed Pinky the phone recorder tape from Clark's office and wondered why Pinky didn't seem to care about the condo fire at Lake Tahoe. "Here's the tape I told you about. There are three messages and they all sound like they're from the same broad. She's talking some sort of shit

I don't understand, so you're on your own. But first, you'd better read the note that was left in your condo. Then I'll tell you about the rest of the LA trip."

Pinky took the paper and read silently. When he finished, he tried hard to act normal, but I could tell that he was mad at me, or pissed off at Willow, or something to somebody.

"We're back." Flo and the woman giggled like a couple of teenage schoolgirls.

I put my arm around Flo's shoulder and said, "I guess it's time for introductions. Pinky, this is Flo. Flo, Pinky. And I don't know this woman's name."

But before the unnamed woman opened her mouth, Flo reached into her purse, pulled out a fistful of paper, and shoved all of them at Pinky. "Glad to meet you, Pinky. Bear told me that you could help me with these IOU's I have from Clark. The total comes to $11,500, and as Bear knows, I'm a woman who can't afford to throw that kind of money away."

Pinky eyed the papers, and then he flashed me his now-I'm-really pissed-off at-you look.

He said, "Mrs. ah . . . Flo, I don't know what Mr. Zabarte promised you, but I haven't a clue who you are talking about. It's late, and I've had a very long, and busy day. I don't know about you, but—"

"Hold it right there, buster! The man I'm talking about is the father of Richard Page, who, if I've put all the pieces together, is the man you are defending for the murder of Clark's brother, Bill."

Leave it to my Flo to cut right through all the crap and call a spade a shovel!

Pinky ignored Flo's bitching and that's not easy to do. He said, "Bear, I have the tape. Once you hand over the box, you are free to go."

Shit, with everything else happening, I forgot to figure out what I was going to do with the cash in that damned box. Real quick, I tried to think up something Pinky would fall for.

Pinky leaned closer, so the girls couldn't hear him, and

whispered, "Bear, I hope for your sake you've brought the metal box from the office, unopened, and with all the cash intact. Because all hell is going to break loose if one dollar is missing."

"Jesus, don't go ballistic. I just forgot to bring it in from my car."

As I walked to my car, I tried to figure out how Pinky could really know how much cash was in that box. I guessed it was possible that his client knew how much. But why would he tell Pinky the exact amount? I wasn't sure, but based on my experience with Pinky before my trial, I knew that they'd spent a lot of time talking together. I mean other than Pinky, and his jailbird clients, who was Richard Page going to talk to? I opened my trunk, and stared at what could have been my ticket to paradise. Finally, after remembering Pinky's power in this town, and what he would do to me if he caught me skimming his money, I picked it up, returned to his office, and dumped the box filled with more than a hundred thousand bucks on his desk.

TWENTY-FIVE

Pinky—Carson City, Nevada

I took a deep breath, and restrained my urge to strangle Bear's female companion. In as pleasant a tone as I could muster under the circumstances, I said, "Flo, as I told you once, I'll look at the notes tomorrow. Right now, my office is closed. Good night."

At that point, Bear walked through the door. He threw the metal box onto my desk. He grabbed Flo's arm and the two marched out of my office.

After Lottie said goodnight, I sat down at her desk and reread the note found at the condo. Cook me like a rotisserie chicken? Cripes! Now I understood why Mabel left. Was it possible that someone threatened her like they did me? I wondered if they told her they were going to barbecue her. Or perhaps they said that they would drop her beloved Puffy into a deep-fat fryer. Experience had taught me that most criminals were not the brightest humans that walked the earth, but that didn't mean that they wouldn't maim, or kill for little reason. If Mabel had been threatened, I didn't blame her for taking the direct route to Montana.

I pushed away from Lottie's desk, walked into my private office, and opened the lower drawer of my desk. I pulled out a bottle of Bombay Sapphire and poured myself a generous portion over the rocks, except I had no rocks. I loved Bombay, when it was combined with a little tonic water over ice, so my glass of straight, lukewarm gin wasn't for pleasure. The slug of fifty percent alcohol was meant to bolster my flagging courage.

I took a large gulp, shuddered, and sat down in my comfortable leather chair. It was obvious that someone wanted me out of the Page murder case, and they were willing to threaten a painful death to get my attention. At least the barbecue idea was a novel approach. I had been threat-

123

ened before. Once by a drug dealer who was pissed off because I hadn't help him beat his drug collar. He seemed to forget that when he was arrested, the police had extracted a five-pound bag of heroin out of the trunk of his car.

Then there was the ungrateful bastard who told me he'd knock my block off when his five years were up—a sentence that I had negotiated down from fifteen.

My third threat came from the pimp who offered to bury five inches of cold steel into my pristine chest when I informed him that, considering his arrest record, which turned out to be longer than one of Castro's speeches, a couple of months in the county jail was the best I could do.

But I had never received a threat from an unknown person or persons. And I had never been told that I would be trussed up like a slab of ribs and cooked over a fire. I had to give the person who wrote the note a couple of points for inventiveness, but to tell the truth, the mental image of me simmering over a bed of red-hot coals was definitely on the creepy side.

I set my drink down. By now I was pretty sure that Richard was not the person who murdered his uncle. However, my beliefs alone would not get the murder charges dropped. As far as Sheriff Durham was concerned, Richard was his man, and Willow was ready to send my client to prison for life, if not execute him. Somehow, this case had slipped beyond constructing a defense to finding the evidence needed to prove my client innocent! I took another sip, and as the warm gin trickled down my throat, a brilliant idea blossomed—a way to prove Richard's innocence. But the plan would cost a lot of money—more money than I would receive from selling the BMW.

That's when my eyes moved to the metal box that Bear had tossed onto my desk. I opened the top, and to my glee, the box was filled to the brim with an impressive pile of cash. I counted the stash and did a quick calculation. Most of the money in that box would cover my expenses, and the rest could be used to keep Richard comfortable during my quixotic quest. I closed the box and dialed Julie's motel.

Her voice on the phone sounded depressed; about what I had expected. "Hi, Pinky. I just got back from the jail, and Richard was very down. I don't know what I can do to pick up his spirits."

Short of a twelve-hour release so he could spend the night in her bed, a feat even I couldn't pull off, I was afraid that Richard's near future would have to remain bleak. "Julie, I'm looking at something that might interest you. Will you be available tomorrow?"

"I'm afraid I'll be stuck here in this motel until they let Richard go."

It was late. I stared at my glass of warm gin and knew that I really didn't have the strength to tell Julie that by the time her boyfriend would be released, Carson City would have declared her motel blighted, and the redevelopment agency would have knocked down the motel and replaced it with a brand-new ten story hotel. "Tomorrow I'll drop by and show you what I'm talking about."

I dialed Willow's cell phone number. She answered on the first ring. "Pinky, I had a feeling you'd be calling me sooner or later. Did Bear give you the note?"

"Yes, but that's not why I called. Are you okay?"

"I'm fine." Suddenly her tone changed. "No, damn it, I'm not fine. Someone set fire to the floor of the living room in my condo because they thought you still owned the place. Pinky, you promised me six months ago that you had transferred the condo title to my name as a single owner. My God, it's been more than a year since our divorce became final!"

"I'm sorry, that was one of those little things I accidentally let slip through the crack."

"Don't tell me that." She was getting so angry that I had to hold the receiver away from my ear. "You didn't change the title on purpose because you thought someday we might reconcile."

I hated it when Willow nailed me like that. But that's why she's at the top of her profession—nailing people to the cross was what my favorite ex-wife did for a living.

I said, "Hey, I said I was sorry. Don't fret sweetheart,

I'll pay for the repairs."

She hesitated, as if she just figured out that she had been yelling like a beer hawker at a baseball game. "I'm sorry I raised my voice."

"Apology accepted."

There was a long pause, and then Willow said, "Pinky, what about the threatening note?"

For a moment I considered how far I could go with Willow. In the old days, in her position as a DA, I had negotiated, bargained, and pleaded with her, to do the best for my clients. But I knew my next words could be construed as stepping over the line. "Sweetheart, I'm ninety-nine percent sure that Richard Page didn't murder his uncle. There's no weapon. There was a cell phone call to the sheriff's office and Richard never owned a cell phone. Your case has more holes than a block of Swiss cheese. Willow, we need to get together and talk about a plan I've come up with. I realize that might place you on the cusp of an ethical dilemma, but—"

She interrupted. "No buts, and no plans, Pinky. I've told you this before, any discussions concerning the Page case must go through Miguel Vaca first. By the way, this afternoon Vaca charged into my office demanding your scalp. It seemed that the court bailiff, his brother-in-law it turns out, told him about the little lie you slipped me concerning Vaca playing golf during working hours. Vaca was so pissed that he insisted I file a complaint against you. Pinky, you've got to understand that—"

I said, "You're a little testy tonight, my love."

"You're damn right I'm testy. And now you are about to ask me to do something that could put my career in jeopardy."

"Willow, do you have the murder weapon?"

She hesitated. "No."

"Do you have the cell phone?"

"No."

"I'll reiterate. We need to talk about my plans, trust me."

"Hey, I've fallen for that line before. Pinky, up to this

point, our phone call could be construed as two attorneys discussing a plea bargain and that's why I'm going to hang up before you go any further."

"Willow, we are both officers of the court, and as such, we both have a responsibility to seek justice."

"Don't tell me what my legal responsibilities are. Goodbye."

She was gone.

I set the phone down and poured myself another glass of lukewarm gin.

As the liquid slipped down my throat, my world turned cold and lonely. I grabbed the phone and dialed Willow's number. After a dozen rings, I gave up. She must have turned off her cell.

I sat back and considered my alternatives. I didn't need Willow's involvement to make my plan work, but having her onboard could make everything so much cleaner. I tried her number again. No answer. So be it! I dialed Bear's home number.

"Hello."

"Bear, my good man, you rushed out of my office so fast that I didn't have the time to tell you what a great job you did for me in LA."

"Pinky, do you know what time it is? I'm—"

"And, Bear, to show my appreciation for your outstanding job, I am going to invite you to my home for a business dinner tomorrow evening at six."

"Pinky, I don't under—"

"Six o'clock sharp. Goodbye."

I hung up the phone.

I was sure that Willow, in a few weeks, would understand that I given her every opportunity to join forces, and that she had forced me to implement my plan without her.

TWENTY-SIX

Pinky—Genoa, Nevada

After a busy morning at the office, a couple stops at court, and a very productive meeting with Richard Page, I stood in my living room and watched Bear's old pick-up approach my driveway. It was six on the dot.

My house was situated on a knoll that overlooked the Genoa Lakes Golf Club and the vast Carson Valley below. I don't play golf. Never felt the inclination to learn the game or had that much time to waste. But I truly appreciated the open grassland and lakes the golf course provided for my vista. However, I wasn't the only non-golfer that appreciated the golf course. Each morning, before the golfers arrived, and every evening, after the players had left the course, a large herd of deer took over the rolling hills of grass. I'm sure inside the deer's tiny brains they thought the golf course had been placed there exclusively for their daily use.

Before Bear had time to push the doorbell, I opened the front door.

As requested, there he stood. However, by his side was that woman he'd brought to the office last night. For a moment I was flummoxed. Her appearance this evening had not been discussed, desired or expected.

I sighed and put on my gracious face. My mother had raised her son to be an affable host, under any and all circumstances. I forced some warmth into my voice. "Good evening. Let me take your coats."

That woman responded, "I need to use the john. Actually I needed to pee before we left Bear's place, but he was afraid we'd be late."

Bear shrugged and said, "That's what I love about Flo. You don't have to wait long to find out more than you ever wanted to know about her."

At least I now knew her name was Flo. I pointed her in the direction of the bathroom, and she hurried down the hall. Once the door closed on the newly redecorated guest bath, a room that she had erroneously described as a john, I took advantage of the moment to talk with Bear.

"Why did you bring her? I invited you, and you alone for a working dinner. You've placed me in an awkward—"

"Nice place you got here, Mr. Delmont." Flo's voice preceded as she burst through the bathroom door. "And sitting on the can you get a terrific view of the mountains. How many square feet have you got in this mansion?"

I took a deep breath and prayed the evening with this she-devil would pass quickly. "I believe a little more than forty-seven hundred. Why? Is that number important to you?"

"Are you kidding? This joint is a palace. Why you could drop Clark's and my house in your living room and still have room to spare. It's just that the place is a little large for one guy. Bear told me that you're single, is that right?"

My marital status was none of her business! I felt a twinge in my gut as I recalled that Willow and I had parted thirteen and a half months ago. Flo was smiling, and that was the moment my distaste for her blossomed into a full bouquet of poison ivy.

Sensing my rising anger, Bear stepped between us. "Flo, I think Pinky and Willow's breakup and the size of his house are a couple of personal things and they have nothing to do with us."

Then Bear addressed me. "Pinky, Flo seems to think that she was put on the earth to burn my ass. It's nice to see that you're here so she has someone else to work on for a while."

"Let's step into the kitchen," I growled, and herded the two through the living room and across the dining room.

Bear spotted two steaks lying on my custom made, John Boos, butcher block. "Pinky, those steaks are big enough, like they're more than a pound each. Just pick out the largest one, cut it in half, and I'll share it with Flo."

I grabbed the cleaver and for a moment, I considered using it on the back of Flo's neck, then I sliced the largest steak in two. "Now that I've resolved the streak dilemma, Bear, you check the potatoes. They're in the oven. Flo, kindly tear the lettuce for the salad. I'll make us some drinks. A gin and tonic for me, a single malt for Bear, and what can I fix for you, Flo?"

Flo glanced at Bear, as if she had to get his approval. "A small glass of red wine for me. I don't drink the hard stuff. It goes straight to my head."

I opened the door of my temperature-controlled wine closet and glanced around. If forced to testify under oath, I'd have to admit that my hand came close to a world-class Bordeaux, but after Flo's earlier personal remarks, a nine-dollar bottle of a serviceable Australian Shiraz was as good as I was going to open for Bear's bitchy companion.

Flo worked on the salad while I poured her wine. Bear moved close and whispered in my ear, "Pinky, hold the wine down to one or two glasses for the night. The hard stuff ain't the only thing that goes straight to Flo's head."

I gave him a nod, and the rest of the evening progressed better than I would have thought possible, considering how badly it had begun.

After dinner, I pulled out my best brandy, and was pouring three snifters when Flo said, "None for me. I still have a little wine left."

Feeling frisky, I considered giving her a short lecture on the fact that brandy is just wine with a large percentage of the water removed, when Bear said, "Pinky, before we start talking about the murder, you need to know that Flo's cool."

Bear's statement seemed to surprise Flo, and caught her with a mouth full of wine. She tried to swallow, and for a moment it seemed as if she had everything under control. But then her cheeks bulged as some of the wine leaked into her lungs. Holding a hand over her mouth she coughed, then again. Suddenly all hell broke loose. I watched in horror as purple Australian Shiraz shot all over my black marble dining table.

Flo jumped up and grabbed a couple of white linen napkins that we had used for dinner. She began to wipe up the wine.

Before I could contain myself, I screamed, "Damn it, don't use one of my best napkins to clean up that mess."

Flo froze, dropped into her chair, and burst into tears.

Bear rushed to her side, wrapped his arms around her, and said, "That's okay, Flo. Pinky didn't mean to yell at you."

Oh yes I did! But I required Bear's services in the near future, so I lied. "Bear's right. It was just an accident that could have happened to anyone. I'm sorry I shouted."

In a valiant attempt to validate my contrition, I ran to the kitchen, grabbed a roll of paper towels, and rushed back to the dining room.

Flo held her hand out and I gave her the whole roll.

While she mopped up the wine, I said, "Flo, do you understand what Bear meant when he said you were cool?"

She sniffed, "No."

I said, "Bear and I are going to discuss a murder case, and what is said during that discussion is off the record, and completely confidential. I'm Richard Page's attorney, and as his lawyer, I have many legal and ethical responsibilities. As of this moment, we are just three friends sitting around a table after eating a fine dinner. Nothing more."

Flo set the paper towel roll down, drained the last of her wine and slammed her glass onto the table so hard that it sounded to me like a plea for more.

I glanced at Bear.

Bear shook his head, and grabbed the brandy glasses. He said, "Pinky, I think we've all had enough to drink. I'll clear the glasses, the dirty paper towels, and be right back."

I almost cried when he took away my full glass of excellent brandy, but I understood his motive. Once he returned, I said, "Do we all understand what I meant when I said that we are just three friends?"

Flo jumped up. "Mr. Delmont, don't talk down to me. You didn't really mean all. You were talking about me. Don't do that again. If you want to ask me a question, just do it. I was going to ask you what you meant, but you didn't give me the chance to open my mouth."

She found it difficult to open her mouth? From my limited experience with her, that happened about as often as it rained in Yuma.

As Flo returned to her chair, I said, "Flo, we're on a first name basis here. Please call me Pinky. Now, as I said, I have professional responsibilities. What I suggested was that I am going to ignore my professional role so we can openly discuss what's going on in the Bill Page murder case without concerning ourselves with ethical questions. To achieve that goal, we need to operate like a reporter when he agrees to keep a conversation or an interview off the record. In other words, what we discuss around this table stays in this room."

Flo smiled at me. "Thank you, Pinky. Now I see why Bear thinks so highly of you."

Bear thinks highly of me? Were we both thinking about the same Bear Zabarte?

I said, "Thank you for your vote of confidence. Now that the ground rules have been established, let's start with the threat on my life. I think the sender of that note wants me off the case because he, or she, wants to see Richard Page convicted of the murder of his uncle. Do we agree to that?"

Bear and Flo nodded. God I love it when I have the jury eating out of my hand.

I said, "So we agree that someone other than Richard Page committed the murder."

Flo's usually busy mouth remained closed, an unexpected, but pleasant condition.

I said, "Fine. Bear, I listened to the tapes you brought back from LA, and the Bill Page murder now takes on an international scope. Here's my plan, and withhold judgment until I am finished. Tomorrow morning, I'll go to court and inform the judge that I'm gravely ill. I'll tell him that my doctor informed me that I might not live through the stress of another murder trial. I'll ask the judge to allow me to withdraw as Richard's attorney. Once the judge accepts my

132

withdrawal, he'll have to turn Richard's defense over to the Public Defender because Richard's broke. Once that geeky PD takes the case, Richard Page is doomed. Even the inept Miguel Vaca could convince a jury to convict."

Flo remained strangely mute, but Bear seemed ready to say something.

I said, "Bear, hold that thought until I've finished. Now that I've been released from my Richard Page responsibility, I'll decide that a month in Hawaii should provide me the rest I need to recover from my near fatal brush of stress."

Bear nodded and sat back. Even he understood where I was headed.

I said, "After my meeting with the judge, I'll ask Lottie to reserve me a seat on the next available flight to Hawaii. My physical departure from Carson City should satisfy the real killer. As soon as he, or she feels comfortable, Bear will make a clandestine visit to the Page ranch. Between your ranch visit, and my trip, I am sure one of us will come up with the evidence that will clear Richard. Everyone with me so far?"

Flo cried, "No!" She jumped up, put her hands behind her back, and started to pace around the table. "I don't like Richard, never did. Known the piss-ant for eleven years. He used to cut my front lawn, and I never thought he did a good job around the flower beds. So I guess I'm not convinced that the police have the wrong man in jail."

I had anticipated her remark. "Flo, I want you to listen to an audio tape I made this afternoon with Richard Page. I asked him to give his side of what happened when he walked into the ranch house."

"Okay, go ahead. But it had better be good."

I placed the tape recorder in the center of the table, and hit the play button. Richard's voice came through loud and clear.

"When no one answered the doorbell, I tried the knob and the door opened. You have to remember that I had driven nearly seven hundred miles, and Uncle Bill had told me he was desperate for his money, so I walked in. The first

133

thing I noticed was a funny smell. I guess I should have recognized it, but I don't own a gun, never even fired one, so the fact that I didn't recognize the smell of gun smoke doesn't surprise me.

"I walked down the dark hall. The only light came from the open door behind me. Then I saw him. For a second I thought Uncle Bill was just lying on the floor. I don't know, like he was playing some kind of a joke or something. Then I saw the pool of blood on the tile. I rushed toward him and stopped when I saw brains where the right side of his forehead should be. As I stared at the body, I called out, 'is anyone here?'

"No one answered. I could see that Uncle Bill was dead. It was creepy. I backed away from his body until I reached the front door. I sat down on the step and tried to figure out what I should do next. I still had the $500,000 check for Uncle Bill in my wallet, but he didn't need money where he was, and Julie was waiting for me in the car.

"I think that's when I realized I had to get out of there fast. My uncle was dead. There was no one else around, and if anyone saw me, they might think I had killed him.

"As quickly as I could, I walked back to the car. I told Julie that no one was home and drove back toward Eureka. I remember seeing a sheriff's car pass us on the highway, but I figured that he didn't know who I was and I was home free."

We heard my voice say, "Now I have a few questions for you, Richard. Did you shoot your uncle?"

"Shit no, didn't you hear me, Pinky? I told you he was lying on the tile with half his head gone when I got there."

"While you were in the ranch house, did you call the Sheriff's office to report that someone had been shot at the Page Ranch and needed help?"

"No. When I was inside, I didn't use the phone."

"Before or after you saw your uncle lying on the floor, did you make a call to anyone with your cell phone?"

"I don't own a cell phone, never have."

"Richard, did you stop by the road, tell Julie you were going to take a piss, and then throw away the murder

134

weapon and your cell phone?"

We all heard Richard's loud sigh from the tape. "Damn it, Pinky. How many times do I have to go over this with you? Yes, I stopped and took a piss. I don't own a gun. I don't own a cell phone, and the only thing I left on that desert dirt was my urine."

I hit the pause button on the recorder. "Okay. If I was trying this case as Richard's defense attorney, I'd turn to the jury and say, I rest my case."

Bear smiled. "Pinky, it's perfect."

Flo said, "I still don't believe him. I watch a ton of cop shows on TV and a murderer will say anything to get off. And another thing, if Richard is as innocent as you say, what happens to him if you and Bear don't find the evidence to clear him? Will you just sit around and let the state of Nevada execute an innocent man? I know I can't do that, and you have to understand that right now."

Damn, this woman was a pain in the ass. I answered her in my most sincere voice. "Relax, Flo, you have heard only half my plan."

One look at her face told me that I hadn't sold her, but I had to move on. "Back to the phone recorder tapes Bear brought back from LA. The woman on the tape was speaking Italian. The first message could be considered endearing, as if she was questioning why her man wasn't lying by her side. By the end of the third message, the tone of her voice had hardened and I'm sure she called him a bastardo."

TWENTY- SEVEN

Bear—Genoa, Nevada

Flo grabbed my arm. "Bear, do you think the cops have the wrong guy? They never make this kind of mistake on TV."

Jesus, I've done some silly shit in my day, but I've never been involved in a crazier deal—with Pinky trying to pretend he's not Richard's attorney, and now Flo asking me if real cops are like some stupid TV show.

I said, "Flo, I know you thought Clark was one of the good guys, but Babe, he was bad news. First, Clark and his brother, Bill, were skimming money from their Pop's estate. I don't know all the details, but from what I learned from an old fart in Bakersfield, Clark and Bill's Pop set up a trust fund that gave him a big income as long as he lived."

Flo said, "What's big?"

I grinned. "Big enough to retire on, Babe, and that's saying a bunch. Based on the SOS checking account, more than a million bucks a year big. But when Clark and Bill's Pop died, those bucks were supposed to go somewhere else, not to Clark or his brother Bill. That Bakersfield guy told me that their Pop had disowned them for one reason or another."

Flo said, "Slow down. That's the part of your story that confuses me. I thought that a son or daughter always inherited their parent's money."

I glanced at Pinky, and I could tell he was dying to say something. "Pinky, do you want to jump in here?"

"Thank you, Bear. Flo, a will, or a trust gives a parent control of their estate beyond the grave. For example, I could put a hundred million dollars into a trust account, and set up a trust to have the income from that account sent to me every year, just like Clark's and Bill's father did. Then after I died, I could, based on my instructions to the trust, have the annual income sent to the Carson City Quilting Society."

Flo's eyes lit up like a progressive quarter-machine when the reels lined up six bars. "Now I get it. Each year, Clark and Bill's Pop lived off the income from his trust, but after he kicked the bucket, that money should have gone to someone else."

I said, "Right. But in this case, the trust bank didn't know that Pop had died because Clark must have told the trust company that his Pop had moved to Clark's house in LA. Every year those checks rolled in. All Clark had to do was forge his Pop's signature. Now, Flo, I know this next part is going to piss you off, so don't get mad and yell at me, but each year, Clark sent close to a half million to some broad living in Italy."

Flo muttered, "And you think that's the woman on the tapes?"

Pinky said, "Yes. Glad to see you finally joined the party."

Flo said, "Jesus Christ! I knew I shouldn't have trusted that bastard. Go on, what happened to the rest of the money?"

I said, "The rest of it went to Bill Page. Then out of the blue, an oak tree falls on Clark and screws up the brothers' perfect scam. At Clark's funeral, Bill told Richard that he needed the money real bad. We don't know why he needed the cash, but a few days later, somebody pumped a bullet into his brain."

Flo thought for a minute and then said, "What about Clark's foundation, SOS. Was it legit?"

I said, "As phony as a three dollar bill. Based on my look at old bank statements, SOS was used to launder money and to skip out of paying income tax on the trust income."

Flo said, "Okay, you've convinced me that Clark was worthless. Now let's go back to that piss-ant, Richard. If he didn't kill his uncle, who did?"

I watched a tiny smile cross Pinky's face. I think that was the question he was hoping Flo would ask.

I said, "Babe, I think that's my half of Pinky's plan. I'll head to Eureka and look for the evidence the cops missed. But, Pinky, before I go, I need to be sure that my job at the Old Globe Saloon will still be there when I'm done in Eureka."

Flo pushed her face into mine. "What job are you talking about? You told me that you were Pinky's full-time investigator."

Oh shit!

Pinky laughed, "Did Bear tell you that?"

Flo flashed me a frosty stare and said, "Yes, he did. Is there more to this story that I should hear?"

Pinky said, "Actually, your boyfriend's a bartender. He went to LA because he had to work off some hours he owed me for defending him against a manslaughter charge a few years ago."

Flo turned toward Pinky and pounded a long index finger into his chest. "Explain to me what you meant by Bear had to work off some hours."

Pinky looked a little intimidated, and I couldn't blame him. When Flo got her feathers up, she was as scary as a bald eagle.

Pinky said, "Well, Bear and I agreed to one thousand hours at the conclusion of his trial. And as of today, he still owes me—"

I watched as Flo grabbed Pinky's silk shirt. In a quick move she lifted him off the floor and twisted his collar so tight that a button popped off, and his face got real pink. "Look buster, I know you're a college graduate, but I guess you forgot that a hundred and fifty years ago Lincoln freed the slaves with the Emancipation Proclamation. Just look at this damn palace you live in. It's not like you can't afford to pay the man for his hard work. From this moment on, if Bear does any more investigative work for you, you'll pay my man a proper salary, or every television and newspaper reporter in Northern Nevada will hear from me that Carson City's top defense attorney is playing ethical games with an innocent man accused of murder."

Pinky's dining room got so quiet and cold that I

thought we'd been transported to the city morgue. Pinky's mouth opened and closed, like a largemouth bass taking his last gasp of air. I was proud of Flo. She had dropped one of Nevada's top lawyers with a couple of words.

I said, "Pinky, Flo was only pulling your leg. I'm sure she wouldn't go to the newspaper—"

Flo twisted Pinky's collar tighter and said, "Oh yes I would, but sweetheart, I won't have to because as of this very moment, Pinky's going to pay you a hundred and fifty a day, plus expenses for your time. Don't worry, Pinky, you don't have to say anything, just a simple nod will tell me that you agree."

Even the great Pinky Delmont didn't win every case. In fact, I once heard him tell a client he was sorry. But this was the first time in my life that I saw Pinky back down.

Pinky had to move his bulging eyes up and down because his head was sort of stuck in Flo's hand.

Pinky's squeaky voice said, "Bear, Flo's right. I've been taking advantage of you, but as of now, you'll receive a hundred and fifty a day, plus expenses. Tomorrow I'll talk with Lottie. She'll set up a payment system. In fact, you'll receive a thousand dollar expense advance for each job and you can reconcile your actual expenses after you submit a voucher."

Flo let go of her death hold on Pinky.

After the red color drained from his face, Pinky stuck his hand toward me and said, "Bear, welcome aboard the J. Pincus Delmont team."

For a second, I felt like the world had stopped spinning and I had lost my mind. I was part of Pinky's legal team!

While I shook Pinky's hand, Flo paced around the table again.

She said, "Pinky, I'm not finished yet. I heard your plan, but you've screwed up. How do you know that broad in Italy, the one who gets all that money, didn't set your condo on fire and write the threatening note?"

Out of the mouths of babes, or in this case, my Babe.

I said, "Pinky, you've got to admit that's a hell of ques-

139

tion. I think most of those Mafia guys were Italian."

Pinky shook his head. "But that's ridiculous."

Flo said, "Ridiculous? Pinky, you jump to conclusions faster than my first husband could finish a quart of vodka."

I could tell that Pinky was thinking hard, but he was having trouble keeping up with Flo. He took a big breath and said, "Perhaps Flo's right. She asked an incisive question and frankly, I don't have the answer. Flo, are you a part of this new investigation package?"

She said, "I'm staying as long as Bear will have me. I guess you could say where he goes I go. If that means I'm part of the package, I guess I am."

Pinky said, "Hold on. Instead of going to Hawaii, I could just as easily take a plane to Rome. Outstanding idea, Flo. And while I'm in Italy, I'll talk with the woman, check out the SOS headquarters, drink wine, and eat some extraordinary food in the process."

Flo said, "I guess Italy's okay with me. Just buckle down and don't spend all your time drinking wine. At least find out where all that money went. Now, before we move on to other items, I want to go on record that Bear and I are getting the short end of this travel deal. We go to Eureka, Nevada, while you get to go to Rome. I've never been to either place, but I don't think Eureka has quite as many tourist attractions as Rome."

I watched Pinky clench his teeth. Then he said, "I'll consider your point for my future travel decisions. Now, I think we've accomplished more than enough for one night. Bear, we'll get together in the morning and lay out a plan."

He got my coat, and Flo's, and walked us to the front door.

Flo started out the door, then she stopped and spun around. "By the way, Pinky, you forgot to tell me what you found out about those IOU's. When will I expect to see some of the $11,500 that that Clark owes me?"

I held my breath as I watched Pinky's face turn red.

"Very soon," he snapped, as he shoved us out of his house.

TWENTY-EIGHT

Pinky—Carson City, Nevada

As I drove to the office the next morning, my thoughts lingered on last night's dinner with Bear and Flo. Now I understood why Richard's father fled to Italy for six months of the year. God knows I'd go anywhere to escape living next door to that she-wolf. Bear seemed to get along with her, but it was pretty obvious that a pair of Flo's attributes had clouded his limited judgment.

When I entered my office, Lottie's smiling face replaced my mental specter of Bear's female companion.

Lottie said, "You look tired. Have a bad night?"

It was amazing what an evening with Flo Sunderland could do to a man.

I said, "I'm fine. You look as bright as a new penny. Lottie, I have a new task for you this morning. I need you to set up some kind of a payment system for Bear Zabarte. On occasion, he'll be doing some investigative work for me."

She said, "Like a part-time employee?"

"Exactly. He's to be paid one hundred and fifty dollars a day plus expenses. To start, he'll need an advance of a thousand dollars. Can you take care of that for me?"

"No problem."

I had appreciated Mabel. She kept the office looking sharp, and polished our desks everyday with Lemon Pledge. But Lottie did all that and more. In fact, at times, she was so damned efficient that it scared me.

I retired to my office and was trying to figure out how I would break the news of my impending departure to Julie and Richard when Lottie buzzed me. "Do you have time to take a call from Ms. Willow Stone?"

I picked up the phone and said, "Willow, before you say a word, I want to tell you how much I missed you at my little social gathering last night."

141

"Cut the bullshit, Pinky. As the District Attorney, I'm informing you that I just received a call from Sheriff Durham. He told me that an hour ago, a Deputy Appleby found the murder weapon and the cell phone."

My stomach did a flip. The frame of Richard Page was accelerating faster than I thought it would. I had to get cracking.

I said, "Let me guess. The good deputy found both of them lying on the ground next to a big red rock, roughly twenty miles south of the ranch on Highway 278."

"The location where the deputy made the find sounds similar. Pinky, how did you know that? Tell me the truth. Are you trying to pull something here? Did you salt the items on the desert?"

"No, and I'm shocked you would think such a thing. That place just happened to be the very spot where Julie told me that Richard stopped to pee after he left the ranch. And that's the identical place I stopped and looked around for the weapon and cell phone after I visited the ranch with Julie a couple of days ago."

Willow paused. "And your little paranoid mind thinks that someone followed you, or somehow knew where you stopped, and then planted those items after you left?"

"My dear, you win the grand prize. Did the Sheriff say why the deputy decided to look near that particular big red rock? I've been there and that hunk of rust colored sandstone is no different from a thousand others that stick out of the ground between Eureka and the Page ranch."

"He did. He told me his office received an anonymous call."

"From the usual untraceable phone no doubt."

"Pinky, are you trying to say that the Sheriff, or his deputy could be involved?"

"I don't know. What about prints on the weapon. Did they find any fingerprints?"

"No. According to Durham the weapon had been wiped clean."

"How about the cell phone. People sign a contract for a year or two of service. My client claims he never—"

"Can't help you there. The instrument was smashed to smithereens. The Sheriff sent me a bag full of shattered plastic, and what I assume are some crushed pieces of electronics."

A cold fear started to fill the cavity where my stomach use to reside. "Willow, that's part of what I wanted to discuss with you last night. There are too many . . . hold on, I went through all that before I asked you to dinner, and you informed me that you didn't want to know what, or how, I was going to extract my client from this dilemma. Something about an ethical quandary, if I recall."

"That's right! And I still don't want to hear about your unprincipled plan. I'm calling now to let you know that we have the murder weapon and the cell phone. Pinky, a cocktail waitress with a briefcase could convict Richard Page of second-degree murder. And once Vaca informs the jury that your client drove seven hundred miles to kill his uncle, he will prove premeditation. Pinky, your perfect record is about to bite the dust."

"Thanks for reminding me of that. Now it's my turn. Over the next few days you'll hear some strange rumors floating around town that I'm mortally ill. The rumors are true. I'm not well and need peace and quiet coupled with time to recuperate. My doctor tells me a month or so of rest should do the trick. The moment I hang up this phone, I'm leaving my office to ask the judge to turn Richard's defense over to Earl Beggarly, that geeky Public Defender. Willow, please remember that when Earl gets nervous, he extracts offensive material from his nostrils. No matter what happens to me, don't shake Earl's right hand."

"Pinky, what do you mean you're ill?"

I hated to lie to my favorite ex-wife, but I would have short-changed a blind beggar to get my client a better chance at freedom. "Willow, my heart is on the verge of failure. It's the stress of all those successful murder trials. My doctor told me I might die if I walked into another courtroom."

"Come on . . . you're pulling my leg . . . Pinky, tell me this is one of your elaborate jokes."

"I'm afraid not. I'll send you a post card from Hawaii."

"Say all you want, Pinky, but I can't believe you'll walk out on a client to save your perfect record. Now if you'll excuse me, I don't know about you, but I have work to do. Good bye."

Willow talked tough, but I detected a genuine level of concern in her voice. I hated to do that to her, but if my ex-wife didn't fall for the scam, nobody else in town would.

I drove to the jail, and I told Richard that I had to turn him over to the PD.

He reacted about the way I had expected.

Richard slammed his fist onto the oak table. "What do you mean you're sick?"

He charged at me and grabbed the lapels of my gray silk jacket. "You can't leave me now."

After some frantic pacing about, he fell into his chair and cried, "I need you, Pinky."

Eventually, once I was sure his histrionics had passed, I adjusted my lapels, and said, "I'm sorry, Richard, but the decision is out of my hands. My doctor told me that if I didn't remove myself from this stress, my heart will fail, and I'll die."

By this point Richard was in tears, and I couldn't blame him. Between sobs he said, "So if you stay you'll die from a heart attack, but if you leave I'll die from the poison the state injects into my arm."

"Richard, don't worry, Earl Beggarly is a capable lawyer, and because he's starting with you from scratch, I'm positive that the judge will give him a couple of weeks, perhaps a month continuance. By then, I might be back. I promise that the moment my plane lands, I'll visit my doctor to see if he'll let me get involved with your case again."

At that point my client could have gone either way. Richard might try to kill me. Or give up. I was relieved to see he took the latter path. My now ex-client crumpled into his chair, dropped his head into his hands, and started to cry. I patted his shoulder and left the room.

Facing Richard had been tough, but telling Julie was almost more than I wanted to cope with. I knocked on her motel room door, tucked the box filled with cash under my arm, and pasted on a gloomy expression.

Julie's smile faded as her eyes absorbed my grim face. While I crossed the threshold to her room, I said, "Julie, my doctor just informed me that I have to drop Richard's case, or I will die from heart failure."

Julie didn't respond with arm-waving dramatics like her boyfriend. She slumped onto her bed, rolled to her side, pulled her knees to her chest, and shrunk into a ball.

I understood Richard's reaction. Julie's physical response puzzled me. She didn't scream—or get angry. She just lay there.

Finally, in a soft voice, she said, "Pinky, yesterday I told you that I trusted you, but that's over now. What will happen to Richard? Or don't you care anymore?"

I explained to her about the continuance. She didn't react to my scrap of hope.

"I'm leaving now."

She didn't move.

I turned toward the exit and had my hand on the door handle when Julie said, "So that's the way this madness is going to play out. Each day I'll go to court until they convict my man. Six months later I'll stand outside the prison and wait for the news that Richard's dead. Hours later, the prison warden will turn over a coffin that contains Richard's lifeless body. This can't be happening. Richard didn't murder his uncle."

Her emotional plea for justice trumped my normally cold heart. Of all my colleagues, acquaintances, and ex-wives, only Willow knew that deep within my soul, lurked a microscopic bit of compassion—a trait I considered a weakness—a part of me that I concealed from the rest of the world at all costs. However, at that moment, Julie had to remain by Richard's side long enough to give Bear and me time to discover who was framing him. As much as I wanted to use some of the cash I held under my arm to cover my mounting expenses, I could see that she was rapidly approaching the point of no return. Before I could close down my receptors, Julie's emotional plea somehow wormed its way into my diminutive reservoir of compassion.

I walked to the table and placed the metal box in the center. "Julie, this box belongs to Richard."

She put her head in her hands. "So what?"

At this point I decided to tell Julie a little lie. If she believed all the money inside belonged to Richard, perhaps her outlook would improve. "My investigator found this box hidden under Richard's childhood bed in his father's house."

Her head remained buried in her arms. "What box are you talking about?"

"The one I told you about yesterday on the phone. Julie, I took the liberty of opening the box—there's a lot of money inside."

She slowly lifted her head.

I said, "Legally, the money belongs to Richard, but if you tell anyone, he'll be required to pay for an attorney, and with the exception of myself, there isn't one in Carson City worth paying for. Live off what's in the box until I return. I can't tell you my plans, but when a man hands you a box filled with two hundred thousand dollars in untraceable cash, I think you can afford to show that man a modicum of trust."

She joined me at the table—opened the box, and her red, swollen eyes widened. "It's . . . .why Pinky, the box is full of money." She stared at the money and tiny smile graced her pretty face. "Just like you said."

Julie was obviously confused and I could understand why. One minute I was selling her boyfriend down the river, and then handing her a metal box filled with bucks.

She said, "I never should have doubted you. I knew that you'd make everything come out right. I'll be waiting for your return."

We hugged—the sort of embrace you get from a favorite aunt, and I left the motel.

It was nearly noon when I returned to my office.

Lottie said, "Pinky, I reserved your flight to Honolulu. You leave tonight at eight. You're booked into an ocean view room at the Royal Hawaiian on Waikiki Beach for a month, and I've rented you a car. This trip seems very sudden to me. Are you going on a vacation?"

"Yes and no. Now I want you to book me a flight this afternoon to Rome via New York and I'll require a rental car in Italy for a month."

Lottie stared at me as if I had just lost my marbles. "I'll take care of that at once, but—"

"Lottie, I need to look as if I'm going to Hawaii so a certain individual, or individuals, will think I'm dropping Richard Page as a client. However, you and I will know that I'm going to Rome to check out the Italian angle to the Page murder."

"But what about your reservations to Hawaii?"

"I won't show up for the flight, and make a standby very happy."

"Will you need a hotel reservation in Rome?"

"Yes, but nothing fancy . Something close to the railroad station. And I want to pick up my rented car at the railroad station."

"How long do you plan on staying in Rome?"

"Two nights. I'll just wing it during the rest of my stay."

Lottie's fingers started to hit some keys and then she stopped. She turned and I noticed a look of apprehension. "Pinky, before I do anything, I have to ask you a question concerning me."

"Go ahead, what's bothering you?"

"I just started working here, and now you're leaving for a month. You won't need to pay me, day after day, to sit here with nothing to do."

"Of course I'll need you. Who'll answer the phones? Who will set up appointments for me so I'll have something to do when I return? Who'll pay Bear for his work? You will, Lottie, that's who. Now that we've settled that, if you need to reach me in Italy, you can call me on my cell phone."

"That won't work. U. S. cell phones use a different protocol than those in Europe. I know how to fix this. You need a laptop. That way we can send each other emails."

"That won't work. I'm a complete idiot when it comes to computers."

She said, "As soon as I take care of all the reservations, I'll go to the Apple store in the mall. They sell a cool little laptop, and Pinky, you'll be sending me an email in an hour."

TWENTY-NINE

Bear—Carson City, Nevada

It was noon when I walked into Pinky's office. Lottie waved me past her desk and into his inner office. He sat behind his big desk poking at a little white box. He looked up and said, "Bear, this little computer is the damnedest thing. Do you own a laptop?"

I shook my head.

"Come over and look at this."

I walked around his desk, leaned over his shoulder, and stared at a little TV screen connected to a bunch of keys with letters, like a typewriter. "Okay, what am I supposed to see?"

Pinky flashed me one of his, boy-are-you-a dumb-shit, looks. "Just watch this."

He hit some of the letters:

`Hello, Lottie.`

Then Pinky squiggled his finger on a little spot in front of the keyboard and I saw the little arrow move to a picture of a paper airplane. He pushed something with his thumb. I heard a click. The words, `Hello, Lottie,` disappeared from the TV screen.

Pinky said, "Now what do you think of that?"

I knew he wanted me to say something smart, but I don't understand anything about computers, so I said, "I know I sound dumb, but I don't have a clue what you just did, and I really don't give a shit."

"Don't worry, Bear, an hour ago I was just as ignorant as you."

Suddenly the white box dinged, sort of like the sound you get when you hit a fancy wine glass with a spoon.

I looked at the screen and saw these words:

`Hello yourself.`

Pinky sat back and said, "Wasn't that something? I

just sent a message to Lottie, and this is her answer."

I turned my head and saw Lottie. She was sitting on the other side of the open door—no more than twenty feet away from Pinky. "Why don't you just walk over and say hello to Lottie in person?"

"Bear, what you don't understand is that I would have received Lottie's answer just as quickly if I had been sitting in Rome."

I shook my head. "Pinky, I don't know what that means or give a shit about computers, but I did notice that you don't have any wires connected to that box. Does it work like a cell phone or something?"

"Between you and me, I don't understand how it works. Lottie called it a wireless laptop."

"So what's that thing called?"

Pinky glared at. "Damn it, Bear, I told you, it's a wireless laptop."

"No, I meant what happened that made those words come and go on that little TV screen?"

"Oh, that's called email. Bear, you need to get one of these laptops so we can send each other emails while I'm in Italy."

I shook my head. "I don't think so. Those things cost a bundle, and once you come home, I won't need to send you email. I can just drop by your office and talk like we're doing now."

What I didn't tell Pinky was that I don't trust anything I can't see, never have, and never will. Someone told me that inside those computers there were all sorts of little digit things—that's what one guy at the bar called them—little digit things—and they're running around inside those computer boxes. Later, a jerk called them x's and o's. Another wise-ass told me they were pluses and minuses. But as far as I could tell, it didn't make a damn bit of difference what you called those little things. They were all invisible, and as I said before, my brain checks out with things I can't see.

Pinky got up and shut the door.

"Bear, trust me, it's just your lack of abstract reasoning that creates your fear of computers. But we don't have time for that now. I instructed Lottie to purchase two laptops for the office, one for me, and the other for you to use when you're in the field. Before you go to Eureka, you will need to come to the office and Lottie will teach you how to send and receive email. Now, before you say anything, the answer to your question is yes. You will be required to learn how to email. The answer to your second question is also yes. You will be paid one hundred and fifty a day while you learn. The answer to your last unasked question is no. You do not have a choice. All members of the J. Pincus Delmont team must be computer literate."

I could see that Pinky was happy that he had trapped me, but I had one final card to play. "Okay boss, I give up. But seeing that Flo is my partner, that makes her a member of my team. We'll both be here first thing tomorrow morning, and I'll promise that between me and Flo, one of us will be able to send and receive email before we go to Eureka."

Pinky smiled. "That's the spirit, Bear. Now, before I fly off to Italy, and you head into Nevada's interior, I want to make sure you understand the importance of our respective tasks. I didn't mention this last night, but whoever shot Bill Page could be anywhere. It is imperative you and Flo work covertly."

"Huh?"

"You will tell no one, and that means no one, where you are going and once you arrive in Eureka, why you are there."

I jerked my head toward the door between Pinky and Lottie. "What about the new broad?"

"Lottie? I'd trust that woman with my life, but she could, inadvertently, mention to a friend that her boss went to Italy, and they could assume I had changed my vacation plans. But we can't afford to have anyone in the state of Nevada know that you and Flo are snooping around Eureka. That's too close to home. Besides, evidence can disappear as quickly as the gun and cell phone appeared by the red rock."

"Huh?"

"The Sheriff found the murder weapon and a smashed cell phone at the precise location I stopped my car off the highway between the Page Ranch and Eureka. Someone must have followed me that day, though I didn't see a car during the drive."

"Jesus, boss, that's kind of spooky. My Pop told me that he saw a lot of weird things happen out on the desert. Do you remember the time he—"

"Bear, I don't have time to listen to any of your father's ridiculous ghost stories today. An innocent man's life depends on one of us uncovering the evidence that will lead the police to the real killer."

"I understand, boss. If we don't find the real killer, your client's ass is grass, and the State of Nevada will be pushing the lawnmower."

"Not exactly the way I would put it, but you obviously understand the severity of the situation. You will tell no one that you are going to Eureka, right?"

"Right." I understood that last part a lot better than the part about those computers. Then I thought about my investigative partner. "Pinky, will Flo be in any danger?"

"Not unless the real murderer discovers you're snooping around Eureka."

"I get it now!"

Pinky's phone buzzed.

"Thank you, Lottie. Send him in."

The door opened and I damn near fell off my chair when Old Jake Dudek walked in. Most people in Carson City knew Jake, because instead of a real hand poking out of his right shirtsleeve, he had a big, shiny, stainless steel hook.

The story around town was that Jake cracked an occasional safe to keep food on his table—until his last job—when something weird happened and the safe door blew his hand clean off. No one ever accused or convicted Jake of doing anything illegal, but short of a few really dumb patsies, everybody knew that's why Jake's got a stainless steel hook instead of a hand hanging down his right side.

Carson City, like most towns, was short on jobs for a one-handed safe cracker. He taught himself how to deal Blackjack, but the casinos in town fired him because his hook scared most of the customers away. After Jake bounced around for a while, he did come up with a job. If you drive east on Highway 50, at about seven-thirty in the morning, you'll see Jake, wearing a bright orange vest and standing by the side of the road. He makes sure the kids get across the busy highway on their way to school. Occasionally, one of the drivers wouldn't slow down fast enough to suit Jake, and he'd hit the driver's front window with his steel hook. That happened to me once, and believe me, after I saw that hook bounce off my windshield, I stopped two hundred feet short of that cross walk. I'd heard that each Halloween, Jake wore a big pirate's hat and pretended to be Captain Hook. The kids loved him, and during Jake's shift, there was never a close call at his crosswalk. It's good to know that after his accident, Jake finally found himself steady work.

I jumped up. "Hi, Jake, how's it hanging?"

He poked his hook in my direction and said, "Good. How's it with you, Bear?"

Pinky said, "Enough of the formalities, we have a lot of work to accomplish, and I have a plane to catch."

Pinky walked to the corner of his office, pulled up the carpet, and I was surprised to see a safe.

Jake sat down on the floor next to the safe and said, "Bear, unless you have better eyes than I do, you have to get a lot closer."

I did, and spent the next two hours, on my knees, while Jake taught me how to crack a AMSEC B3800 floor safe!

THIRTY

Bear—Eureka, Nevada

The sun had almost set by the time Flo and I checked into the Eureka Tumbleweed Inn. Once I got the bags inside the room, Flo started on her dumb nesting thing while I turned on the TV to ESPN. I was in luck. I found a baseball game. It was the bottom of the ninth. The Yankees were playing the Red Sox at Fenway Park.

"Bear, I've stacked your clean underpants, socks, and tee shirts in the second drawer."

I had turned on the game just in time to see the best part. Boston had a runner at second. There were two outs and the score was tied.

"Your toothbrush and shaving gear are on the shelf above the sink."

The batter hits a line drive single to left field. The Yankee outfielder grabs the ball on one hop, and throws a frozen rope toward the catcher at home.

"I've set the computer up. Are you ready to send an email to Pinky?"

The throw flies past the shortstop. The runner heads for the plate and he's running as fast as he can. It's going to be a bang-bang play at home.

All of a sudden the TV screen went black. I looked up. Flo was waving the power cord at me. "Damn it, Bear, I've done everything but sweep the floor. All you had to do was answer a simple question, but your eyes were glued to the damn TV."

I growled and plugged the cord back in. "Don't ever do that again. There was going to be a close play at home. Don't you understand, that's one of the coolest plays in baseball?"

Flo pulled the cord out again. "I'll keep pulling the plug until you answer my question. Are you ready to send Pinky his email?"

Damn! She sure liked to burn my ass. I'd almost forgotten about the email to Pinky. For days I had worked real hard to learn as much as I could while Lottie told us which buttons to push, and how to make that little damn arrow go where we wanted it to go. Flo took lots of notes, and it looked to me like she caught on fast. Like I said, I tried hard, but everything Lottie said sounded like Russian, or something.

Hoping to catch an instant replay of the close play at Fenway. I plugged the cord back in and said, "I'm turning the TV back on. After I see if the guy was safe or out, I'll answer your question."

Flo plopped down on the bed and pulled out a magazine. "Whatever. Do what you want. Just understand that I'm not going to be the only member of this team doing any work."

The TV picture showed a new Ford Escort driving through the mountains.

I glanced at Flo. She was reading her magazine.

Then I looked back at the TV. Now a Toyota Camry was driving on the desert. Damn, I must of missed the replay. "Okay, what did you want to know about that email thing?"

"For the last time, what are you going to say to Pinky in his email?"

I shrugged. "I don't have a clue."

Flo said, "All right, I'll write the email this time, but tomorrow it's your turn."

She talked as she typed:

```
Dear Pinky,
We arrived and checked into the Tumbleweed
Inn in Eureka. Tomorrow we'll go to the County
Recorder's office as planned. Let us know
what's happening in Rome.
Bear and Flo
```

I said, "Sounds good, Babe. Now let's go see if there's a place to eat in this burg."

Flo closed the lid of the computer and we headed down-town.

Finding a good place to eat in most towns shouldn't be a tough job, but Eureka was a different kind of place. The burg was nothing more than a few old buildings hanging on both sides of Highway 50. As we walked along, I saw that most of the storefronts on the south side of 50 were boarded up. I spotted a Chinese restaurant, but the windows were so dirty I couldn't tell if the joint was open. With front windows that grimy, I'd hate to think what the kitchen floor looked like.

A block later we came to the Owl Bar and Steak House. I stuck my head in the door and saw two old farts nursing a beer at the bar. Except for them, the joint was empty.

The bartender waved to me. "Howdy! Come on in, the water's fine."

I pulled on Flo's arm and she pulled back. "Did you forget? I don't like bars. Let's go back to the Chinese place."

I said, "I want a drink first. Then we can get the lay of the land from the bartender."

"All right, but only one drink."

Inside, the Owl was set up more like a bar and casino than a steakhouse. The bar was on the left. Along the right wall sat a line of slots and an empty Blackjack table covered with a thin layer of dust. At the back of the room, I spotted a few empty tables. I whispered to Flo, "This place is deader than my Grandma. I'll bet those old coots at the bar have been working on those beers since noon."

We sat on a couple of stools and I said, "A glass of the house red for the lady and a Gold Label on the rocks for me."

The bartender, a lanky six footer, looked almost old enough to cash his first social security check. His hair was sort of gray, and his wrinkled, ruddy face came from working too many hours under the hot Nevada sun. He said, "Sorry fella, we don't stock Gold. Will Black Label do?"

"If that's all you got." I scanned the near empty room and said, "Are we late or early for the big party."

The bartender looked up and snickered. "Where're you

from?"

"Originally Elko, but lately I hang at Carson City."

He nodded, like me telling him where I came from explained why his town was so dead. "I guess you could say you're late for the last big gold strike, and a little too early for the next one."

I laid a twenty on the bar. He grabbed it and said, "That'll be $9.50."

I said, "Keep the change."

I wasn't trying to impress him. Hell, we Basques don't spend a lot of energy trying to impress people because the Basques are an impressive bunch without trying. But as an old bartender, I knew how much I depended on tips, and I was pretty sure that a tip that large would turn this dipshit into a friend for life. And besides, Pinky was picking up the expenses.

I said, "Business slow?"

"Yup, and it's bound to stay that way until the price of gold goes up. But you folks are from Carson City. Your economy doesn't have to worry about a gold mine closing. Nope, big government is the one business that never slows down. I appreciate the generous tip."

"You're welcome. My name's Benate Zabarte, but my friends call me Bear. I used to tend bar at The Old Globe in downtown Carson City. The next time you're in the big city, stop by the place and if I'm there, I'll buy you one."

I offered my hand over the bar. He shook it. The bartender didn't cough up his name, but he topped up Flo's wine and my glass of scotch, a courtesy generally extended only to fellow bartenders.

I said, "Perhaps you can help us. Flo and I are thinking about buying a ranch in this area. Know anybody that can show us around?"

The bartender grinned so hard that his face popped a couple of new wrinkles. He reached into his shirt pocket, and pulled out a card. "My name's Albert Good, but my friends call me Goodie. As you can tell from my card, I'm the top agent with The Lonely Highway Real Estate, Inc. And you're in luck, Bear, I just happen to specialize in

157

ranch properties."

I said, "Flo and I are staying at the Tumbleweed Inn down the block. We'd like to look at some ranches tomorrow. I know it's a rush, but would you be available?"

"Available? First thing in the morning I'll stop by the office and check the listings. How about I pick you and your wife up at ten."

"I'm not his wife," barked Flo. "And I could use some more red wine."

Goodie filled her glass to the brim and said, "Is there anything else I can offer you, Mrs. . . . . ah . . . Flo?"

She knocked down half the glass and said, "Yes, your opinion of that Chinese restaurant across the road."

Goodie shook his head. "In a few words—bad—no good—I'd say the worst dive east of the Sierra. Most of the crap they serve in there comes out of a can. I can't think of any local that's eaten in that joint in the past year."

I said, "How do they stay in business?"

He snorted, "Tourists like yourself who aren't smart enough to ask their friendly bartender."

"Any other place to eat in town?"

"Besides where you're sitting right now? Nope."

On Goodie's recommendation, we ate dinner at the Owl. I ordered the rib eye steak and Flo had the fried chicken. My steak wasn't bad, but it wasn't great either. After Flo's third glass of wine, I gulped down the last of my steak, pulled her away from the table, and managed to get her back to our motel room in one piece.

The next morning, in the motel lobby, we grazed over a giant breakfast spread of rolls, doughnuts, muffins, cereal, juice, and coffee. Actually, it looked good to me, but for some stupid reason, Flo didn't go for it. She pissed and moaned to everyone sitting within shouting distance that the motel I had checked her into wasn't good enough to have a swimming pool. Then she grabbed a bran muffin, took a tiny bite, made a nasty face, and put the muffin back on the table.

I wanted to smack her one, but I calmed down and said, "Babe, I'm sorry they don't have a pool, but this is the only motel in Eureka. And besides, we're not here on vacation. We have work to do."

Flo picked up a banana, squeezed it hard, shook her head, and tossed it back into the basket of fresh fruit. "Humph, I thought this trip would be more like Bakersfield where you went out and did whatever it was you did, while I worked on my tan by the pool."

Damn it, ever since I had met this woman, I had tried hard to ignore her nasty side, because she had so many other nice parts. But after pulling the plug on my TV last night, and now this swimming pool crap, Flo's bitchy self was really starting to piss me off.

I said, "No, Flo, this is not like the Bakersfield trip. I thought you knew that after what we talked about at Pinky's house. From now on, I don't work alone. We're partners in this investigation."

I didn't want Flo to go back to LA, but a man can't back down to his woman every time she complains and still be a man.

She started her crying thing again, but this morning I didn't fall for her act.

"Flo, if our deal doesn't fit your picture, then you'd better go back to the room, pack your bag, and head back to La-La land."

Flo grabbed an apple and looked like she was going to throw it at me. A guy who had just set a glazed doughnut on his plate, took one look at her, set his plate and doughnut down, and edged away from the breakfast bar.

Then Flo started to blubber real loud. The rest of the room stopped chewing and stared at us. I had to say something real fast or this whole trip would blow up in my face. In fact everything would fall apart. I'd let Pinky down. I'd never lie on top of Flo's luscious body again. I'd throw away a job that paid me a hundred and fifty a day, plus expenses. I'd never get close to Flo's big tits again. An innocent man might die. And worst of all, I'd run out of clean socks and underwear the day after tomorrow.

I couldn't just sit there and let all that bad shit happen. I wrapped my arms around her and said, "Flo, don't cry. I'm sorry I snapped at you. If you want to stay at the motel and watch Jeopardy on TV all day long that's good with me."

Her tears stopped. Flo wiped her eyes, gave me a kiss, and said, "I'll go with you and help investigate things. However, the next time we go out of town, I trust you'll pick a better motel—one with a pool."

I smiled at Flo. She smiled back. The guy who set his glazed doughnut down came back, but this time he worked at the far end of the breakfast spread.

We found a table and I wolfed down three of those great, old-fashioned doughnuts covered with a thick layer of chocolate icing before the lobby door opened. Goodie barged in and shouted, "Flo, Bear, my car's parked out front and I'm raring to go."

Flo snapped, "Hold your horses, Goodie." She sipped her coffee with her little finger held up, like she thought she was the Queen of England. "I haven't touched a morsel of my breakfast yet, and I refuse to let a common real estate agent rush me through the most important meal of my day."

THIRTY-ONE

Pinky—Rome, Italy

The wheels of my Boeing 757 touched down on the
Leonardo da Vinci runway at nine-fifteen in the morning.
Even in first class, the shortage of bona fide comfort was
exhausting. By the time I exited the plane, my stiff muscles
were on their way to complete rebellion, while my brain had
turned into mush.

After forcing my sluggish self through customs, I
pulled my aching body onto the train that connected the
airport with downtown Rome. As the train pulled away
from the airport, my eyes closed and the clicking wheels
took me back twenty-five years—when I was young, poor,
and an untested lawyer—a condition totally opposite to my
present financial, and professional situation. The train
lurched abruptly and returned me from my nostalgic day-
dream. I sat up and conducted an internal review of my decision to go to Italy. Could Bear and Flo have handled the
Italian angle? Absolutely not! The thought of Bear crashing
about Italy brought up a genuine chuckle. And God knows
that Flo wouldn't be much help as a translator. Besides, according to Sheriff Durham, I was persona non grata in his
county. If not Bear and Flo, who else could look for evidence
at the Page ranch? Convinced I had made the proper choice,
I enjoyed the rest of the ride through the outskirts of the
Eternal City.

Rome's train terminal looked, smelled, and sounded
the same as I recalled—blaring loudspeakers—befuddled
tourists—milling businessmen—busy housewives—noisy
children—all jumping on and off their wonderfully efficient
rail system.

In the middle of the chaos, I inhaled the general madness that permeated the terminal. America has a host of
outstanding sights, but I had forgotten the excitement I had

161

felt standing in the Rome train station all those years ago.

I grabbed my suitcase and fought my way across the street through an outrageous stream of taxis, cars, and scooters. Lottie had booked me a room at the Hotel del Sole and included a map from the train station to the front door of the hotel. I frowned as I saw that the main entrance was a heavy metal gate with a collection of buttons on the wall to my right. I selected the one that said Hotel del Sole and pushed.

The metal gate clicked. I walked through and stopped. Where was the hotel lobby? I stood in the middle of a large, atrium-like room. Muted morning light streamed through a filthy glass roof six stories above. On my left and right stood doors to businesses. In the center of the space was a stairway that wrapped around an old-fashioned elevator. But I didn't see a hotel lobby.

A door to my left popped open and a man who looked to be from the Middle East passed by me, and said, *"Buon Giorno."*

That's when my mushy brain woke up and noticed the sign posted on the elevator. The Hotel del Sole lobby was upstairs—located on the fifth floor—just like many of the small hotels throughout Europe that are situated near railroad terminals.

I pulled open the small doors on the claustrophobic elevator, and with the wild abandon of a fool or an exhausted traveler, I stepped into the tiny lift, closed the doors, and pushed the button for the fifth floor.

The elevator clanked and groaned upward, finally coming to a halt with an unsettling lurch. I opened the door and was startled by a man who stood no more than two feet away.

A dusting of gray covered his wrinkled jaw, and cigarette smoke dribbled from his nose like a leaky faucet. *"Buon Giorno."*

I said, "Good morning. My name is . . . ."

"Mr. Delmont?"

"That's correct, but how did you know?"

"I received an email from someone named Lottie to

remind me that you would be arriving soon. When I saw you step off the elevator, I could tell that you were an American, and assumed that you were Mr. Delmont. Welcome to Roma. Please come in and sign the register."

I followed him through the door into a dimly lit area no larger than a closet. The man stepped behind a three-foot wide counter, and pulled out a ledger-type book so old that it could have been on loan from Caesar's personal library. On my left, I saw people crowded around tables that lined the wall. They ignored me, buttered their rolls, and drank their coffee.

I reminded myself to relax and go with the flow. I was checking into a small European hotel, not the giant Silver Legacy in Reno.

The man behind the counter said, "The email reserved a room for two nights at 85 per night. I have put you into one of our finest rooms on the fourth floor." He pointed at the ancient book. "Please sign here. Then you must pay in cash for both nights."

I said, "I would rather pay by credit card."

He frowned. "That's not possible."

It became obvious to me that the Italians had business taxes, and he wanted to keep our little transaction off the books.

I said, "Fine, but first I have to find an ATM."

"I understand, Mr. Delmont, but as soon as you have the money, come upstairs to the fifth floor. If I am not available, just give the 170 to my wife or my mother. Now one more item before we go downstairs to your room, I need your passport. There is a law in Italy that . . ."

"No problem. I've traveled in your country before. I know that each hotel must register the passports of their guests."

He smiled. "Thank you for your understanding. I have had many, how do you say . . . . arguments . . . . that is the word, arguments with Americans concerning their passports. Now, if you will follow me, I will take you to the fourth floor and show you your room."

The walls of the tiny reception area were so close that

I backed out of the lobby into the atrium. After I entered the elevator, I held the door open for the man.

He shook his head, "No thank you, Mr. Delmont. I'll walk down."

I wasn't sure if he was politely trying to tell me that the elevator was too small for the two of us, or that he didn't feel like dying today. I closed the door and listened to the various moans and clanks as the box jerked down one flight. By the time I opened the elevator, the man was waiting for me by a door marked with a large brass four.

Before he opened the door, he held out a large ring with some keys. "These are your keys. You will use the large key to open this door. The smaller key opens your room door, and the very small brass one you will use to open the metal gate at the street entrance. You see, we do not answer the buzzer after 11:00 pm."

He unlocked the door and I stepped into a spacious, cheery room with five tables, each one surrounded with four chairs. In the center of each table was a white vase that contained a single pink carnation. "Mr. Delmont, this is your breakfast room."

Then the man unlocked the door to 4A, my room.

After we entered, he said, "Mr. Delmont, as you can see, this is one of my premium accommodations with a television and a sink."

A sink? I glanced around looking for the door to the bathroom.

Leaving me by the bed, he walked back to the breakfast room and said, "Each morning, Christina, the fourth floor attendant, will serve you breakfast. Your bathroom is across this room."

"What, there's been a terrible mistake. I can't possibly stay in a room without a private bath."

"I'm sorry, Mr. Delmont, all my rooms with a private bath are taken. A this time of the year Roma is filled with tourists. If you . . . ."

A door across the breakfast area opened and a woman blessed with stunning beauty walked through. Did I say stunning beauty? Upon further inspection beautiful was an understatement. I guessed she was in her early twenties. I had trouble pulling my gaze off her. Momentarily struck dumb, I nodded at the vision and smiled.

She smiled back and said, "*Buon Giorno.*"

The man said, "Ah, this is Christina. She will make up your room each day, and if you need an extra towel, or blanket, she will help you."

My gaze remained on the young Italian beauty as I said, "Normally, I would not consider sharing a bathroom with other hotel guests, but due to the heavy influx of tourists, I will lower my standards for the next two days. Good morning, Christina. Do you speak English?"

"Yes, I do. I work on this floor because this is where Mr. Luchitti places all of his English-speaking guests."

She blinked her dark eyes at me. Not in a cheap, come-hither way, but like the girl next door. My heart jumped two beats.

I said, "Mr. Luchitti is a smart man."

She blushed, started to return to her room, and then she turned back. "Will that be all, Mr. Luchitti?

He looked at me, as if to ask me the same question.

I said, "Christina, what is your full name?"

"Romano," she replied. "My full name is Christina Maria Romano."

It had been a long journey, but her response made it easy for me to turn on my one hundred watt charm. "If my memory of Latin serves me, Christina was derived from the Latin name, Christianus, and that means a follower of Christ. Romano means one who lives in Rome. So if I desire a second cup of coffee tomorrow morning, should I call you, One Who Believes In Christ, or would you rather I call you, The One Who Believes In Christ And Comes From Rome?"

She tittered, and our stares lingered for a moment longer than they should have.

Mr. Luchitti frowned and cleared his throat. "I will leave you now. Please remember to pay me the 170 before you go to bed tonight. That way the business part of your visit will be completed, and you can enjoy the rest of your trip to Roma in peace."

"Mr. Luchitti, before you leave, could you recommend a good place where I can eat that's close to the hotel. By dinner time, I'll be on my last legs."

Mr. Luchitti frowned. "Last legs? Non capisco."

Christina said, "Mr. Delmont is very tired from his long journey."

Mr. Luchitti nodded. "Now I understand."

I said, "I would appreciate any dining suggestions you can give me."

Mr. Luchitti thought for a moment, and said, "I believe Roberto's on Via Dell Cavour will suit your needs. Now, Mr. Delmont, if you'll excuse me, I have other duties to attend to. Good day."

Christina gave me a short curtsy and disappeared behind her door.

I considered how lucky I was to have a fourth floor room at The Hotel del Sole. I had two days in Rome to recover from jet lag, time to visit a few old haunts, and tomorrow, I would get closer to Christina while she served my breakfast.

THIRTY-TWO

Pinky—Rome, Italy

I closed my door and gave my premium room a quick once-over. A single word came to mind, parsimonious. At least the floor looked clean. I turned on the tiny TV. It was black and white! The set picked up five channels and everyone spoke Italian. So much for CNN news. I sat on the bed and fought back the urge to lie down. I had to sync my circadian rhythms to Italian time as rapidly as possible. To accomplish that task, I knew I must get off that bed and do something at once!

I unpacked and visited the communal bathroom. A few moments later I slipped my laptop into its backpack and headed down the creaky elevator to the railroad terminal. If I was going to stay awake, I had to get moving, and the city of Rome was the place to be.

I found an ATM, and extracted 400 Euros from what has to be considered as man's greatest invention since Saran Wrap. Then I dropped by the Hertz counter to be sure my rental car would be waiting for me the day after tomorrow. Now I had one final task to complete before I became a full-fledged tourist; find one of those Internet places that Lottie had told me about so I could send her my first email.

I willed some starch into my rubbery legs and marched out of the terminal, determined to remain vertical until the sun set into the west.

The day turned out to be so damned glorious that, I'm ashamed to admit, I completely forgot about my client who was moldering in the Carson City jail. A blue sky, warm temperature, and wandering through the ancient streets of the eternal city made me forget everything but the moment.

I hit all the usual tourist haunts, the Coliseum, the Forum, and on my way to the Pantheon, I spotted one of those Internet places. The owner spoke English and offered

167

to configure—that's what he called it—configure my computer so I could send emails from my laptop. Lottie had warned me that I might have trouble finding someone who would take the time to help me, but she was incorrect.

When I opened my mail program, the little laptop dinged and indicated that I had two unopened messages.

The first one was from Lottie.

```
Pinky
Hope you had a good flight. Please respond
after you read this email. That way I will
know you have arrived safely and I'll know
that you understand how to use your laptop.
Lottie.
```

Momentarily stung by her lack of confidence in me, I hit the reply button and up popped a blank page with her email address already filled in. I liked the way this email system worked.

I typed:

```
Lottie
Arrived this morning. Hotel fine. My car
is ready for me to pick up. Rome is beautiful.
As you can see from this response, I under-
stand how to use my laptop. Is everything good
at the office?
Pinky
```

I didn't mention that the Internet shop owner configured my laptop. The less Lottie knew about my ignorance the better.

The other email came from Bear.

```
Dear Pinky.
We arrived and are checked into the Tum-
bleweed Inn. Tomorrow we'll go to the County
Recorder's office as planned. Let us know
what's happening in Rome.
Bear and Flo
```

168

My God, even Bear had figured out how to send email! I hit the reply button:

```
Bear
Arrived in Rome safe and sound. The city
is beautiful. Now get to work and come up with
some solid evidence.
Pinky
```

Now my final task was to remain on my feet for the rest of the day. I paid the man for my online time, replaced the laptop into the pack and started toward the door.

The Internet man said, "*Scusilo*, are you planning to go to Trevi Fountain?"

"Yes."

"Then you must be careful walking around with your backpack like that. Tourists see Rome . . . ah . . . *vetri colorati rosa* . . . What is the English?"

My grasp of Italian was shameful. I said, "I'd like to help, but . . ."

"Ah-ha, now I have it. Tourists see Rome through rose-colored glasses. Many bad persons hang about the fountain, and they will know what you have inside your pack. To be safe," he spun his index finger in a circle, "Wear your backpack in front."

I placed both arms through the straps, pulled the pack toward my chest, and looked at my reflection in the storefront glass. "But I look foolish this way."

The Internet man tapped his glasses. "*Vetri colorati rosa.*"

I didn't recall anyone giving me a warning like that during my last visit! I said, "Are you trying to tell me that it is not safe to walk the streets of Rome any more?"

"No, but you are a tourist, correct?"

I nodded.

"*Signore*, there are good people and bad people in Rome, but to the tourist, they all look alike."

"Thanks for your advice, and for the help with my computer."

He smiled. "*Arrivederci.*"

169

I couldn't believe that Rome was as bad as he claimed, but I pulled the pack close to my chest and walked out of his shop looking like a woman in her seventh month of pregnancy. I said, *"Arrivederci."*

The Trevi Fountain was a ten-minute walk away and all visitors to Rome were told to go there and throw a coin in—to guarantee their return to the eternal city. I'm not a superstitious man, but twenty-five years ago I had followed the tradition and I had returned, so the guarantee must work.

After I finished the coin tossing ritual, I caught a bus, and headed to the Vatican Museum where I spent the rest of the day wandering through the world's greatest art collections.

By the time the Roman sky had shifted from a brilliant azure to shadowy indigo, my legs had taken on the consistency of cooked pasta, long past the al dente stage, and my brain was functioning on autopilot. I grabbed a bus, got off near Via Dell Cavour, and one block later I spotted Roberto's. The moment I entered the restaurant, I saw a familiar figure seated at a table at the back of the room. Christina Romano was sitting alone and nibbling a breadstick.

For a moment the words *vetri colorati rosa* niggled at me, but as I approached Christina's table, the area below my belt had effectively shut down all warning alarms.

I said, *"Buona sera."*

She looked up and seemed genuinely surprised to see me standing next to her. She set her bread stick down. "Mr. Delmont . . . I'm . . . I'm . . ."

I said, *"Buona sera,* Christina Romano."

Christina absently ran her hand through her lovely hair. *"Buona sera,* Mr. Delmont."

I gestured toward the empty chair and said, "Are you dining alone?"

In the soft light of the restaurant, Christina looked even more beautiful than she had the first time I had seen her. In place of her work uniform, she had donned a pair of brown leather pants, a simple white blouse, and draped around her neck was one of those colorful scarves that European women use so successfully to encourage a second look from the opposite sex.

"*Si, signore.*" She blushed. "I am alone."

Then, as if she suddenly realized there was an empty chair next to her, she said, "Would you care to join me, Mr. Delmont?"

"I'd love to. Do you eat here often?"

She blushed and smiled again. I noticed that when she smiled, small dimples formed just below her full cheeks.

"This is my favorite place to eat, but I do not go out very often. I have a *piastra calda* . . . a little stove in my room where I usually fix some pasta, or soup."

"Christina, since you have eaten here before, and you are familiar with what the chef does best, would you be so kind as to order for the both of us?"

Her dark eyes sparkled like sunlight reflecting off the finest onyx. "I would be pleased to do that."

A waiter came to our table and Christina said, "*Specialità della casa per due, per favore.*"

Our waiter, an elderly gentleman, scribbled something on a pad. For a moment he looked at the two of us, then he leaned close to me and whispered his *vino favorito* into my ear. I nodded and in a few moments, he poured two glasses of a Chianti classico that blended perfectly with the finest dinner I had ever eaten in Rome. The antipasto consisted of veal meatballs, pickled peppers and onions—sweet sausage—fried zucchini and baked eggplant. The second course followed with a plate of pesto pasta. An hour passed before we took our first bites of Veal and Chicken Romano.

After two hours, the sumptuous feast and company had restored my rubbery legs, cleared my foggy brain, and washed away the fact that I hadn't slept in a real bed for days.

The waiter presented the check, and after warding off Christina's protestations, I took care of the bill.

Rome on a summer evening can be a heady, romantic place. As we strolled back to the hotel in the balmy night air, people passed us, arm in arm, hand in hand, like lovers have walked through the ancient streets for centuries. Occasionally our hands would brush together, but each time, Christina would quickly pull her hand away.

When we approached the steps of Hotel del Sole, a part of me wanted to ask her to join me in my room, but will power can only carry a man so far. I knew that this night, beyond our chance meeting at the restaurant, and an accidental bump of hands, nothing else was going to happen between us.

I had a wonderful dream that night. I heard a knock on my door and Christina call my name. I opened the door. Moonlight flowed through Christina's white, lace nightgown and highlighted the magnificent curves of her body. For a moment, embracing on my threshold, we kissed gently. That was all the invitation I needed. I pulled her into my room.

THIRTY-THREE

Pinky— Rome. Italy

About eight the next morning, I sat down at the table nearest my room. Christina served me a shy smile, a small pot of coffee, and a basket with two rolls, butter and jam.

I said, "*Grazie.*"

She nodded, and quickly moved toward a British couple that had just exited from their room.

Suddenly, the door to the atrium flew open with a force that caused the solid wooden slab to crash against the wall.

A very old man, sporting many days of white stubble, stormed into the breakfast area. He glanced around, spotted me, and spouted an Italian curse in my direction.

When I was functioning at the peak of my linguistic power, and if the speaker spoke very slowly, I could make my way through a reasonable amount of the language. However, most Italian's spat out their words at the speed of light, and I didn't have a clue as to what the old man was saying, or why he was pointing at me, except I could tell he was pissed off.

Then the old man charged me. I jumped up and ducked behind Christina.

He pounded both fists on my table. The contents of my coffee cup jumped into the basket filled with rolls and butter.

Christina jumped forward, wrapped her arms around the old man, and screamed over his tirade, "Nonno Luchitti is very upset because you didn't pay for your room. He is afraid you are going to . . . . ah"

"Skip?" I offered while I peeked around her shoulder.

She nodded while continuing to shield me from the berserk elder.

"Who is he?" I yelled over the man's never-ending

173

stream of Italian oaths.

"Mr. Luchitti's father."

"Now I understand. Tell Nonno to calm down. I was so tired last night that I forgot to pay for the room. I'll get him his money immediately."

While Christina relayed my message, I ran to my room, extracted 170 Euros from my money belt, and returned to the breakfast area. By this time, all the previously closed doors, 4B, 4E and 4F, were wide open and the area was filled with curious spectators.

I handed the old man his money.

He gave me a cold stare, counted each bill with dramatic hand gestures, and after a final nasty remark that I didn't want to understand, he pushed his way through the curious throng and left the breakfast room.

I waved at the audience and said, "Show's over folks. Nothing happened, just a simple misunderstanding."

While the people returned to their rooms or their morning repast, I whispered to Christina, "What did he call me?"

"A thief, and a few other things that I won't repeat, but you need to know that Nonno Luchitti is very old, and not . . . . ah"

I twirled my index finger around my temple. "Not all there?"

She smiled. "Exactly. Let me clean the table, replace your breakfast, and then serve the rest of the guests."

After I finished eating, I stalled for time, slowly sipping my coffee, and waited until the last guest, a single woman who looked like an English schoolteacher on sabbatical, pushed away from her table and returned to her room. I caught Christina's eye. She shook her head.

Not sure what her problem was, I left my table and returned to my room. Five minutes later, I heard a light knock. I opened the door and she entered.

"Mr. Delmont, what happened last night was—"

I smiled. "Wonderful."

"Please, do not make a joke."

I looked at her angelic face and could see that she was

174

upset about something.

"I'm sorry, Christina. What's wrong?"

"As I tried to say, what happened last night was very unusual for me."

"I understand. We had a grand dinner together. The food—the wine—Christina, what happened last night is why Rome is called the eternal city."

She walked over to the sink, picked up my dirty towel and the trash can. "Thank you, Mr. Delmont."

"Christina, do you want us to act as if we had never met last night?"

She nodded and rushed toward the door.

I said, "Please, don't go. I need to talk with you."

She shook her head violently.

I had thought our dinner was marvelous, but for some reason, Christina acted as if she had been violated in some way.

I said, "Please hear me out. I came to Italy because I have to transact some important business. That scene with the old man convinced me that my Italian is very weak. To complete my business, I will need help with the Italian language from a person I can trust. Someone like you."

She put her hand on the door handle and started to twist the handle. "No. I'm sorry, but that is out of the question."

"Do you understand the English meaning of hitting on you?"

"I think so. It means that a man is interested in a woman."

"That's correct. Christina, I'm not trying to hit on you. I'm making you a simple business proposition. I need your help, and I will pay you three times what you would make working here."

The moment she heard my offer of three times her salary, her fingers relaxed and slipped off the handle.

She said, "I have to leave now to complete my morning duties. If you truly want to discuss business, meet me in two hours. I'll be in the railroad terminal building, next to track platform 21, at the little stand drinking a coffee."

THIRTY-FOUR

Bear— Eureka. Nevada

Goodie herded us toward his car, a tired gold Cadillac convertible. He sat me in the front, and put Flo in the back. "Everybody buckled up and settled down?"

Flo snorted, "Whatever."

Goodie said, "Bear, what do you think of this Caddy? It's a classic."

It was big, ugly, and the only thing it missed was a set of long horns nailed onto the front hood. But I thought we should start out friends, so I said, "What year is it?"

"A '71, and Bear, they don't make 'em like this anymore."

Goodie was just the kind of patsy who'd think that the biggest engine in town was a good thing. His car was so huge that he'd need two tugboats to guide his gold boat to the curb, "Yup, it's a real classic. Flo, will you be happy sitting in the back?"

"First a motel without a pool. Next I'm relegated to the back of the bus. At least you gave me enough time to finish a little breakfast."

Flo was doing her usual morning grouchy stuff, but we had work to do so I ignored her. "Let's go, Goodie."

He fired up the engine. A cloud of dark gray smoke billowed from the rear of the gold boat and we lumbered west on Highway 50. It took us no more than thirty seconds to clear the city limits of Eureka.

Last night, while listening to Flo grunt and snort, I had come up with a cool plan to see the Page ranch. Now it was time to see if my idea worked. "Goodie, how many places do you have for us to look at?"

"I brought five outstanding ranch opportunities. I have big ones and I have small ones. The biggest one—"

"Goodie, at the bar last night I forgot to tell you that I

176

was born and raised in Elko. I guess I'm only interested in ranch property north of here, between Eureka and Highway 80. You know, like I'd feel closer to home. Maybe a ranch off Highway 278."

Without a grab-your-ass-I'm-turning-around-warning, Goodie cranked the wheel and floored the gas pedal of that monster car. The gas sucking V8 under the Caddy's hood roared like a wounded lion and the car made as close to a one-eighty as it could. The rear wheels screeched as they bit into the blacktop. With a cloud of sand and black smoke, we started back to town.

Goodie, said, "Shit, Bear, you should'a told me. I only brought two ranches off 278. I could stop by the office and find a few more."

I knew that Goodie was a fellow bartender and all, so I should treat him nice, but I didn't really give a shit about any of his ranches off of Highway 278. I needed a ticket onto the Page Ranch, and Goodie had the key to the box office. "That's okay, Goodie. I'm sure those two will be enough. If not, we can do this all over again tomorrow."

I heard a voice from the back seat mutter, "Bear, I draw the line at your suggestion. One day in this back seat is as much as I can stand."

The bellowing V8 must have hurt Goodie's hearing, because he nodded and said, "Sounds good to me. Bear, you and your woman—"

Flo smacked Goodie hard on the back of head and snapped, "I told you last night. I'm not his woman. We're partners in our work, that's all."

"Sorry, Ma'am."

Flo did have her way!

Goodie slammed on the brakes at an intersection. The Caddy skidded sideways inside a cloud of gray smoke kicked up by the brakes and tires. He said, "Sorry folks, I almost missed the turn. Okay, we're now entering the scenic section of Highway 278. It'll be about ten minutes before we reach our first stop, so sit back and enjoy the view."

For what seemed like a lot more than ten minutes, I stared out the window at nothing but dirt and rocks. Maybe

I missed something, but I didn't see anything that looked scenic. A hundred yards ahead, I spotted a mailbox on the west side of the road. Goodie slowed down and hung a left. After a couple miles of kidney busting dirt road, the Caddy stopped at what looked like a pile of old adobe bricks.

We all got out of the gold boat. Flo frowned, and started to say something, but I shook my head and she clammed up.

Goodie waved his arm and said, "Just take in that sweeping vista."

I did a 360 and all I saw was the same wasteland I had stared at for the last fifteen minutes. Then my eyes settled on the pile of adobe bricks.

Goodie said, "I know the ranch house looks a touch run down, but with a little TLC, that place could look like Martha Stewart herself lived here."

Martha Stewart? A million bucks, and ten years of back-breaking labor might make this place livable. I wanted to smack Goodie for thinking I was that dumb, but at this point I needed him more than he needed me. I said, "Goodie, I think the ranch house is a little run down and I'm not one of those do-it-yourself guys."

"Bear, I knew that. I just wanted to start you at the bottom, so the rest of the places will—"

I pushed Flo back into the backseat and said, "Let's go."

We returned to 278 and headed north. Around the sixty-mile mark, I spotted two rock pillars on the right and watched the Page Ranch sign flash by.

Flo leaned forward and tapped my shoulder. "Bear, didn't that sign—"

I pushed Flo back into her seat and yelled in Goodie's right ear, "HOW FAR TO THE NEXT STOP?"

Flo punched my arm, but she sat back and dummied up.

"A couple of miles north," he said, like he didn't notice that I had just screamed in his ear.

About a mile passed. He said, "Zabarte's a Basque name, right?"

After hearing tales of Basque persecution from my mother, both in Nevada and Spain, I wasn't sure where Goodie was heading. I tightened my right fist and said, "Yes, I'm Basque."

"Then you'll love the next place. Your neighbors are related to that rich Basque who owns that big hotel in Sparks, east of Reno. I'd bet if you buy this ranch, your new neighbors will get you free tickets to one of those big name shows."

Now that should seal the ranch deal sight unseen. Flo and I will buy a broken down ranch in this god-forsaken badlands because we'll get two free tickets to a show at The Nugget. That was the second time I wanted to smack Goodie one, this time a right on the jaw, but I calmed down and said, "Out here I'm sure good neighbors are really important."

Goodie turned off 278 and the Caddy cruised down a smoother ranch road, but this time I watched a giant rooster tail of dust chase us. Goodie stopped—the cloud of dust caught up—and poured through the old convertible top like it was made out of fish net.

Flo coughed and said, "Let me out of here. I can't breathe."

It wasn't that bad, but it wasn't any fun either. I opened my door. Me and Flo jumped out of the dust storm on wheels.

Goodie, trying to act casual, said, "Sorry about that little leak, Flo. I have a man lined up to fix it next week. What do you think about this ranch house, Bear."

Flo glared at me. I glared back and tried to brush some of the dust off her shoulders.

Without really looking, I answered Goodie's question. "It looks better than the last one."

Flo pushed my hand away and climbed back into the car.

I joined Goodie on a quick tour. He was right, the closer I got to the place, the better it looked. I had to come up with a quick reason to move on. I said, "How many acres?"

"I know that last night you told me you were looking for a spread with at least five hundred acres."

"Goodie, answer my question. How many acres?"

He dropped his head. "Only forty."

This was my lucky day, the ranch was too small. "God damn it, you told me that—"

"Bear, I'm sorry, but I had five places selected for your exclusive viewing before you changed the search area."

"So that's all you have today?"

A look of pure panic covered Goodie's face. As far as he was concerned, I was an honest-to-god customer, and if he didn't come up with something real quick, he was going to lose a big commission. Goodie's real estate life had reached the point of the starving coyote with no food in sight. It was time to offer him a rib-eye steak. I said, "Are you sure there's nothing coming onto the market—something so damn good that you want to save it for yourself?"

He shrugged, "Well, there's a ranch down the road a piece. But it's not on the market at this time. The owner . . . . he . . . . ah . . . . he just recently passed away. The estate will be tied up in probate for a while. But the size of the spread is 640 acres and would be perfect for you and Flo. The ranch house is a classic. I can drive you by, but you have to remember that I'm not officially offering the property to you, this is just a little look-see."

"Sounds good to me. Are you game, Flo?"

"So now you want my opinion." She looked at my face and saw I wasn't smiling. She said, "Okay, one more stop and then back to the motel. I want to spend the rest of the day at the spa."

Goodie said, "Sounds like fun."

"Humph!"

In a few minutes we turned east off 278 and passed underneath the sign of the Page Ranch.

Again, Flo leaned forward. She said, "Bear, isn't this the—"

I gave her my nastiest look and she shut her trap. I said, "Goodie, Flo's father, God rest his soul, her father's first name was Page. So even though he's been gone for twenty years, every time she see that name, she sort of chokes up, emotionally I mean."

He looked at her through his rear view mirror. "I'm sorry, Flo. Actually Page is the last name. The guy who owned this spread was named Bill Page."

Flo punched my shoulder hard and said, "I knew all that. What I don't understand is—"

I turned and gave Flo my second nastiest look. She did that little pouty thing with her lower lip, but at least she shut up. I was glad she did what I wanted her to do, but I had a feeling that any hope of getting my hands on her later were slipping away with each nasty stare.

Goodie hit the brakes and jumped out. "Wait here. I need to make sure that no one's around."

In a minute, he came back and said, "We can't go around the front way, but we can walk around the back if you want to give the house a once over."

Flo's expression had turned to a full-blown snit. She said, "You go ahead. It's obvious that I'm not wanted."

I followed Goodie around the back of the house. I peeked into a couple of windows and told Goodie the things he wanted to hear—like nice place—and solid roof—the kind of shit you'll tell a real estate man to keep him happy. When we finally got back to his car, I never let on that I saw the wad of crime tape pasted across the front door.

On the way back to 278, I said, "Goodie, me and Flo are interested in the Page Ranch. I know you told me that the place wouldn't be on the market for a while, but we'd be willing to wait a few months. Before we make an offer, though, I'll need an official map, the kind that comes from the County Recorder's Office, to show me the real acreage and boundaries."

"Bear, I knew all along that I was dealing with a shrewd businessman. I'll pick up the maps, and the other paperwork, and give them to you when you stop by The Owl for dinner. And don't forget, tonight, the drinks are on me."

THIRTY-FIVE

Pinky—Rome, Italy

I was on my second cup of coffee, and beginning to think I had been stood up, when I felt a gentle tap on my shoulder.

Christina sat down next to me and ordered a coffee from a skinny kid behind the counter. "Mr. Delmont, I have come, although a part of me said I should not do this. What did you want to talk to me about?"

In the mid-morning light, Christina's visage reminded me of Monticello's Birth of Venus that hung in the Galleria degli Uffizi in Florence.

I smiled. "Christina, I am honored that you trusted me enough to come."

"I am here, Mr. Delmont, but please do not make my attendance into more than you should. I have only a short time before I must return to the hotel so please explain your business proposition."

"Before I do that, we need to address each other as equals. In America, friends call each other by their first names."

"I understand that, but earlier you said that we would be business colleagues, not friends, no?"

I said, "Yes, that is correct. But in my country, even business colleagues, those that respect each other, address each other by their first names."

That stopped her cold. For a moment, she seemed to consider the possibility that I had told the truth—that our two countries could have different business customs.

I said, "You wouldn't expect me to call you Ms. Romano, each and every time I addressed you? I think not. Business associates need to address each other on a first name basis."

She nodded. "Now I understand. Yes, you may call me

Christina."

"Fine, and from now on you will call me Pinky."

A bemused expression crossed her face. "Do you mean pink—the color between red and white?"

"Actually, Pinky, not Pink. My given name is Pincus, and my business colleagues in America have shorten Pincus to Pinky."

Christina smiled, thrust her hand toward me, and said, "Hello, Pinky Delmont. Now would you explain to me what sort of a business arrangement you are proposing?"

"I have very important news to give to a woman. According to my information, she lives in an area that I'm unfamiliar with—in the Maremma—and the largest city of the district is called Grosetto."

Her lovely face lit up. "Pinky, I know the area well. The Maremma is in southern *Tuscano,* next to the Ligurian Sea. I have an aunt who lives near the city of Grosetto. When I grew up, during each summer, my mother's sister would take me to the beach near a wonderful town called Castiglione della Pescaia. The water was warm, the sand soft, and the air sweet. I love those memories."

"According to my information, the woman I need to talk with lives near a town called Vetulonia."

Her mouth dropped open. "Pinky, Vetulonia was one of the eight major cities of the Etruscan empire. When I was a little girl, the aunt who lives near Grosetto told me stories about the Etruscan warriors who had been buried in tombs near the village of Vetulonia."

"How big is Vetulonia?"

"I have never been there, but my aunt told me it is very small, perhaps three hundred people."

"So I'm in luck. You're familiar with the area where we need to go. How far is Vetulonia from Rome?"

She sat back and frowned. "Pinky, slow down. You just said we. I have not yet decided that I will accept your business proposition. What have I done that tells you to make that assumption?"

"I'm sorry. I thought after our date last night, that you'd want to—"

183

Christina's voice turned cold enough to freeze the coffee in my cup. "Mr. Delmont, I am not that type of woman. Our dinner last night was not a date! It was just a chance meeting."

Now I got it. She was going to play the hard-to-get game.

I said, "I apologize. Now, if you can't trust me enough to go with me, can you at least answer a few questions?"

She glanced at her watch. "Go ahead, but I have only a minute before I must leave."

"How far is Vetulonia from Rome?"

She said, "Three, perhaps four hours by train. It all depends if you take the express or—"

"I've rented a car so we'll, excuse me, I'll be driving. How long will that take me?"

"Two hours, perhaps. I'm sure that you can drive that distance much faster than taking the train."

"Good."

But I still hadn't come up with a way to get her to commit to the trip. Since college, I had dated, and married, a succession of beautiful women. Christina Romano fit my profile perfectly. Plus she could translate. I had to do or say something to increase her confidence in me.

I took a slow sip of coffee. In Carson City I played poker one night a week with some of the men from the court. There were times when I had to call a bluff, and there were times when I had to give up the hand and throw in my cards. I decided that it was time to call her bluff. "Christina, I want you be my business associate, but if you won't believe my motives are pure, would you help find someone else who will go with me to Vetulonia? I still have the language problem, and I'm sure one of your friends will find a good use for a thousand American dollars."

Christina tried hard to retain her passive expression, but I saw a minuscule twitch below her right eye, a give-a-way 'tell' that she wanted to get her hands on my money.

"Pinky, don't rush me. Let me ask Mr. Luchitti if he will give me the time off. If he agrees, I will go with you to Vetulonia."

In my gut, I knew that if I packaged the right incentives, the prim and proper Christina Romano would come around to my way of thinking.

I said, "Wonderful. Now, all you need to do, once we reach Vetulonia, is to translate my information for the woman."

Christina's eyes narrowed slightly, as if she had picked up something from the tone of my voice that had sounded an alarm. "I will translate for you, but, Pinky, I feel there is something very important about the information that you are not telling me."

My possible companion was way too smart to work as a maid. I couldn't tell her everything, but she knew that I hadn't come thousands of miles to discuss pasta-cooking techniques with Maria Gotelli. "You're right, my meeting with the woman could be touchy."

Her eyebrows shot up. "I do not understand touchy. Why do you feel the need to touch the *signora*?"

"I'm sorry. I used an American colloquialism. What I meant to say was, what the woman hears from you could be difficult for her to accept. Also, and this is very important, everything you tell her must remain confidential."

"Ah, so everything must remain in my head, no?"

"Now that was a refreshing way to define confidentiality. Will that present a problem for you?"

"No, but I am still concerned about the ultimate objective of your trip to Vetulonia. You must understand that I will not become involved in any situations that I would not discuss with my parents."

I decided to level with her. "Christina, I came to Italy to tell a woman named Maria Gotelli that her husband is dead."

"Oh."

"But that's not the worst part. Her husband was married to another woman in California."

"*Il mio dio.*" She crossed herself, and said, "The California wife, does she know about *Signora Gotelli*?"

"No."

There was no reason to inform Christina that the California wife was also dead, because that fact wasn't important. But her question had reminded me that if the California wife had died before Clark had married his Italian wife, then the lady living in Vetulonia could be Clark Page's legal heir. But if Clark had married the Italian wife before the California wife died, then the Italian marriage was null and void. Either way, the legal conundrum could generate legal fees for an Italian lawyer well into the next century.

Christina said, "I am sorry, but I am not sure I can tell another woman that sort of news. Pinky, why are you doing this? What kind of work do you do in America? You sound to me like you are a lawyer . . . the word in Italian is *avvocato*."

"Guilty as charged. Why the question? Will my being a lawyer cause you a problem?"

"No, but in my country, many *avvacatos* have been known to take large liberties with the law."

"Imagine that." I forced a stern tone to my voice. "Nothing of that sort would ever happen in my country."

Christina sighed, "I'm glad you told me that. My parents would die if I was ever involved in anything illegal."

"Not to worry. So, will you still go with me?"

"It all depends on Mr. Luchitti, *la mia sporgenza* . . . he's my boss. Pinky, I need my job as a maid. I clean rooms and scrub the toilet so I can earn money to finish my education."

I knew that there was more to Christina than the dark eyed, beautiful hotel maid in Rome. "What's your major?"

"*Scusilo*? I am sorry, I do not understand your question."

"When you complete your studies, what will your new job be?"

She nodded, "*Commercio internazionale* . . . you would call it international business."

"How many more years left in school?"

"This is my final year. Lancia, the Italian car manufacturer, has offered me a position in their international marketing division."

God knew that I'd buy a Lancia from her. I said, "Do

you know what you are going to tell Mr. Luchitti?"

A conspiratorial smile graced her lovely face. "Yes. I will tell him that I have been given a special assignment from the university."

Christina was as clever as she was beautiful.

I said, "And your assignment will require you to leave Rome for a couple of days?"

"That is correct."

I offered her my hand and said, "So do we have a deal?"

"Yes, I believe we have agreed upon a business arrangement."

THIRTY-SIX

Bear—Eureka, Nevada

Goodie dropped us off at the motel with the dream of a giant commission filling up his pea-sized brain. He gunned the engine before Flo had closed her back door. I don't think the patsy noticed the door was still open when he started his big u-turn, but he would the next time he washed his car. His right-rear door crashed into the mailbox that sat in front of the dirty-windowed Chinese restaurant. Dented door and all, clouds of gray smoke bellowed from the Caddy's exhaust as Goodie made a beeline to the County Recorder's office.

Flo said, "What the hell was that loud noise?"

"Goodie just crunched his rear door into a mailbox, but I don't think it registered."

She said, "Humph. I'm not surprised. He didn't strike me as very bright. What's your take?"

"Flo, you have a way of peeling a guy down until all that's left is bone. To answer your question, I think he's a nice enough guy, but I wouldn't want him investing any of my excess money."

"As if you had any to invest. I'm going to put on my swimsuit and head to the spa. Want to join me?"

Flo had been cooped up in the back seat all day with only a couple of flare-ups. She had allowed me to do my thing, so I needed to thank her in some way for her good behavior. Besides, she was going to put her suit on, and that meant taking her clothes off. I'd win no matter what happened. "Thanks for the invite, but I might not make it past the part where you get naked."

Flo kissed me and said, "Bear, you're nothing but an animal. And I don't want you to change a thing."

Three hours later, and that included about an hour soaking in the hot water at the spa, we dressed and walked the block to The Owl.

The minute Goodie saw us come through the door, his face lit up like a pinball machine adding up a million points. He grabbed a wine glass for Flo, gave her some red, and poured me four fingers of Black Label.

As soon as we settled our butts on the bar stools, Goodie said, "Here are the maps you wanted. You and Flo take all the time you want, and when you make up your mind, just give me a call."

I sipped my scotch and acted cool. "Thanks. We'll do our best to come to a fast decision, but don't sit by the phone. We still have to talk with our lawyer and check with the bank. You've been around the track a few times and know how hard-ass some of those people can be."

"Tell me about it. Bear, I've had deals that took a year, one dragged on for two years. Don't worry, I'm cool." Goodie reached over the bar and shook my hand.

To tell the truth, I felt a little bad taking advantage of him that way, but if I nailed this job for Pinky, I wouldn't be tending bar anymore. I guess I really didn't give a shit if a fellow bartender got screwed out of a little time and a few gallons of gas.

What I wanted to do was head back to the motel and spread out the Page Ranch map. Instead, I hung around through two more drinks, and another so-so dinner. Jesus, if The Owl was the best place to eat in this town, just how bad was that Chinese joint?

Finally, I herded Flo back down the sidewalk into our room. As usual, after downing four glasses of red wine, she was lights-out the minute her head hit the pillow. Ignoring her grunts, I laid the map of the Page ranch on the table.

The map was really fuzzy, like it was a copy, of a copy, of a copy. The ranch acreage was a perfect six hundred and forty acre square with Highway 278 marking the west border. The ranch road, located near the south property line, was clearly marked and ended about where the ranch house should be. A north-south dry creek bed marked the east border. I leaned closer and pulled the lamp down. If I squinted hard, I could just make out a faint line that went

189

right through the center of the map. I grabbed the motel pen and darkened the line. It split the six hundred and forty acres in half. At one time, it looked like the section had been two three hundred and twenty acre parcels. I got real close, checked out the northern parcel and noticed two faded lines near the north property border. The lines started at Highway 278, went straight toward the eastern property border, and then angled due south, near to the end of the Page Ranch road. Flo snorted. I looked at the bed and thought about getting close to her warm body. Then I remembered how worried Pinky was before he got on the airplane to Italy.

He had said, "Bear, one thing that keeps nagging at me is the fact that the deputy only saw Richard's car traveling south on Highway 278. If there was another killer, where did he go? How did he escape? There are no maintained cross roads on that section of Highway 278. Besides, that area is so desolate that even a deputy sheriff could spot a turtle sitting on the asphalt a mile away."

I told him, "Boss, we don't know how the real murderer escaped. That's why you're paying me big bucks to find the answer."

Pinky got mad. "Damn it, don't call me boss, and stop reminding me how much I'm paying you. I must have been drunk when I agreed to that outlandish amount."

Flo made an extra loud snort. Then it hit me. The other road might be the answer to Pinky's question. If there was a second road to and from the ranch house, and if that road was still drivable, the real killer could have used that road, driven north on 278 to Highway 80, and the deputy, Richard, or his girlfriend would never have seen the murderer's car.

I got up and pulled back the curtains. The moon was full and there was more than enough moonlight for a trip to the Page ranch.

I went over to the bed and kissed Flo on her forehead. "Wake up Sleeping Beauty, we have work to do."

"Huh."

"Come on, get dressed. We have to head out to the

Page ranch."

Flo pushed her face close to the clock by the bed. "Are you crazy? It's the middle of the night. We can do that when the sun comes up." As the last words fell out of her mouth, her head hit the pillow and she snorted herself back to sleep.

I shook her shoulder. "Come on, Flo, wake up. I know it's late. But we're like spies, and sometimes spies sneak around the desert in the moonlight."

She opened one eye, saw I wasn't kidding, and rolled her beautiful body out of bed. "All right. I'm up, but you better have a damn good reason."

After she threw on some clothes I pushed her into the car. Flo laid her head back and pretended to sleep while I drove to the junction of 50 and 278. "Flo, here's the reason. Pinky told me that we have to find evidence to prove someone besides Richard had the opportunity to murder his uncle."

Her eyes stayed closed. She said, "Okay, but you still haven't told me why we're driving around this God-forsaken wilderness at this hour!"

"While you were sleeping, I looked at the map and spotted what might be another road to the Page Ranch. If I'm right, somebody could have used that road to drive to the ranch, shoot Bill Page, and then leave unseen."

Flo opened her eyes and stared at me. "Okay, maybe you're not nuts. I get it. Now let me go back to sleep."

I wasn't sure she got everything, but I did and that was all that counted. I let her saw logs while I drove through the moonlit night. About a mile before we got to the Page Ranch road, I killed my headlights and slowed down. That would have been dangerous on most roads, but I hadn't seen another car since we left Eureka, so I wasn't worried.

A few minutes passed, and then we rolled past the rock posts at the entrance to the Page ranch road. I stopped and checked out the speedometer. The secret road would be nearly a mile a way. I punched the gas for eight tenths of a mile and then slowed down to 5 MPH. After two minutes of

191

crawling along, I spotted fresh tire ruts on my right. I jabbed at Flo, and said. "Wake up, we're here."

She woke up, and looked around. "Shit, how can you tell?"

"See those tire ruts in front of the car?"

She leaned forward and nodded.

"That's what I was looking for. We're going to follow those ruts. I think they'll lead us to the Page Ranch."

"You're kidding. All the way to the ranch house?"

"Never been surer of anything in my life."

I turned off the highway and even with the bright moonlight; I couldn't see more than twenty feet in front of the car.

"Bear, if you don't turn your headlights on, you need to slow down."

"Just sit back and relax."

"How can I relax? Have you lost your mind? We could crash into a rock. You could drive us into a ditch. Or you could come across Basa Faun like your father did."

"Shit, Flo, Basa Faun was just one of my Pop's old stories."

"I knew that," she snapped.

After we had driven real slow for a long time, the ground started to rise. The ruts turned right and ended at an old building.

"I thought you told me that this road would go to the Page Ranch."

I could always depend on Flo to burn my ass. "Cut me a little slack, damn it. I'm getting out to look around. Are you coming?"

"No! Not until you can show the Page Ranch."

I was sorry I had dragged Flo into this. But Pinky had told me that she had to be with me, to be some sort of a colobilating witness, I think he called it, in case we did find something important.

I said, "Okay, but as soon as I find something, you're going to roll your butt out of this car. Don't forget, this is a partnership."

She put her head back, closed her eyes, and said,

"Whatever."

God, she could be frustrating at times. I got out and walked to the building. There were two big doors with wooden handles on each door. They didn't look like they were locked. I pulled on the handles and the doors opened without a peep. Now that was really strange because the building looked older than dirt. I rubbed my fingers against the closest door hinge, took a whiff, and walked back to the car.

"Flo, wake up. We've got work to do."

She opened one eye. "Did you actually find something?"

"Yup, WD-40."

"What's that?"

"Someone used WD-40, that spray-oil-in-a-can, on the door hinges to make them work without squeaking. My guess is that it's the man, or woman, who pumped a bullet into Bill Page's head, so drag your butt out of the car! We've got work to do."

Flo shivered. I wasn't sure if her chill came from the cool air, or the fact that we were about to walk into a spooky looking building in the middle of the night.

I said, "Hold on a minute."

I popped the trunk and took out a canvas bag.

Flo said, "What's that?"

"Just some investigative tools Pinky told me I might need."

We walked into the building. Moonlight poked through holes in the roof and gaps in the walls, and the inside wasn't much darker than outside. One glance told me that the building used to be a barn. Above, was a loft filled with the smelly remains of rotting hay. To the right there were a couple of broken down horse stalls. In front of us was an empty room with a window and a door. When I reached the window, my heart started to jump around because below I could see the ridge of a roofline. "Take a look over here, Flo. There's a house down there, and I'd bet my ass that's the Page place."

We were both standing there looking at the roof when

193

Flo said, "Do you pick-up something besides moldy alfalfa?"

I took a sniff. She was right. The smell was a mixture of skanky underpants, singed hair, and burnt sugar.

Flo spotted it first. "Down there, near your left foot. There are three of them. They look like dog turds, but dog turds don't smell like that."

I crouched down, set the canvas bag on the dirt, and checked out our find. They weren't dog turds. Dog shit doesn't smell that bad. What Flo had found were three cigar butts—about two inches long—leftovers from some cheap, nasty cigars. "Flo, do you have some of those tissue packs you always carry around with you?"

"Of course I do. I use them on a regular basis to blow my nose, why?"

I held my hand out and said, "I need two brand-new, unopened packs."

"Well so do I, and you didn't answer my question. Why do you need my tissues?"

Jesus, she was a pistol. I took a deep breath to stop from grabbing her purse and beating her over the head.

I said, "Look, Pinky told me there's this stuff called DNA. Everybody's got it and you can track people by their DNA. It's like fingerprints, only it's a whole bunch better."

Flo snorted, "DNA evidence didn't do much good in the OJ case."

"I know that, and Pinky told me that DNA evidence has come a long way since the OJ trial."

"So what does all this DNA talk have to do with you needing my packs of tissues?"

"Pinky said that DNA floats around inside of us, but it leaks out on things like spit and blood—stuff like that."

"Yuck."

"Check out these butts, Flo. Whoever smoked those cigars, sucked on those butts like they were locked onto their momma's tit. The ends of those butts are black and they're full of dried spit."

"Double yuck."

"But I can't pick them up because I might get my DNA on them. That's why I need two of your tissue packs."

194

"Now why didn't you tell me that in the first place?"

Flo reached into her purse and handed me two of her prized possessions. I opened both packs, took out all the tissues and gave her back all but three. I used the tissues to pick up each butt and I stuffed the ugly things into the empty plastic pack covers.

I said, "As soon as we get back to town, we can find a real plastic bag and seal up the tissues and butts. Now come over here and look out this window. You can see the roof from here."

"Why didn't you and I see this building when we were here this afternoon?"

"Well, you didn't get out of the car, and when I walked around the ranch house, I was looking in the windows."

"What about Pinky? Didn't he go to the ranch house?"

"Maybe he didn't notice, like me. But I think the real reason we didn't see it is that the barn is behind the crest of the hill. You'd have to stand on the roof of the ranch house to see the window we are looking out of."

Flo stood on her toes and said, "I guess you're right. Do you think this is the place where the real killer hid out?"

"Hell yes, and I'm willing to bet Richard Page's life on it. Let's walk down the hill to the house, but be careful. It's steep and we can't see very well."

Flo grabbed my arm.

"Hang on," I said, "and don't let go."

After a few steps, I stopped. "Look, from here, even at night, you can see the ranch road that leads up to the house. Let's say for a second that I'm right. Somebody wants Bill Page dead, and somehow, don't ask me how, that person finds out that Bill's nephew, Richard, is on his way from LA. All he has to do is use the secret road we used, and wait here until he sees Richard's car on the regular ranch road. Then the killer runs down to the house, shoots Bill, and runs out the back door as Richard walks through the front. Next, our cigar smoking killer high-tails it back to Highway 278, again using the secret road, and drives north to Highway 80. Shit, Flo, it's the perfect crime, except the murdering bastard didn't plan on bumping up against a couple of sharp investigators like you and me."

Flo frowned. "Wait a minute. Why would Bill Page just sit there and calmly wait for a bullet with his name on it?"

"Jesus, I don't have that part figured out yet." I waved the tissue packet at her and said, "At least give me credit for what I've figured out so far."

Flo shivered. "Right, Bear, you're wonderful. Now can we return to the motel?"

I grabbed the canvas bag. "'Fraid not, Babe. We're going into that ranch house 'cause we still have to crack a safe."

THIRTY-SEVEN

Pinky—Castiglione della Pescaia, Italy

Christina left me a curt, business-like note informing me that her boss had given her the next three days off to complete her university assignment.

The next morning I returned to the car rental agency, signed an indecipherable stack of papers, and a few moments later, picked up the lovely Christina who had been waiting for me in front of the terminal.

It took me an hour using all of my driving skills to battle through the millions of scooters and cars that congest the narrow streets of Rome. Eventually, I ended up on the same route selected by Lucius Aurelia when he constructed Via Aurelia in 241 BC. Two hundred years later, Caesar used the Aurelia to march his Roman legions north to conquer Gaul.

As my powerful Maserati Quattroporte cruised at nearly a hundred miles per hour, I said, "I'm sure that Lancia makes a very nice car, but you have to admit that nothing beats a Maserati."

"That is true. I have never ridden in such a car."

I ran my hands over the leather-wrapped steering wheel and smiled with satisfaction. The Maserati was indeed the ideal way to view the Italian countryside. A powerful engine moved to my command. A beautiful woman sat at my side. I was one day away from solving the Italian mystery surrounding the Page murder. Simply stated, the life of J. Pincus Delmont couldn't get much better.

After a couple of hours, we skirted around Grosetto, a sort of county seat for the Maremma district, and entered southern Tuscany.

I said, "Is this the area where your aunt lives?"

"Yes. She would take me and my cousin Paulo to the beach."

I said, "Sorry we don't have time to stop by."

"I understand. I think you called it a tight schedule?"

"That's correct. However, based on your love of the beach next to the Ligurian Sea, we could get a room in Castiglione della Pescaia. According to the highway sign, we'll be there in a few minutes."

Christina turned toward me and frowned. "Pinky, this is a business trip."

"I'm sorry. What I meant to say was that we need to book two rooms in Castiglione della Pescaia."

"Pinky, please don't make that mistake again." Christina's tone was cold, as if she was really upset with me. "You made an improper assumption, but this time I will accept your apology. Please remember that I am a simple Italian girl from the country."

Hold on, I thought. Hadn't Christina told me that she was from Rome? No, that was not correct. She had told me that her last name was Romano, and I was the one who'd said that Romano meant someone from Rome.

She said. "I know this is more of a cost for you, but I would not feel comfortable in the same hotel room."

"Money's not a problem. Go ahead and book two rooms."

The road narrowed as we entered the town. Like most towns and cities in Tuscany, Castiglione della Pescaia was an amalgamation of new and old structures with most of the old section encased by the new—similar to the way a puff pastry wraps around a fine beef fillet in a classic Beef Wellington. The new part of town hugged the coast. The older section consisted of ancient stucco buildings anchored to the near vertical cliffs. Above everything and everyone, stood the ubiquitous church atop the tallest peak.

Christina selected one of the modern hotels on the beach side of town. Inside twenty minutes we were both safe and sound in our respective rooms.

Even though a few citizens of Carson City might consider me a devious person—a man unworthy of their trust—there was no way that J. Pinkus Delmont would ever take advantage of a woman who had the slightest question con-

198

cerning what she was about to do. However, I was fully confident that sooner or later, the lovely Christina would succumb to my charms.

I picked up the phone near my bed and dialed her room. "Hi. It's too late to head to Vetulonia, but I need some help with my computer. Would you mind?"

"Mind what?"

"Coming to my room to set up my computer so I can send and receive email. Or if you rather, we can go to the beach for a swim."

"I'll help you with the computer first, then we can go to the beach. I'll be there in a minute."

I pulled my laptop out of the backpack and set it on the desk. It took Christina five minutes to knock on my door, but who was counting?

Christina connected the laptop to a phone jack and fiddled around with the keys. She frowned and dialed the front desk. "*Pronto. Posso inviare della posta elettronicada qui?*" She listened intently for a moment. "*Ah DSL. Grazie.*"

I said, "What was that all about?"

"I requested the dial up number, but they told me this was a modern hotel. I should use the DSL jack at the back of the desk."

She plugged the laptop into a jack by the lamp, pushed a couple of keys, and said, "There you are. Do you want to download your email now?"

"No, I'd rather go to the beach."

Christina smiled. "I'd like that too."

This was going to be easier than I thought. "I'm going to put on my bathing suit. I'll see you on the beach as soon as I change—"

Christina waved and walked to my door. "*Ciao.*"

"*Ciao.*"

Ten minutes later, I joined my 'business partner' on the sand, but I was the only one wearing a bathing suit. "Christina, I had hoped we'd take a quick swim before dinner."

"Pinky, I did not feel . . . . ah—"

"Comfortable?" I smiled, but my facial expression belied how I felt. I had wanted to see more of the lovely Christina, and our little beach-wear party was the perfect excuse. "In America my suggestion to swim would be proper, but here in Italy, I see that I may have over stepped the bounds of propriety."

Christina leaned over, removed her sandals, and said, "Thank you for understanding."

At least barefooted, we strolled along the edge of the water and talked about the many differences between our countries. The air was warm, with just a whisper of breeze. Gentle, cool waves bathed our feet. About a half-mile from our hotel, we sat down and watched the fiery orange ball slip into the blue water. At that point, I was ready for anything.

Christina broke the magic spell when she said, "I think we should to return to the hotel. I am very hungry."

"I agree," but I don't believe we were thinking about the same kind of hunger.

We dined outside under a full, cream-colored moon. After a magnificent meal, and nearly two bottles of wine, I escorted Christina back to her room.

She slipped her key into the door. "Pinky, thank you for a wonderful dinner. You made me feel very special."

I made my move. "Thank you. I . . . ."

Christina backed into her room, said, "Good night," and closed the door.

Chagrined, and a touch humiliated, I returned to my room. After nursing two glasses of brandy, I recovered enough to check my email.

There was one from Lottie, the only female close to me that I could depend on.

Pinky:
How's everything in Italy? I haven't heard from Bear, or have any idea where he is. I may need to get in touch with him to replenish his $1000 advance. Can you help me?
Lottie

I was pleased to note that Lottie was alert, but Bear's

stealth modus operandi meant more to me than his running short of money. I sent Bear a scathing email to remind him that an innocent man depended on him.

Work completed, I crawled into my bed fully assured that sometime tomorrow evening the desirable, but very hesitant Christina, would end up happily lying at my side.

THIRTY- EIGHT

Bear—Eureka, Nevada

I jogged down the slope to the ranch house. Flo yelled, "Did you just say we are going to crack a safe? That's illegal. I'm not going to be a part—"

As I disappeared into the darkness, Flo's loud bitching changed to fear. "Bear, don't leave me here alone in the dark . . . Bear, I can't see you. Where did you go?"

I pulled out a flashlight and turned it on for a second. "I'm down here, but if you don't stop ragging at me—"

In the moonlight, I watched her gorgeous body walk toward me. When she got close, she grabbed my arm and held on tight. "Don't leave me like that again. I'm afraid of the dark."

I kissed her. "I'm sorry, Babe. I didn't know that. Now let's go in."

I popped the door lock with a credit card and we walked into what looked like the kitchen.

Flo sobbed, "Can we turn the light on?"

"No. We can't take the risk of a neighbor seeing anything." To tell the truth, I didn't think there was another human being within a hundred miles, but I liked having Flo scared—she was quiet, and nice to be around when she was scared.

I said, "You stay right where you are and I'll try to find the hall."

"Okay," she whimpered.

I opened the door closest to me, and waited for a second so my eyes adjusted to the dim light. I was looking into a big pantry filled with canned goods and flour.

I backed into the dark kitchen and opened the door on the left. I peered into what looked like the insides of a black dog.

I said, "I think this must be the hallway. Follow me."

202

Flo grabbed my arm. "Don't leave me."

I handed her the canvas bag. "Carry this bag so I can slide my left hand against the wall."

"Why?"

"I'm trying to feel the door, damn it."

Using my left hand like I was a blind guy with a white cane, we crept down the black hall and after five or six steps, my hand bumped into a door.

"I think this must be the office."

We moved inside and I closed the door. I pushed the light part of the flashlight against the floor and turned it on for a second. I saw a blue carpet, just like Pinky had told me, and Flo set the canvas bag on the carpet. I said, "Flo, I'm going to turn on this flashlight for a three count. I want you to look around. If there are any windows, tell me if they are covered. Ready?"

"Yes."

I clicked on the flashlight and counted, "One, two, three."

When the light went off, it was doubly dark, but I had spotted a window and it looked like it was covered with something.

I said, "What did you see?"

"We are standing next to a desk. To my right is a window nicely decorated with a cream colored drape. The floor is covered with wall-to-wall blue carpet. Personally, I don't feel that the carpet and the drape are the correct color combination for this room, but—"

"Yeah, I saw all that crap too."

I flipped the flashlight on and set it on the desk. "Flo, I want you to stay right where you are. I'm going outside and find this window. Once I find it, I'll tap on the glass and you need to tap back. I want to be sure that none of the light is leaking through the drape."

She shivered. "Bear, please don't leave me alone. Bill Page was murdered in this house."

"Don't worry, he was shot down the hall."

For a tough broad, Flo sure was squirrelly when it came to the dark and dead bodies. "Trust me, Babe, nothing happened in this room. You'll be safe."

"Okay, but don't be gone long."

"I'll move as fast as I can."

It took me a minute to find the window and tap. Flo tapped her side, and I hustled back to the office.

She said, "Was there any light leaking out?"

"Nope. We're as snug as a bug in a rug. Flip the light switch. Maybe they left the power on."

Flo tried, but nothing happened. That was okay. I didn't want the power company wondering why an empty house was using electricity.

I said, "Hand me the canvas bag."

The way Flo threw the bag to me told me, that for some dumb reason, she was pissed off at me again. "Bear, I just realized that we broke into this home. That has to be against the law even in Nevada. We need to leave at once."

"Not until I've opened the safe."

"So now you're going to compound our first offense of breaking and entering and crack open a safe. Next thing you'll tell me is that we are going to steal the contents of the safe."

"You got it."

"That's it. Count me out. My mother didn't raise me to be a burglar. I'm not going to be a part of your criminal activity."

I'd had a feeling she'd get back on her high horse sooner or later. "Look, Flo, we have a job to do for Pinky. There might be something inside that safe that will save Richard Page from the needle. I'm going to do this. You have two choices—stay with me, or head back up that hill—alone. I don't have time to argue with you."

Flo stood up and started toward the door. Then she stopped. "All right. I'll stay, but you be sure to tell Pinky that I stayed under protest."

Now what the shit did that mean? "I'll do that. Now get over here and hold the flashlight steady. I've only opened this kind of safe once before."

As Jake had warned me, those flashlight batteries wore down faster than chips disappeared off a craps table.

Flo went through three sets of D cells before I finally cracked the damn thing.

She said, "Bear, I apologize that I doubted your word. After watching you screw around for the last hour, it's obvious to me that you'd starve to death if you depended on cracking safes for a living."

"Thanks, I think. Now stand back so we can see what Bill Page wanted to keep from nosey people like us."

First, I dragged out the deed to the ranch. Next a couple of bankbooks. I dropped them into the canvas bag.

The last thing in the safe was a small notebook. I flipped it open and saw a couple of pages filled with letters and numbers. The rest of the sheets were blank.

I said, "Flo, do you think this notebook is important? What do those numbers and letters mean?"

She leaned over my shoulder. "They could be passwords, those things people use for their computers to keep their data secure from crooks like you."

We both looked at the desk. There was a computer.

I said, "If we had power, we could check out your password idea, but there's no power."

Flo jumped up, "I know what we can do. We can take the computer back to our motel."

Flo picked up the keyboard and mouse and dropped them into the canvas bag. That left the computer and the heavy monitor screen part for me. They both looked really heavy and the car was parked at the top of the hill, on the other side of the barn.

I closed the safe and replaced the carpet. Then I picked up the computer, monitor and pushed Flo out the door of the office. "Babe, I'll carry all this crap, but if your crazy idea doesn't work, I'm not listening to you anymore."

THIRTY-NINE

Pinky—Vetulonia, Italy

The following morning, before consuming my room service breakfast of coffee and rolls, I checked for new emails.

```
Pinky,
Willow called to tell me that Richard
Page's Public Defender has agreed to a man-
slaughter plea with Deputy DA Vaca. I reminded
her that on the advice of your doctor, Richard
Page was not your client. Willow told me that
Vaca will present the plea agreement to the
judge first thing tomorrow morning.
Lottie
```

I didn't like what I read, but in reality, there wasn't a damn thing I could do about it. Once the judge accepted the PD's plea agreement, Richard's goose was cooked. And where was Bear in this picture? What about the proof he was going to find on the Page ranch? Bear's continued failure was further confirmation that I never should have hired a marginal bartender in the first place.

The phone rang.

"Good morning, Pinky, are you ready to go to Vetulonia?"

The sound of Christina's lilting voice pushed Carson City, Bear's failure, and Richard's pending ten to twenty year sentence from my thoughts. "Yes, I'll be in the lobby in five minutes."

We met in the lobby. She wore a white dress that showed off her outstanding figure.

I was about to suggest we forget the drive to Vetulonia and spend the day on the beach when an image of Richard Page rotting in the state penitentiary crept into my mind.

"Are you ready to go to work?"

She returned a shy smile. "Yes."

Without further ado, we walked to the car and began what should have been a short drive to Vetulonia.

In general, the Italian road system was one of the best in Europe, as long as you knew where you were going, and stayed on one of the major arteries. All the important highways were well marked, but the secondary roads were another story. They lacked directional signs, and took the uninformed onto tangents that defied the standard points on a compass. It didn't take long for me to figure out that Christina was confused, so what should have been an easy jaunt turned into a forced march.

Christina, her lovely face buried in a road atlas, cried out directions. "Slow down—no, I was wrong. We should have gone to the right— slow down, I can't figure out which way to turn —take the next right, no, make that left."

Frustrated, I cried, "I thought you told me you knew the area?"

The genesis of tears formed in the corners of her soft brown eyes. "I was a child back then. If you would drive slower, everything would be easier."

"All right, I'll slow down."

A few minutes after I took my foot off the accelerator, Christina said, "Pinky, I know this town. We are in Grilli. I remember we used to eat at a nice restaurant here. Take the right fork out of town and the next time the road splits I think you must take the left side. Then we should be on the road to Vetulonia. The village sits on the top of that hill."

I took a right, then the next left and to my surprise, she was correct. The road immediately started up an incline.

We drove in silence as I allowed my annoyance toward Christina's poor navigation to subside. I was paying her a substantial sum for her claimed expertise and I expected commensurate results.

The powerful engine pulled us up the tree-covered mountain, but the road was so curvy and narrow that I had little time to dwell on the surroundings—rows of olive trees, some young, some old, some abandoned—native oaks, dry grass, and wild berries—an abandoned building with half its ramparts reduced to a pile of rubble—ancient rock walls partitioning off empty pastures.

As we continued our climb, I expected to spot the buildings of Vetulonia around every turn, but all I saw was more road and more Tuscan landscape.

Eventually, just as I was about to tell Christina that she must have told me to take a wrong turn, the road widened and swept to the left. I hit the brakes. We had finally arrived at the entrance to Vetulonia. The tiny village consisted of two rows of stucco buildings that lined either side of the road, a road that petered out at a small church near the top of the hill.

"If I recall, you told me that your aunt described Vetulonia as small. Christina, I'm sure your aunt is a wonderful woman, but she is prone to understatement. This won't take as long as I thought. I'll drive up the hill to the church and turn around. Remember, we're looking for a sign, or something that announces the Save One Sinner foundation."

Christina nodded. She seemed reserved today, I thought, but once we returned to the hotel I was positive I would perk her up.

A cobblestone courtyard fronted the church and allowed me to make a u-turn. Prior to starting back down the hill, I set the parking brake. "Before we begin, I need to set down a few ground rules."

Again she nodded.

"First, I will decide what questions to ask of the woman, and when to ask them. You must translate the exact question even if you feel that I am being harsh. This is very important, Christina. Deciding on the intent, and pace behind my questions is not part of your job. Do I make myself clear?"

"I think so."

"Also, please do not interrupt me or make suggestions concerning how I conduct the interrogation."

She hesitated, as if she were just beginning to understand that the work could be unpleasant.

I said, "Christina, what I ask this woman might recall bad memories. You have to ignore any emotional behavior on her behalf."

"I will do my job, but I cannot understand how you can turn your back on a woman's grief."

"Long ago I learned to maintain an aloofness from any anguish that might develop in this type of situation."

As I reached for the hand brake, I noticed half a dozen men who lined the wall on my left. They pointed at my Maserati and seemed to be laughing at something.

I said, "What's the joke with those fellows?"

"I think they are laughing at your fancy car. Many people living in *Tuscano* do not understand why city people waste large sums of money on expensive cars."

"Don't they have something to do besides making fun of my car?"

"Of course they do. They have their work. They raise their families. For centuries, the people of *Tuscano* have lived a slower, quieter life. The Italian's call it *La dolce far niente*."

"Translate, please."

"It means the art of doing nothing. The people of *Tuscano* have refined how to savor every moment of life on earth."

She was lecturing me, and I did not like that. I had hired Christina to translate, not editorialize. However, I needed her at my side, both now and later at the hotel, so I decided to let it slide.

I released the hand brake and the car started to roll back down the hill. "Now keep your eyes open."

After we had traveled no more than a couple of hundred feet, Christina cried out, "There on the right. See the sign over the door, *Salvezza dal Peccato*? That translates into salvation from the sin. I am sure that's the place you looking for."

I pulled the car over and got out. By now, most of the windows and doors of the adjoining buildings had opened, and half the population of the village, including the out-of-work men from the top of the hill, watched our every move.

At the moment, we were the only show in town.

I knocked. The door opened and a woman in her late thirties poked her head out. She had a simple, pretty face, but I picked up heavy lines and coal-like shadows under her eyes. She said, "*Buon giorno.*"

I waved to Christina for linguistic assistance. "Find out her name and ask if we can speak with her husband."

Christina looked shocked but asked my questions in Italian.

Eventually she said to me, "Her name is Maria Gotelli. When her husband, Antonio Gotelli, is in Italy, he spends part of his day at this office, but most of the day he works on their farm on the valley floor. She has not heard from her husband for some time and she fears something could have happened to him. Pinky, I think this would be the perfect opportunity for you to tell her about his death, but before you say anything, I must summon the local priest."

"Christina, not five minutes ago I told you not to interrupt the flow of my questions. We don't have time to wait around to find a priest. I need to learn more about Maria's life with Antonio. Continue."

Maria's sad tale informed me that Clark Page had led two completely different lives; one in America where he kept his family poor and struggling, and one in Italy where he lived on a farm with his Italian family. It turned out that Maria was the mother of a boy of five—more interesting news to pass on to my client once I returned to Carson City.

She explained that their farm in the valley was potentially profitable, with fifty acres planted in olive trees. However, according to Maria, it would take a few more years before the young trees would produce a full crop. Until that time, the farm would be financially dependent on the money that Antonio brought with him from America.

Christina said, "This year, she and Antonio had hoped to pay off a loan from the bank. Then they will be able to embrace," she paused for emphasis, "*La dolce far niente.*"

I sloughed off Christina's needle. What I had learned so far was interesting, but I still didn't know if Maria was involved in the murder of William Page. I reached into my briefcase and extracted a picture of Clark Page. "Is this Antonio?"

Maria's expression jumped with joy. "*Si.*"

There was a murmur from the villagers who were watching us.

I leaned forward and said, "Madam, it is my sad duty to inform you that your husband is deceased."

I could see that Maria wasn't sure what I had said to her.

I said, "Translate, please."

"Pinky, I insist we summon the priest."

She had pushed me too far. "Christina, do the job I'm paying you to do."

Christina's anger toward me was palpable, but she told Maria her husband was dead.

The crowd gasped as Maria collapsed into my arms.

"See, I told you we needed to call a priest."

I carried the unconscious woman into the *Salvezza dal Peccato* office and set her into one of the few chairs in the room.

After a moment, her eyelids fluttered. Maria struggled to straighten up. "*La mia vita finito,*" she groaned.

I said, "That I understood. She said her life was over."

Christina nodded, "Yes, and now that her husband is dead, the bank will take the farm."

At that point, I was ninety-nine percent sure that Maria Gotelli knew nothing about Clark Page's crimes or the murder of his brother. I said, "I'm sorry about the bank. After all the bills are paid, and if there is any money left in Antonio's American estate, I will make sure the money is sent to Maria."

I knew that I didn't have the right to tell Maria that, but I had a few questions left and I needed both women on my side.

Christina translated my statement, and Maria was able to compose herself.

I said, "When did you marry, Antonio?"

Maria's expression was puzzled.

Christina translated.

Maria thought for a moment and said, *"Dieci anni fa."*

"Ten years ago."

That cleared up the question concerning Clark's estate. He had married Maria while his American wife was alive. Maria's marriage was null and void. So any money left in Clark's estate would go to Richard, not Maria.

I said, "Ask her if she knew a man named Clark Page."

Christina said, "Pinky, she looks very weak. If you keep asking her questions, I fear you are going to make her ill."

"Christina, do you recall what I said at the top of the hill?"

"Yes."

"Then ask her the question."

Christina said, *"Conoscete un uomo chiamato,* Clark Page?"

Maria shook her head.

I said, "William Page?"

"No."

I said, "Richard Page?"

"No, perchè?"

I said, "Because those men knew your husband."

Maria grabbed Christina's arm, pulled her close, and mumbled something.

Christina said, "She wants to know how Antonio died."

"It was an accident."

Christina translated.

Maria said something else.

Christina said, "Where is he buried?"

"Los Angeles."

Maria grabbed my arm and said something.

"She wants to know if a priest gave him his last rights."

"I don't know, but I doubt it."

Christina translated my answer. Maria dropped to the floor, grabbed her sides and started to moan.

"Pinky, we must stop now!"

"I agree. Go to the car. I'll be out in a moment."

212

I had my answers. Clark Page and Antonio Gotelli were the same man. There was no obvious Italian connection to the Page murder. So except for the company of the lovely Christina, the trip to Italy had been a total waste of my time and Richard's money.

I took out a couple of hundred Euros, laid the bills on the desk, and said, "*Arrivederci, Signora.*"

Outside in the bright sunlight, I pushed the crowd away from my car, fired up the powerful Maserati V8 engine, and left the village of Vetulonia.

I was pleased with my day's work. I had achieved my goals in a very short time, but I could see that my lovely business partner was not happy with a few of my tactics. She stared out the window as we drove down the hill toward our hotel.

I said, "I'm sorry I didn't stop to get a priest, but I needed to gauge the honesty of Maria's answers to my questions."

"Is that the way you ask questions in America?"

"Yes."

"Then you are no better than the Italian lawyers."

"Christina, any lawyer worth his salt would have done what I did, but you could be right, sometimes in the heat of battle, I forget myself. Will you accept my apology?"

She didn't respond.

I said, "What time is it?"

"Two thirty."

"Great, we'll have time for another walk on the beach before dinner. Doesn't that sound like fun?"

She hesitated, then turned and gave me a shy smile. "Yes, some fresh air on the beach sounds good."

I said, "You did good work back there."

"But I thought you were mad at me."

I said, "No, I wasn't mad. Believe me, you did a fine job today and I have a little surprise for you."

Our car rolled into the hotel parking lot. I set the brake and took out my wallet. "Instead of our agreed upon one thousand American dollars, I'm going to give you one thousand Euros. I'm fully aware that at the present exchange rate, that will work out to a bonus of two hundred American dollars. Christina, I trust that will make up for my asperity."

Christina took the stack of fifty Euro bills and stared at them. It was as if she had never held that much money at one time in her life. "Pinky, now I will go to my room and change into my bathing suit. Let us meet on the beach in an hour."

I watched her walk across the parking lot. Then I jumped out of the car and ran to my room. I took a quick shower, and put on my bathing suit. We'd meet on the beach in forty-five minutes. I set a bottle of Pinot Grigio in the sink and drizzled cold water to chill the wine down.

I glanced at my watch. Forty-one minutes left. I sat down at the desk and checked my email. Nothing! I sent Bear the following:

    Leaving Italy as soon as I return to Rome.
    What are you doing? Richard Page will soon be
    in the penitentiary and you've dropped the
    ball. As your employer, I require an immediate
    email response or I will be forced to take
    disciplinary action.
    Pinky

I hit send and checked my watch. I'd meet Christina in thirty-eight minutes. I poured myself four fingers of brandy and downed half the glass in a single gulp. I sat down in an overstuffed chair, and with each sip of the golden elixir, my pending tryst with Christina took a backseat to exhaustion and alcohol. I laid my head back and closed my eyes. The sound of my empty glass bouncing off the carpet jolted me awake. I glanced at my watch. Oh my God, I was twenty minutes late for our meeting. Had I slept through her knock? I called her room. The phone rang fifteen times before I gave up. She must still be waiting for me at the beach. I ran to the sand. Christina was nowhere in sight. Puzzled, I returned to the main desk.

"Excuse me, I was suppose to meet Christina Romano a half hour ago. I called her room and received no answer.

Did she leave a message for me at the desk?"

The clerk glanced at his register. "The lady in room 32A? I'm sorry, Mr. Delmont, Miss Romano checked out over an hour ago."

It took all my years of courtroom experience to maintain my outward calm. "Thank you. I must have confused the time." I looked at my watch. "As soon as I complete packing, I will be checking out. Have the concierge book me a flight from Rome to New York—any airline that departs Da Vinci six hours from now."

"As you wish, Mr. Delmont."

Fifteen minutes later, as my Maserati hurtled south toward Rome, I struggled to control my rage toward the woman who had treated me with utter disdain. As each mile flew past, a cold truth replaced my angst. Were the last two days real, or were they an elaborate scheme to make me think there was no Italian connection? Somehow I had to find an answer to that question in the next few hours.

Many miles later, after I returned my rental car, I stood in the Rome rail terminal. During the drive, I had considered going to the police. But what would that accomplish? I had hired a woman to do translation work. Once the work was completed, I paid her. Then she unexpectedly left my employment. Wake up and smell the coffee, Pinky, you have been conned. The only question left was why?

I had a couple of hours before my flight. I was sure that Christina wouldn't return to the hotel, so where could I look? That's when Roberto's popped into my head. Christina had told me that she ate there occasionally. If she had made a mistake and told me the truth, perhaps someone at the restaurant knew her.

I checked my luggage into a locker and briskly walked the few blocks to the restaurant. The same old waiter who had served us that night stood in the back of the near empty dining area.

I ran up to him and said, "*Scusilo.*"

"*Si?*"

I said, "*Ah . . . Sto cercando . . .*"

215

"Perhaps I can be of some assistance? I am the owner of Roberto's."

The voice came from the shadows behind the waiter. A large man dressed in a gray, double-breasted suit emerged.

I said, "Thank you. I'm looking for a woman I dined with at this restaurant a few nights ago."

The gray suit whispered to the old waiter.

The old man leaned close and scrutinized my face. His breath, with its tang of garlic made my eyes water.

He pursed his lips and shrugged.

I pointed to a table at the waiter's right. "We sat at that table. She ordered the house specialties and I ordered the waiter's wine selection."

The suited man repeated my statement. This time a glimmer of recognition flashed across the old man's eyes.

"And I left the waiter a thirty percent tip."

The gray suit turned toward me, as if to question my sanity.

I sighed, "Yes. A thirty percent tip."

The suit passed on my statement. The old man looked to the owner. The gray suit nodded.

The waiter said, "*Si, Christina Luchitti.*"

The last name hit me like a stream of water shooting from a fire hose. The con had started the moment I had entered the Hotel del Sole.

I yelled, "*Grazie,*" and ran out of the restaurant.

I jogged the three blocks to the Hotel del Sol and arrived at the heavy metal gate that guarded the entrance. I caught my breath while I briefly considered how to enter without pushing the button. Suddenly, the gate popped open. A man walked through, and unannounced, I entered into the building. I eschewed the elevator and sprinted up the five flights. The front door was open and the tiny lobby was unmanned. The breakfast tables on the left were empty. I glanced around, spotted a call bell and pounded it with all the fury of my pent up rage.

A door behind the counter opened and Mr. Luchitti, a white napkin tucked into his shirt, cautiously stepped through.

"Ah, Mr. Delmont. How may I help you?"

"You can begin by dropping the friendly crap and telling me what's been going on."

"I'm not sure—"

"Let's start with the woman who you pretended was the fourth floor maid. It turns out her name is not Romano, but Luchitti. Now do you understand my question?"

"Mr. Delmont. Please calm yourself. We have a few guests that sleep during the day. Yes, you are correct, Christina is my daughter. Now, if you will excuse me, I am in the middle of my dinner, so—"

"Hold it right there, buster. That doesn't explain a damn thing. First, did you know who I was before I arrived?"

"Of course I knew. You had a reservation under the name of Delmont for two nights."

"But why did Christina go with me to Vetulonia?"

"Because you paid her one thousand American dollars to do translation work. That was the amount you agreed upon, correct?"

"Mr. Luchitti, why did you and your daughter con me?"

"Mr. Delmont, I do not understand the word con. If you are asking me why we tricked you, I will answer that question. After the answer, I will return to my dinner and you will leave my hotel. Do you agree?"

I wanted to reach across the counter and grab the son of a bitch by the neck, and had I been back home in Carson City, I would have done so. However, at the moment I was standing on the fifth floor of a seedy hotel in Rome, and I was a lone American minnow swimming in a sea full of Italian sharks.

I said, "Yes, I agree. Now answer my question."

"Prior to your arrival, I received an email offering me five thousand American dollars to track your activities during your stay in Italy. Mr. Delmont, although my hotel looks prosperous, Rome is a very expensive place to conduct business. Also, I have the heavy financial burden that comes from supporting a father with dementia. Five thou-

217

sand American dollars would help me cover all of my extraordinary expenses, so I replied that I would accept the offer, but only if the sender wired me the money before your arrival. A few minutes later a second email arrived stating that Western Union had a limit of $2999.99 on the amount of money that could be transferred in a single transaction. However, the email stated, to prove good faith on their part, the sender had transferred twenty-five hundred American dollars to my name via Western Union. That email further stated that the final payment of twenty-five hundred American dollars would be made to me on the following day. I went to the Telex office and picked up the first half of the payment. I was not concerned at that point, because if the second payment wasn't made, I would contact Christina and tell her to return home. I emailed the sender and agreed to monitor your activities. Your question confirms to me that you know the rest of the story. I received the final payment of $2500 and my obligation is concluded. Good afternoon, Mr. Delmont."

"But wait, who sent you the email. Who wired you the five thousand dollars? And why did Christina suddenly disappear from the hotel?"

Luchitti reach down behind the counter and pulled out a stack of paper. "Christina returned home because I received an email this morning telling me that my services were no longer required. The first few sheets are copies of the emails I received requesting and terminating my services. The others are receipts from Western Union for two wire transfers of twenty-five hundred dollars. Now I insist you leave at once, or I will call the police."

I grabbed the papers from his hand and stormed down the stairs. When I reached the second floor landing, I stopped and looked at the email address of the sender. My legs gave way and I sat down on the stairs. The email address belonged to me: `pinky@silverstrike.com`.

Stunned and confused, I forced myself to look at the Western Union receipts. They both stated that J. Pincus Delmont, Carson City, Nevada, had transferred twenty-five hundred dollars to Paulo Luchitti, Rome, Italy.

My brain was in such a turmoil that I don't recall riding the train to the airport, or boarding the plane. However, by the time my plane landed in New York, the Italian female devil, 'Lucrezia' Luchitti, and her father's deviousness had been successfully banished to the darkest niche of my mind.

FORTY

Bear—Eureka, Nevada

By the time we started back to the car, the moon had gone behind a mountain, and the night was darker than a black cat at midnight. I stumbled up the hill with Flo whimpering on one arm with the TV and that plastic computer box under the other. Ten feet short of the car, Flo stepped into a rabbit hole, or something. She let out a squeal and refused to budge. I had to set the damned computer down and carry her to the car. What with Flo claiming she had a bum ankle, and my stumbling over rocks in the dark, it took me two more trips to carry all the computer crap to the car.

As soon as I started back to the paved highway, I could tell the return trip was going to be a lot tougher. During the drive in, following the old road was easy, but by now, with most of the moonlight gone, just holding the front wheels in the ruts was a real bitch. A couple of hundred feet before we reached the highway, the right wheel dug in the sand, the steering wheel jerked out of my hands, and the right fender crunched into a big boulder.

Flo, who I thought was asleep, surprised me with, "Don't worry about the car, Bear. That's a work related accident. Pinky's responsible for all the repair work."

"You don't know Pinky as well as I do. The Chicago Cubs will get into the World Series before he'll pay for that fender."

"Bear, you can't let that pip-squeak shyster take advantage of you all the time."

I was sweating like a pig from struggling with the steering wheel and fighting to stay awake, but I knew Flo was right. "Okay, I'll ask him to pay for it when he gets back from Italy."

"You do that. Now I'm going to sleep. Wake me up

when we're in the motel parking lot."

When I pulled the car into our parking slot, it was nearly four in the morning. Flo, her ankle still hurting, made me help her into the room. Then I dragged in all the rest of the crap. By this time, I was beginning to think that tending bar wasn't such a bad job.

Flo, who hadn't done a thing all night tougher than hold a flashlight, kept telling me how tired she was as she pulled her sweatshirt off over her head.

I was pooped, but she sure knew how to wake me up.

Flo jumped under the covers, and said, "Don't even think what I can see you're thinking. I need some sleep. Good night."

I picked up her sweatshirt and tossed it in the corner with the other dirty clothes. "I hope the 'Do Not Disturb' sign keeps the maid out."

"Whatever."

I dropped my pants and shirt on top of Flo's sweatshirt, smiled, and crawled into bed.

The sign did its job and we slept until ten. After a little fooling around in the shower, Flo said, "I never told you this before, but my second ex-husband ran a small business. He took care of the customer side, while I did the books on our computer. I got pretty good at manipulating numbers. All we have to do is get Bill Page's computer system connected. I'm sure that I can figure out what he was trying to keep secret."

We got dressed and Flo started to plug the thing together. I tried to help, but the more I did, the more she got pissed off.

"Bear, you're buzzing around me like a blind bee trying to find a flower. Go get me coffee and something to eat from the lobby."

"Okay, Babe."

I walked to the front desk, and as I headed toward the food spread, the man behind the counter said, "Mr. Zabarte, the normal check out time is eleven. Were you planning on staying another night?"

"Good question. I don't think so, but I'm not sure. I'll

221

grab some coffee, a couple of donuts, and check with the missus."

Back in the room, the sour look on Flo's face told me that she was stumped. I pushed a cup of coffee in her direction. "Having trouble?"

"I can't find the cable to connect the monitor to the processor. The computer's running, but without a picture, we're dead."

I handed Flo a donut.

"Damn it, why did you bring me one of those chocolate fat pills? I wanted a bran muffin."

Shit, two days ago she didn't like the bran muffins. I took a big bite out of my donut and noticed a computer cable on the floor.

"Flo, if you're looking for one of those cable cord things, there's one by the TV."

Squealing like a pig in shit, Flo ran across the room. "That's the one I'm missing." Then she snatched the half-eaten donut out of my hand. "Hey, don't take all of my breakfast."

I didn't notice a limp. "Glad to see your ankle feels better."

"Thanks." She plugged in the missing cord. The computer screen lit up. On the right side I saw three little boxes.

Flo giggled. "That's what I hoped we see. Those are programs."

"Flo, why is the color of this guy's computer screen orange? The screen on our computer's blue."

Flo had the same look my Mom shot me the one time I brought home a bad report card. "It's orange because that's what Bill Page wanted the color of his screen to be."

"Oh." I thought my question was pretty good, and would show Flo that I was beginning to catch on to all that computer crap. I reached into my pocket and pulled out another chocolate donut.

Flo said, "We need to open the accounting program."

With a mouth full of sticky chocolate icing, I said, "Whatever you say, Babe."

222

The screen sort of jumped. The color stayed orange, but now there was a single skinny box in the center. Flo reached for the notebook that I had lifted from the safe. She typed in a pot full of letters and numbers. The screen jumped again. But this time it looked like a white paper with lots of little boxes, and the boxes were filled with numbers.

Flo wrapped her arms around my leg. "We did it. No, I did it, but who's counting."

"Babe, the guy at the desk asked me if we are going to stay another night."

"Go back to the lobby, get me a couple of poppy-seed muffins, and tell him that we'll be out of this dump in an hour."

Fifty minutes later, after Flo unhooked the computer, I set our bags on the back seat of the car. Then I dragged, for the third time, all the computer crap to the trunk and covered everything with a blanket.

As we drove back to Carson City, I said, "You were pretty good with that computer. What kind of business did your husband have?"

"He ran a dry cleaning business. I did the books for six years. Bear, if you spent that much time staring at a monitor, you'd be computer literate too."

"I don't know about that. Pinky once told me that I missed something he called abject seasoning. That's why I'm a dumb-shit around computers."

"I think he said abstract reasoning, but you're not a dumb-shit! You have more street smarts than anyone I've ever known. The next time I hear Pinky say something like that to you, I'm going to kick his fancy ass."

I squeezed her knee, and hoped for Pinky's sake, he wouldn't call me a dumb-shit around her, 'cause once Flo says it, she'll do it.

It was four in the afternoon by the time we hit the eastern edge of Carson City. I drove straight to Pinky's office to see if Lottie could help me make out that expenses thing.

The door was locked and the parking lot was empty.

I drove to our apartment. While I grabbed the first load of computer crap, Flo said, "I want to catch the last of today's rays by the pool. Care to join me?"

"We've got to carry all this stuff to the apartment. How about helping me?"

"I don't think my ankle is up to heavy lifting. I'll see you at the pool."

Ten minutes later, I grabbed a towel and lay down next to the best body in Nevada, if not the whole U. S. of A.

Flo, her eyes covered with a fancy sun mask, said, "I've been thinking about how the killer escaped undetected. After the murderer shot Bill Page, and he escaped over your secret road, he'd end up on Highway 278, right?"

"Yup."

"And we don't think he went south, so where does he end up when he drives north?"

I turned onto my side and there were two cute teens lying on their backs about ten feet the other side of Flo. They both had those tiny bathing suits, not much bigger than a couple of large band-aids.

"Bear, you didn't answer my question. Where would he go?"

"Oh yeah . . . he would hit Interstate 80. Why?"

"And once the killer reached 80, which way would he go?"

Damn if Flo didn't take the cake. "Babe, you're great. You just helped me come up with one of those hunch things. While you put the computer back together, I've got to make a quick trip to the Reno airport."

"But I'm not ready to put the computer back together. I'm very happy lying in the sun, thank you." Then after a second, she said, "What do you need at the airport?"

"To check out that hunch."

"See there? That's what I told you. Bear, no matter what that midget lawyer tells you, you're not a dumb-shit."

Ten minutes later, on the way to the airport, my cell phone rang.

"Bear, this is Willow. Have you heard from Pinky?"

I was afraid to answer her question. "Hi, Willow, just

224

a minute. I have to pull the car over."

I had just seen a cool show on TV where an FBI investigator told how he could listen in on all cell phone calls, and 'cause I was talking to Willow on my cell phone—actually, it was Pinky's cell phone—and Pinky's trip to Rome was supposed to be a secret, I didn't want to blab anything that I didn't want the rest of the world to hear.

I set the brake, and said, "I can't say right now. We'll talk later about you-know-who."

"You-know-who? Are you talking about Pinky? Bear, focus for a minute. He called me from Philadelphia and asked me to pick him up at the airport. His plane arrives in a couple of hours. Could you do me a favor and pick him up?"

"Sure, I'm on my way to the airport."

"Thanks. I'm extremely busy."

"Give me his flight number and I'll get him for you."

Willow said, "Hold on, why were you going to the airport?"

"To check out a hunch. I've got some very, very important information to give you that I can't talk about now. We'll meet later tonight at you-know-who's house. He'll call you with the time. Then I'll bring you up to speed on everything."

"Bear, I don't have a clue what you are talking about, but . . . did you just say we're going to meet tonight at you-know-who's house?"

"Yup."

"I can't. I have to attend a fund raiser for my future campaign."

"Willow, this meeting's a matter of life and death for a second you-know-who."

"A second you-know who? I give up. What time?"

"I'll have the first you-know-who home by eight. Willow, before you hang up, I have an important question to ask."

"Go ahead."

"Did anyone check the wrists of the dead you-know-who to see if there were any marks? Like he'd been tied up

225

before he was shot?"

"The dead you-know-who's wrists? Damn it, will you stop talking in riddles . . . oh, I get it now, that dead you-know-who. The guy who was shot in the head out in lonely land."

I smiled. "You got it!"

"Bear, that's an excellent question, and I don't know the answer." She paused. "I'll see what I can find out and let you know when we meet tonight at the home of the first you-know-who. Bye now."

Ten minutes later I reached the airport ,and parked in a police zone, 'cause after my phone call with Willow, I figured I was sort of on official business for the Carson City DA.

I was pretty sure that I'd find my cousin sitting behind the counter of the Reno-Way car rental agency scanning the latest Playboy. I rounded the corner of the baggage claim area and there he was.

John closed the magazine without offering me a peek at the latest Playmate of the month. "Bear, what brings you here today? Need a car? Because you're a relative, I can let you have a Mercedes for the price of an Escort."

"No thanks. I'm looking for information."

John was my cousin on my mother's side. I'm a couple of years older, and when we were kids, we used to terrorize the Elko countryside together. John was the closest thing I had to a brother.

He said, "Ask away."

"First, I'm doing investigative work for a big-time Carson City lawyer on a murder case so, from now on, everything we talk about is strictly confidential. Got it?"

John sat up straight. "Wow, Bear, that's really cool. Did you quit your bartending job at the Old Globe?"

John always looked up to me, like I was his hero. "Yup, I'm a full time investigator now." That wasn't exactly telling him the truth, but it was close enough. "But you haven't promised me that from now on, everything between us is confidential."

John's face got all scrunched, like working on a murder case had spooked him. "Wow, whatever you say, cuz."

"Okay. I'm looking for the name of a guy, at least I think he's a guy, who flew into Reno ten days ago. He rented a car, and returned the car the same day or the following day."

"Do you know the name of the person?"

"No."

"Do you know where he or she came from?"

"Nope."

"Do you know what time their plane landed?"

"No."

John shook his head. "Jesus, cuz, you don't want much, do you?"

I knew John's question was one of those funny kinds that I wasn't supposed to answer. I kept my trap shut and waited.

He said, "You aren't kidding, are you?"

"Nope."

"Shit, Bear, I don't have time to go through all those records, and I'll have to stop to take care of customers."

"All you have to do is show me how to do it. I have a couple of hours to kill."

"But what if the jerk didn't rent the car from me? I'm not sure all the other agencies will let you dig through their records."

"John, forget all that shit. Just show me where to look."

He fiddled with his computer for a minute. "Okay. Here are all the rentals we made ten days ago."

I sat down. It took me a few seconds to figure out how to handle that dumb little arrow that slides around the screen. I came up with two possibilities, but they were both females. John printed out both rental agreements for me.

"Okay, John, I'm ready to hit the next agency."

John looked twenty feet away, at the Sierra Rental counter and said, "Hold on. First I need to grease the wheels for you."

At the fifth rental agency, and about twenty-five minutes before Pinky's plane was scheduled to land, I found the rental record of a jerk named Armen Bedrosian. He flew into Reno on a flight from Fresno at seven in the morning of the day Bill Page was murdered. He rented a full-sized Buick for a full week, and returned the car inside twenty-four hours. Why did I think he was our guy? Because of the note added to the rental agreement by a lady named Mary Jane Arlett, Customer Agent number 2377:

When Mr. Bedrosian returned his vehicle, an inspection of the wheel wells and undercarriage noted major damage along with dirt and other desert debris indicating that Mr. Bedrosian had taken his rented vehicle off-road, a direct violation of his rental agreement.

When I questioned Mr. Bedrosian about the damage, he acknowledged that he had driven the Buick off-road. He also agreed that he had initialed the section of his rental agreement that stated rented cars were not allowed to be driven off paved roads.

At that point, I informed Mr. Bedrosian that the next day we would do a comprehensive vehicle inspection. Mr. Bedrosian acknowledged he would be responsible for any, and all the damage to the vehicle. I further informed Mr. Bedrosian that if the full amount was not paid within thirty days, his credit card would be charged plus the twenty-five percent penalty stipulated in the contract.

I printed out a copy of the rental agreement with the note.

I headed to the bar and ordered an over priced single malt using Pinky's expense money. I raised my glass and thought, Pinky, you remember me—the guy you called a dumb-shit bartender—well this dumb-shit just came up with the name and address of the guy who murdered Bill Page.

FORTY-ONE

Pinky—Carson City, Nevada

Underneath my black, satin sleep mask, I avoided conversing with my seat mates, and slept as much as I could to alleviate the boredom one faced during long flights. By the time the wheels touched down at the Reno Airport, I felt relatively together and ready to do battle with Willow.

I grabbed my backpack from the overhead compartment and debarked the plane. The last person I expected to greet me was Bear Zabarte, but there he was. I was set to vent my spleen at Willow, for her premature plea agreement, but Bear would work in a pinch. I'd chastise him roundly for his failure to email me as I had demanded.

He waved a big paw and said, "Hi, Pinky, glad you're home."

"No happier than I am. However, I'm surprised you had the courage to show your face. Bear, after your initial digital missive, I never received further communication. Did you forget how to email?"

Bear said, "Hey, we were busting our butts out there night and day."

"I'm sure you worked no harder than I, and I found the time to email. But that's water under the bridge."

"Pinky, I think Flo and me found some important shit at the ranch house. I'll fill you in on everything while we drive back to Carson City."

"I'm afraid you'll have to define 'important shit' for me. After a week in Italy, it will take me awhile to pick up the dialect of Carson City English."

Bear said, "No boss, really, Flo and me found—"

I interrupted, "Don't call me boss. After we stop by my office, you'll have plenty of time to bore me with all your little discoveries. First and foremost, I need to determine the latest information concerning Vaca's plea agreement."

229

Bear said, "That reminds me. I rolled by your office a couple of hours ago. The place was closed tighter than a bull's ass at fly time."

"That's strange. Are you sure? Lottie always started early and stayed late. That's not like her."

"Like I said, the place was closed."

In the hour it took us to return to Carson City, I regaled Bear with fascinating narratives of Rome, Tuscany, and the natural beauty of my Italian translator. Of course, I eliminated the jarring conclusion to my trip. Occasionally, Bear would try to interrupt me, but I forged ahead because I knew his plebeian views of Eureka, Nevada, would pale when compared to my colorful descriptions of Rome and the Italian countryside.

As Bear had warned me, my office was dark. However, it was seven in the evening, and way past Lottie's normal departure time.

I said, "Let's go in. I need to check on my court schedule ."

I didn't really need to check anything, but after the disastrous finish to my week in Italy, I needed grounding— I wanted to stand close to something familiar, besides Bear Zabarte. I unlocked the door, keyed in the security code, and flipped on the lights. At first glance, everything looked normal, and then I noticed the thick layer of dust that covered Lottie's work area. I checked my office and it was covered with the identical patina.

I said, "Bear, that's strange. Lottie sent me an email from this office about twenty-four hours ago. Come here and look at the top of her desk. There must be at least three days worth of . . . ."

"Mr. Delmont?"

My heart jumped at the sound of the unknown voice. I turned and looked into the face of a stranger who stood at the front door to my office.

I ducked behind the ample girth of Bear. "Who wants to know?"

"My name is Louis Loomer. I own the Rapid Replacement Temp Agency. Mr. Delmont, we met six months ago at

230

a Chamber mixer. Remember, we both drink the same gin?"

I barely recalled his face, but he looked safe enough. "Now I remember. We're both Bombay Sapphire men."

"Right. Mr. Delmont, I just saw your light and I was curious about something that's been bothering me for some time."

I fought back the urge to tell him I was exhausted and didn't give a damn concerning his internal confusion. But you never know when you might be talking with a potential client. "How may I help you, Mr. Loomer?"

"A couple of weeks ago you called my office and requested a temporary secretarial replacement."

Now I remembered who he was. He ran the local temp agency. I moved out from behind the formidable wall of my bodyguard. "Yes, I made that call. Is there a problem?"

"My agency is very small. Frankly, I can't afford to lose a potential customer. I understand that my replacement didn't arrive as soon as I had promised, but—"

"Mr. Loomer, I must apologize, but I just returned from a tedious trans-Atlantic flight, and my brain is a little fried. Frankly, I don't know what you're talking about. I'm not a potential customer. I was a happy customer. Discounting a bit of confusion over the past few days that girl you sent me was outstanding. Why, Lottie accomplished more in—"

"Excuse my interruption, Mr. Delmont, but when my replacement arrived, a young woman in your office told my girl that the job had already been filled."

My exhaustion abruptly disappeared. "But you sent me Lottie—I'm sorry, Loretta Evans. Are you trying to tell me that Lottie didn't come from your agency?"

"I am the sole proprietor of my agency and I've never had a woman named Lottie, or Loretta Evans, as a member of my staff. I'm afraid you've been deceived. Should I send someone to your office first thing tomorrow morning?"

I've been deceived? Oh my God, that would be twice in two days. When I was young, an older colleague had warned me that sooner or later I would reach a point in my legal career when I would lose that fine edge—the superior intellect that pushed me to the pinnacle of my professional world. Was it possible that I had reached that tipping point so soon?

And if Lottie hadn't come from Loomer's agency, who was she? Where did she come from? And why? My weary body turned to mush and I slumped into Lottie's chair. I tapped the last of my reservoir of inner strength to continue. "No, Mr. Loomer, but thank you for your kind offer. However, I'm pleased you stopped by this evening. In fact, you've just supplied an answer to a nagging question that's been bothering me for weeks."

Loomer said, "Good evening, Mr. Delmont, and don't forget, Rapid Replacement stands ready to supply all your future needs."

Once the door closed, Bear said, "What was that all about?"

"Come into my office. We'll share a glass of warm gin, and I'll tell you how a young woman bamboozled me."

Bear said, "Okay, but before you do that, you need to hear what Flo and me found at the ranch."

After I listened to Bear's tale of secret roads and cigar butts, I felt like I'd been emasculated with a dull butter knife. While I had aimlessly wandered about Italy, and let myself be conned by a beautiful woman, a simple Basque bartender and a blonde bimbo with big boobs, had come up with enough evidence to establish doubt in a jury. I downed the half-empty glass of gin and searched for enough self-worth to keep going. "Bear, those cigar butts you brought back could save my client."

"And don't forget the computer."

I poured myself a second glass of gin. "I'll have to review the computer data very carefully. Juries have trouble comprehending complex evidence. Do you know what kind of records Flo found?"

"Nope. Oh, I almost forgot. Just before your plane landed, I—"

I cut him off with a wave of my hand. "Before you continue, I have to call Willow. She betrayed me with a plea agreement and—"

Bear interrupted, "I wouldn't do that, boss. That's another thing I almost forgot. I told Willow we'd meet at your place at eight to go over what we found in Eureka and Italy."

"Fine. That will offer me the opportunity to extract the proper retribution for her act of treachery. Bear, that woman waited until I was out of the country, and then she encouraged her minion, Miguel Vaca, to make a deal with the Public Defender, something she would never have tried if I had remained in Carson City."

From the empty expression on Bear's round face, I was positive that he didn't understand a word I had just told him. "Now, where were we?"

Bear said, "We're going to drink some gin while you tell me how you were bamboozled"

"I hired Lottie without checking her background. God, that woman pulled the wool over my eyes. She was privy to every move I made with Richard Page. She transcribed my notes and interviews with him, and my visit with his girlfriend. She knew everything I did concerning the Page murder from day one."

"That was pretty dumb all right. Did she know you're flying home today?"

I thought back to the emails between us. "No, I sent an email to you, but for some reason I didn't send one to Lottie."

"That's good. She thinks you're still in Italy."

He was right! "My God, we need to turn the lights out and get out of this place before she drives by and figures out I'm back."

I grabbed my laptop and we immediately left my office. Bear drove his truck through the fading light to his apartment.

Flo joined us, and the instant she had clicked her seat belt, she started biting at me as if we hadn't spent the last week separated by thousands of miles.

"Pinky, I just got around to reading your last email informing us that you were coming home, along with your threat of disciplinary action. Silly me, I would have thought saving your client from execution would trump a forgotten email."

"And I'm delighted to see you as well, Flo." For the life of me, I couldn't comprehend how Bear could stand to be near that banshee.

Bear slammed his big foot onto the accelerator and I was tossed into that she-wolf by my side. During the silent drive, I tried to understand why Lottie had inserted herself into my operation. When Bear pulled into my driveway, I spotted Willow's car and my anger transferred from Lottie to my ex-wife, one of the few females who could still cause my heart to skip a beat.

Bear carried in my bags.

Willow met me in the hall. She presented her cheek for a platonic kiss. I ignored her offer, and said, "After you thrust your knife in my back with the plea agreement, I'm surprised you have the courage to face me."

"Pinky, the plea agreement was my way to flush you out of your hiding place. Don't worry, I have Vaca on a short leash. I won't let him present anything to the judge as long as you tell me what you and Bear were doing—unless you are concerned that knowledge could get us both disbarred."

"Bear's heard most of this, so he can fetch a bottle of wine while I bring you up to the present."

I explained to her about the possible Italian connection to the Page murder, and my suspicion that there was undiscovered evidence at the Page Ranch. As I finished telling her how we had split into two teams, Bear returned with a bottle of a '94 California cabernet and four glasses.

Willow said, "Okay, so you went to Italy. What did you find?"

"In a few words, nothing. Italy was a waste of time and money. However, I'm pleased to report that Bear and Flo discovered a modicum of new physical evidence at the ranch."

Flo, her wine glass already empty, cried, "A modicum of evidence? If that isn't the understatement of the year. Willow, we not only figured out how Bill Page was murdered, we know the killer wasn't Richard Page, the little-

piss-ant you were ready to send to the Nevada State penitentiary!"

FORTY-TWO

Bear—Genoa, Nevada

Willow gave Flo one of her patented, you've-got-to-be-kidding-me looks. "Flo, I know that you and Bear are sure you found something important, but I can't accept that the two of you uncovered evidence missed by a team of professional law enforcement officers."

Flo handed me the plat map of the Page Ranch, and hissed, "Bear, show this broad what a couple of dumb, non-professional types came up with."

While I spread the map on the dining room table, Flo reached into her purse and pulled out the plastic sandwich bag with the three cigar butts.

Willow said, "Wait a minute, Bear. I trust you found all this evidence in a legal manner. Otherwise, some, or all of it might not be admissible in court."

I said, "Willow, Pinky pays us to find stuff, not worry about all that legal mumbo-jumbo."

Willow didn't seem to have a comeback. I decided to tell her, but for her sake, I thought that I had better soft pedal the breaking and entering part, and the safe I cracked. "Okay, this is what we did, and how we did it. Flo and I conned a local real estate guy named Goodie into driving us out to Bill Page's ranch because he thought we wanted to buy the place."

Flo gulped down her second glass of wine. "Like we'd be dumb enough to pay real money for that pile of rocks and sand."

I said, "Come on, Flo, some of the folks in that part of Nevada like their rocks and sand."

She snorted, "That doesn't mean I have to."

Pinky said, "Go on, Bear, tell us what happened after your visit with the real estate salesman."

"The next day, Goodie gave me a map and I noticed an

old road. You can just see the faint lines on the map right here, about a mile north of the ranch road we had used the day before. Real late that night—"

Flo said, "Bear, it was two the following morning when you dragged me out of bed, like you didn't care that most civilized people were asleep."

"Right, around two. The road ended up at an old barn. You can't see the barn from the house, but from the barn, you can spot the roof of the ranch house."

Willow frowned. "You'll have to excuse my ignorance, but what makes your secret road and an old barn so important?"

"Remember how the deputy saw Richard's car heading south, toward Eureka, on Highway 278? If the real killer went north on 278, the deputy would never have seen him or his car."

Willow leaned forward and started to question me, like I was a bad guy on trial. "Not good enough. What evidence do you have that proves the real killer used that road, and what's the barn got to do with the murder?"

I said, "That barn was really old, but the hinges had recently been oiled, I think by the killer to keep from making any noise. And we found something lying on the floor by a window that overlooked the ranch house."

Flo said, "That's where I come in. If I hadn't carried more than my normal two packs of tissues in my purse, Bear wouldn't have had the plastic to wrap up those vile cigar butts."

I said, "Flo's right. The something we found on the floor was three cigar butts. I wrapped them up using Flo's tissue plastic just like she said, and when we got home, I put everything inside a plastic sandwich bag. That way, Willow, you can check the dark, slimy part for that DNA stuff."

Willow sat back and looked at Pinky.

He shrugged.

Flo said, "We're sure the real killer stood by that window and smoked those cigars while he waited. Willow, I don't know about you, but I never could understand how a woman could come close to a man who chewed on those nasty things."

I said, "Flo, we're trying to explain a murder here, not to listen to your carrying on about cigar smokers."

She glared at me. "Whatever."

"Then we went into the house—"

Willow said, "Stop right there. How did you get into the house?"

I was afraid she'd ask that. "The back door was unlocked?"

"I find that hard to believe. Are you sure?"

Flo jumped in. "Willow, do you want to find the real killer, or ask a bunch of stupid questions?"

Willow said, "Flo, I've taken an oath to uphold the law. However, I see we have an empty bottle of wine. I'm going into the kitchen to find a full one. While I'm gone, you three can discuss anything you want."

As soon as she left, I said, "Pinky, I used a credit card to pop the back door. Then we hit the office and cracked the safe. Inside the safe we found a note pad with a bunch of passwords. Before we left, I grabbed Page's computer and brought it back to my apartment. If you want, Flo can fill you in on what she found inside his computer."

Willow returned and filled everyone's glass. I took a sip. No matter how much Pinky tried to convince me, all of his expensive wine tasted like sour grape juice. I'm a single malt guy, but Willow was pouring wine, and as my Mom always told me, beggars can't be choosers.

Pinky said, "Willow, at this point, it's probably best you don't know the details concerning how Bear and Flo found the evidence, but—"

Willow interrupted. "I'll listen to what they found, but they must understand that any and all evidence they gathered illegally will be declared inadmissible by a judge."

I was pretty sure I understood what she told me, so I nodded.

Flo said, "That's okay with me. I can't wait till you get one of your experts to look over those printouts. I may be nothing but a simple bookkeeper, but from what I could see,

Bill Page was like laundering money, and skimming off a large pile for himself."

Willow shook her head and took a sip of wine. She seemed to be worrying about something, but I wasn't sure what.

Pinky said, "Bear, run your complete murder theory by Willow. That might help clear things up."

I said, "Okay. Bill Page was skimming. He got caught. Oh, Pinky, I almost forgot. Just before your plane landed, after checking a bunch of car rental records, I found out the real killer's name is Armen Bedrosian."

Pinky set his glass of wine down and put his head in his hands. "Is there a reason you didn't tell me that important piece of information before now?"

"I tried to, but you were so busy with your cool stories about Rome and all those other Italian towns that you didn't give me a chance."

Willow said, "I'm almost afraid to ask this, but what makes you think that's the killer's name?"

"I'll get to that in a second. Some of this is a guess, but all the pieces fit. Bill Page gets caught skimming and now he owes somebody big bucks. That somebody hires Armen Bedrosian to snuff him. Bedrosian flies to Reno and rents a car. Bedrosian may know how to kill people, but he's a real dumb-shit about a lot of normal stuff. First, he rents a full-sized Buick instead of a four-wheeled SUV like I would. Then he drives east on Highway 80 all the way to Highway 278, because he doesn't know about the cut-off at Fallon. He takes the abandoned ranch road instead of the real road and ends up at the barn above the ranch house. I think he wanted to use the old road so he could get the drop on Page. It's not as easy to surprise a guy if you have to knock on his front door. Anyway, he uses the old road and that's why I noticed his car rental contract. The dummy kicked the shit out of his big old Buick by driving it over the desert.

"Now the next part of my story is sort of made up, because I wasn't there, but I think it's pretty close to what really happened. Bedrosian parks his car at the barn, pulls out his gun and walks down the hill to the house. He gets the drop on Bill Page and tells him he's been paid to take him out. Bill begs the hood not to kill him because his nephew, Richard Page, is on his way from LA with a fat check. But Bedrosian's a hired gun, and hired guns don't know from checks—they live in a world of cash. He ties up Bill, sits down and waits. When he spots a cloud of dust heading toward the ranch house, Bedrosian blows off half of Bill's head, pulls off the ropes, and hightails it up the hill to the barn. He waits until Richard gets out of his car, then he calls the Sheriff's office on his cell phone. He tells them there's been a shooting at the Page Ranch, and he returns using the only route he knows to the Reno Airport. He turns in his car to the rental agency and gets hassled because of the damage to the Buick's undercarriage. All we have left to do is match the DNA off those cigar butts with Armen Bedrosian, and Richard Page is a free man."

Pinky set his wine glass down and clapped his hands. "Bravo, my good man, bravo."

Willow said, "I agree. Bear, as you requested this afternoon, I had the coroner check the victim's wrists and he picked up some faint indications of rope marks. Now, I hate to throw cold water on this picnic, but we need to slow everything down for a minute."

I said, "Why?"

"If Flo's brief analysis of the printouts is correct, and Bill Page was skimming money, it is very likely he was working for organized crime."

Flo said, "What's that got to do with anything?"

Willow sat back. "If this was a mob hit, and if Bedrosian was the hired gun, once we go public, Bedrosian will be fitted for a pair of concrete shoes and vanish forever into a large body of water."

Pinky nodded. "Willow's right. The minute the mob hears the cops are looking for Bedrosian, his goose is cooked."

Flo said, "Frankly, I don't care a whit about a man who makes his living killing people. Good riddance, I say."

Willow said, "You don't understand, Flo. If Bedrosian disappears before we can get a sample of his DNA, Bear's theory is just a theory. Without proof, like a DNA match, Richard Page is no better off than he was a week ago, and as we all know, that's not good."

Pinky said, "It's obvious to me that we need to find Bedrosian."

I said, "But that shouldn't be a big problem. The guy flew in from Fresno. I have his home address on the rental contract. All we have to do is make sure he really lives there, and then ask the police to arrest him."

Willow said, "Sorry, Bear, but that won't work. We're in the State of Nevada, not California. Without more evidence than your theory, I'll never convince a California judge to extradite Bedrosian to Nevada. I could request help from the Feds. If a murderer crosses a state line to kill a man, that's a federal offense."

Pinky said, "True, but once this becomes a federal case, the prosecution will end up in a federal court."

Willow said, "That's right, and I won't prosecute the case."

Flo said, "And you won't be able to tell the public how you saved an innocent man from execution just before your election."

I said, "Flo, I think you've had enough wine for the night. Willow, how can we pull this thing off?"

Flo said, "I'm sorry, Willow, that wasn't very lady-like of me. Bear's right. How can we clear Richard Page?"

Willow thought for a minute. "Let's assume the cigar butts you brought back from the Page Ranch are uncontaminated. We'll need a sample of Bedrosian's DNA. If his sample matches the cigar butts, California would extradite him faster than Pinky can pull the cork on another bottle of this outstanding cabernet."

We waited while Pinky got another bottle and opened it up.

I said, "Pinky, could I have a single malt instead?"

"My good man, this cabernet is one of the finest in the world."

"I know all that crap, but—"

Pinky said, "As you wish. That will leave more for

241

me."

After Pinky dumped my wine into his glass, I said, "Pinky, do you think this is this a good time to tell Willow what you found out about Lottie?"

Pinky's head drooped like a puppy that had just been caught peeing on the carpet. "You do that for me while I dig up a bottle of single malt."

I told them about our meeting with the owner of the temp agency a couple of hours earlier.

Pinky returned and poured four fingers of scotch into my glass.

Flo said, "Lottie was a spy? Who'd want to spy on Pinky?"

Pinky said, "Flo, during the torturous ride from your apartment, the reason became clear to me. For the moment, let's assume that Bear's elaborate scenario is correct. If Richard hadn't stumbled into his uncle's murder, the Page killing would be an unsolved crime. That's not the best solution for a mob hit because unsolved murder cases remain open forever. However, once the state convicts Richard Page for the murder, or manslaughter for that matter, the case is closed and the real killer is home free. And don't forget, my old secretary left because someone threatened her. That's precisely when Lottie showed up. And that note threatening to roast me over a fire, like the one set in my condo living room. Think of it, every day Lottie would transcribe my recorded notes, and every night she could inform her people of each move I made concerning Richard's defense."

I said, "You know, I'll bet she made us buy those damn laptops so she'd know what we were doing while we were away from Carson City."

Pinky sat back and I could see he was thinking hard, so hard that he stopped drinking his wine for a minute. "My God, you're right. I sent Lottie many emails from Italy. I told her I had arrived. Then I sent her one that told her I had hired a translator and we were going to spend a few days in a town on the Ligurian Sea to talk with Clark Page's Italian woman."

Willow sat up. "You spent a few days by the Ligurian

242

Sea with a translator? Flo, how much do you want to bet that the translator was female, good-looking, and under thirty?"

Flo snorted, "Considering the man involved, no bet. But hold on here, we're missing something important. Pinky, all you have to do is pull out your laptop this very minute and send Lottie an email. You can tell her how much you're enjoying lying on the beach with your paramour, whoops, translator."

Pinky blushed! Damn, I'd never seen him do that before.

Pinky said, "Flo, I can't do that. Lottie would know that I'm sending the email from my house."

Flo snorted again, "And you keep trying to convince Bear he's stupid. Pinky, an email doesn't tell the reader where you are when you send it. Hell, Lottie could have sent your emails while perched on your fancy john down the hall."

Willow said, "Flo, I see what you mean. Pinky, you and Bear need to send Lottie an email at once."

Now I was lost. "Why?"

Willow said, "Pinky needs to send Lottie an email and tell her that he's going to stay in Italy for another week. Bear needs to send Lottie an email telling her that he didn't find anything at the Page Ranch and he's going to stick around Eureka for a while. With any luck, the bad guys, as you so aptly call them, will sit back and wait for the judge to accept the manslaughter plea arrangement."

I said, "I see what you mean. It's like Pinky never left Italy, right?"

Pinky said, "My God, you're right. In fact, no one outside of this room knows I've returned home."

I hated to be the jerk that threw water on Pinky's bonfire, but sometimes that's my job. "Except for Mr. Loomer."

Pinky's face turned white, and for a second he looked like he was going to barf on his fancy marble table. "You're right, Bear, except for Mr. Loomer. Damn, that means that until this mess is cleaned up, I can't be seen in town, or even in my office. I'll have to lie low until you and Flo come up with a way to extract that DNA sample from Bedrosian."

"Boss, you don't have to sit here and wait. You can come with Flo and me. Nobody knows what you look like in Fresno. Of course, we'd have to get two rooms at the motel, because Flo and I will need some privacy."

I saw Pinky shoot a look at Willow, like he was fishing around to see if she wanted to come with us.

Willow must have caught Pinky's look. "Sorry, Pinky, I can't do it. Too many trials coming up."

Pinky didn't look happy. In fact, he looked like he'd just lost his best friend, but I knew that was dumb, 'cause except for Willow, Pinky didn't have any friends.

Flo said, "Hold on a minute. We can't both send emails to Lottie at the same time. That would look set up. Pinky, you do yours first. Then I'll follow you in an hour or so."

Poor old Pinky was looking worse by the minute. "Flo, I hate to admit this, but I don't know how to send an email."

We all said, "What?"

Pinky waited, like he hoped that maybe the need to answer our question would just go away. Finally, he said, "I know that Lottie taught me how to send emails before I went to Italy, but never understood what the hell she was talking about. My translation . . . . ah . . . . person initiated of all my emails."

That surprised me. I knew that I was a dumb-shit about computers, but Pinky had told me he was cool with those digit things.

I said, "What about the first email you sent to Flo and me from Rome? Did the translation lady do that one too?"

"No, a man at an Internet center sent that one."

Flo jumped up and said, "Okay, that's water under the bridge. Pinky, give me your laptop. I'll send the damn email to Lottie."

Willow said, "But first, I think we need to hear more about the woman who did Pinky's translation work. Just how young was she?"

Pinky jumped up, and as he ran out of the dining room, he yelled, "Willow, I'll answer that question after I find my laptop. As Flo so aptly pointed out, that email must be sent at once."

By the time Flo finished the letter and hit the send button, I thought Willow had forgotten that Pinky never answered her question, and I wasn't going to be the jerk to remind her.

Flo said, "In thirty minutes, I'll send Lottie a message and tell her that Bear and I are going to spend a few more days in Eureka looking for gold."

Pinky stood and held his glass up, like he wanted to do one of those toasted things. "Bear, first thing tomorrow morning, after I pack some clean clothes, we're off to Fresno."

I heard what he said, but I could tell that Pinky was bummed out.

First, Willow wasn't going. Second, he didn't get along with Flo. But mostly, I think he was bent out of shape because we had stopped treating him like he was the leader of the pack. That's a hard thing for a guy like Pinky to face, 'cause when you're suddenly not the lead dog, all the air you breathe is filled with the farts from the dogs in front of you.

FORTY-THREE

Bear—Genoa, Nevada

I said, "Okay, Pinky. We'll bunk down for a couple of hours and then drive west. You've already said that you're tired, and Flo and me are pooped from the little sleep we got last night."

Pinky said, "Thank you, Bear. You and Flo can take the guest room down the hall. Willow and I will—"

Willow shook her head. "No we won't. Pinky, after I explain to you how to take a DNA sample, Willow is going home. You need rest. And don't think I've forgotten about that woman translator. The minute you return from Fresno, I'll expect an hour by hour, day by day, and night by night, explanation."

I could see that there was still some bad stuff between them, and I thanked my lucky stars that I had my Flo. I said, "I'll set our alarm for five. That should give us enough time to get some sleep and still get to Fresno by noon."

Flo jabbed my ribs. "What makes you think you're going to go to sleep right away?"

I grinned. "Hey, that sounds good to me, and besides, I'll sleep better after. Good night."

We headed to the guest room and left Pinky and Willow talking quietly in the hall. The guest room was bigger, and better furnished than my whole apartment. After a quick scan of the fancy digs, I turned the light off.

"Hey, turn the light back on. I want to take a closer look at the furniture."

Flo pulled her sweater over her head.

"Okay, but first, I just want to look at you in the moonlight."

"Bear, you're so sweet."

Flo wrapped her arms around my head and held me close to her soft skin. Then she pushed me away and said,

246

"Give me one good reason why Pinky needs to come with us to Fresno? We could do a lot better without him."

I pulled her down on my lap. "Flo, Pinky's in pretty bad shape right now. He needs family, and I guess we're as close to him as his family ever was."

"But he's a pain in the ass, and I don't like him."

"That's okay. No rule in the world says you got to like every member of your family. There're lots of times when I want to kick him in the balls, but then he does something good, like keeping my ass out of jail. Babe, think what you want, but during my trial, Pinky was the only guy in town who stuck by me."

"He was your lawyer, damn it, and he turned you into a slave for his work. I don't see how that comes close to a family relationship."

"Trust me, Babe. If you're staring at twenty years in the slam, your lawyer becomes your mother and father, all rolled up into one package. Pinky goes with us to Fresno, and you'll try to be nice to him, right?"

She sat there so long that my legs started to go numb. "All right. He goes, but when he gets to be a pain, and he will, I can't guarantee I'll always be nice."

"That's all a guy can ask for. Now, let's get naked and have some fun."

Five hours later, the alarm bell beat at me to wake up. I jumped into the shower, and when I came out, Flo staggered by.

I yelled through the steam, "I'm going to hide your towel and wait until you come out. That way I'll have to lick the water off you to get you dry."

Flo opened the shower door, reached down and gave me a loving squeeze. "You need to jump in. I could use some help scrubbing some of my hard to reach parts."

By the time we got to the kitchen, Pinky had set out three cups of coffee and a big platter of bran muffins.

"You two took an exceedingly long shower."

Flo smiled. "We do that a lot."

Pinky glared at Flo. I knew that Willow had gone home after teaching Pinky about that DNA crap, and that

Pinky had spent a lonely night, and I guessed that he thought our long shower was sort of rubbing his nose in it. I said, "The bran muffins look good."

Pinky said, "I found them in the freezer and heated them up."

Flo took a tiny bite. "I should have known. There's a definite freezer burn taste."

Pinky started to edge toward the knife rack, so I said, "It's only about two hundred and fifty miles to Fresno. If we leave soon, we'll be there around noon."

Pinky moved away from the knives, and said, "Yes, about noon."

I smiled. "Then it's settled, we leave in fifteen minutes. One more thing, are we all going to squeeze into my pick-up, or will we take your car?"

Pinky took a bite of muffin, frowned, and spit it out. "We'll take my Jag. That way Flo will have the back seat all to herself."

Flo smiled. "I've never ridden in a Jaguar before. Thank you, Pinky."

I wasn't positive, but I was pretty sure that Pinky hadn't put Flo in the back seat to make her happy. I think he didn't want her sitting next to him for the half-day drive to Fresno. But you never know, maybe they were learning how to get along.

Flo slept most of the drive, but once we reached the outskirts of Fresno, she woke up, leaned over the seat, and started to tell Pinky all the things she knew were important to look for in a motel.

Pinky stopped at the first two joints we saw off Highway 99. They both looked pretty nice to me. They weren't great, but we only needed a place to crash for a couple of nights. But each time, after Flo checked out the pool, she marched back and said, "Not a chance."

After the second motel, Pinky shot her a look that would have dropped a bull moose in its tracks. "Flo, we're checking into the next motel I stop at, and I don't care if the God damn pool water is olive green and as thick as a bowl of split pea soup."

Five minutes later, around twelve-fifteen, we pulled into the parking lot of the Golden Raisin Inn.

While Pinky and me checked in, Flo left to look at the pool. When the man behind the desk handed me my key, Flo walked into the office, grinning from ear to ear. "Bear, you found the perfect motel. They have a giant pool, a great deck, and fancy lounge chairs with cushioned blue pads," She turned and glared at Pinky. "And the water's crystal clear."

Pinky didn't say a word, and walked to his room, number 202. Flo and me were next door in 204. Flo charged around and did her usual nesting thing. Then she threw on her bathing suit, grabbed a towel, and headed for the pool.

About the time our door closed, my phone rang. It was Pinky.

"Is she gone?"

"Yup."

"Fine, we have the rest of the afternoon. Let's see if we can figure out where Armen Bedrosian lives."

"Okay. Come on over. The door is open."

By the time Pinky arrived, I had the car rental form spread out on the table next to the phone directory.

I said, "According to his rental form, he lives at 278 Peachland Way."

I grabbed the phone directory and flipped past the A's to the B's. "And according to the phone directory . . . Jesus, there he is. The stupid son-of-a-bitch is listed at the same address."

Pinky said, "Why would a hired gun use his real name and address on that car rental form?"

"Why not? If the dumb-shit hadn't gone off the road with his Buick, I'd have never found him."

Pinky frowned. I could tell that he wasn't convinced. He said, "Maybe he's the wrong Armen Bedrosian. There are a lot of Armenians living in the Fresno area."

"I heard that somewhere. Why do they all want to live here?"

"They felt the land around Fresno reminded them of their homeland. They called the surrounding area Yettem,

249

or the Garden of Eden."

I looked out my window at the flat countryside. All I saw was rows of grapes, lots of sand, and nothing much else. "I guess there's no telling what turns some people on. You ready to go?"

"Yes. Will Flo be joining us?"

"Nah, she'll be by the pool all afternoon. Don't get me wrong, if this was an important trip, she'd come along, but we don't need her right now."

Pinky's lips moved, but I couldn't hear him because right then about fifty motorcycles roared into the parking lot below our rooms. The noise from all those bikes sounded like a jet airplane taking off.

Pinky said, "What a clamor. Let's go."

"Right."

I walked down the stairs ahead of Pinky and saw a big guy sitting on the hood of Pinky's spotless Jag. He had long hair, a full beard, and he was wearing a jacket with a Hell's Angels emblem on the back. Oh shit! I glanced around and spotted three more Hell's Angels jackets standing by an open motel room door. Jesus, I thought, I'll bet there are more of them inside the room.

Before Pinky noticed the big guy sitting on his car, I grabbed his arm, and said, "Boss, we need to check for mail in the office." Then I sort of lifted him off the ground and carried him past the scary dude.

Pinky tried to get away, but it didn't do any good. "Bear, you set me down this minute. Why are we going to the office? We don't have any mail waiting there. We just checked in thirty minutes ago."

By the time we reached the office, the big guy had jumped off the Jag's hood and gone into the room. I set Pinky down.

Pinky looked at me like I had gone loony or something. "What the hell got into you, Bear?"

"Nothing. Let's go."

After Pinky drove the Jag away from the motel, I said, "Didn't you see those Hell's Angels all over the parking lot?"

"I was aware of the excruciating racket created by the

numerous motorcycles, but no, I did not tumble to the fact that those gentlemen were members of that club. Why, was that important?"

Jesus, my boss was as smart as a whip in court, but on the street, the poor jerk acted like a newborn baby. "They were Hell's Angels, damn it. First, for no reason, they'll pound you into hamburger, then they'll drop their pants, and tell you to kiss their ass."

"Oh yes, the Hell's Angels. I've heard of them. After all, I did see that old Marlon Brando movie, but Bear, that movie came out many, many years ago. Are you positive the Hell's Angels organization still exists?"

"Yes I am, and one of the biggest ones I ever saw was trimming his toe nails while he was sitting on the hood of your Jag."

"My Jag? God damn it, he didn't do any damage did he?"

"Pinky, that's why I moved you past the guy. If you had told that dude to get off your car, I could have fit what was left of you into your suitcase and still have enough room leftover for twenty pounds of oranges."

Pinky grunted, like he was trying to act tough, but I think secretly, he was glad that I had saved his sorry butt.

"Fine. Now, we need to discuss our plan for this afternoon's activities. Last night, while you and Flo were . . . ah . . . I laid out a simple strategy that I am positive will provide us with a sample of Mr. Bedrosian's DNA. Bear, I took the liberty of making you a copy."

He reached into his coat pocket and pulled out a sheet of paper.

"Pinky . . ."

Pinky flashed me one of his nasty grins. I think he was trying take back the lead spot, but when my life goes on the line, like right now, I don't give a shit whose feelings get hurt. I'd never been inside the city limits of Fresno. I didn't know anything about the place—like what part of town was safe, and what wasn't. I didn't know where the hoods hang out, and what cops they have in their pocket. "Boss, we're looking for a man who snuffs people for a living

251

and we don't know what he looks like. I don't mind telling you that I'm a little spooked."

"My good man, you have nothing to worry about. That's why I took the liberty of laying out a plan. We'll both be working off the same page, so to speak. You have all the details in your hands, and I'm sure once you read my—"

"Pinky, you can take your plan and stick it where the sun don't shine. As far as I'm concerned, we're just going to nose around."

"Bear, speak to me in a language I understand. I don't even know what nosing around means. Long ago I learned to never go into court without detailed preparation. I never ask a question that I don't know the answer to. I never—"

I turned and glared at Pinky. "Damn it, we're not going into court. We're going to case the house of a hired gun."

Pinky squirmed on his soft leather seat for a second. "All right, I'll concede that point. You're right, we're not going to court. And I will admit that I'm a neophyte when it comes to accosting a murderer at his domicile, so this time I'll defer to your untested method. However, I reserve the right to implement my strategy, if and when I determine your plan indicates any sign of failure. Now that we're agreed, define nosing around."

Pinky doesn't usually give in this easily, I thought. But maybe being trapped in a car with Flo sort of wore him down. "Okay. This is what happens when I nose around. I look for a way to do something that I didn't know how to do before I started. Sort of like the way I conned Goodie into taking Flo and me to the Page ranch. Or the way I got the old coot in Bakersfield to give me all that information about Teddy Roosevelt Page. I don't have a plan. I just go somewhere, nose around, and figure out what I need to do next to come up with the shit I need. Understand?"

"It sounds very shaky to me, but as I said, for the moment, I'll defer to your expertise. Now, what do we need to do to implement your plan?"

"Damn it, I told you I don't have a plan."

"Bear, don't become tied up over a question of semantics. What do we do next?"

I yelled, "Pull into that gas station on the right."

Pinky said, "Now that wasn't so hard, was it? I just filled up the tank, so why are we going to a gas station?"

Damn it, if he asked me one more stupid question, I was going to turn him over to the Hell's Angels. "I need to buy something, and check out a map so we can find our how to get to Peachland Way."

Pinky pulled into the station and stayed in the car while I bought a six-pack and two big bags of chips. I wasn't hungry or thirsty, but for what I had in mind we needed a bag full of stuff, and I'd get around to drinking the beer and eating the chips later. I was surprised to find that Peachland Way was only a couple of blocks from the gas station.

We left the station and I took Pinky through a couple of quick lefts and rights and told him to park the Jag around the corner from Bedrosian's address. I said, "We'll get out here, walk around the block, and get the lay of the land."

Pinky nodded. "Good idea. That way, perhaps, if he's not home and his house is not protected by an alarm system, we can go around back and peek in his windows. Now I'm beginning to understand what nosing around means."

Jesus, what a dip. "Why not knock on the front door and ask Bedrosian if he'll open his mouth so you can rub the inside of his cheek with a cotton swab."

"But that would be dangerous."

"So would going into his backyard and peeking in his windows. Look, we can't afford to let Bedrosian know we're looking for him. If that happened, we'd both end up dead. From now on, just do what I tell you to do and nothing more."

"Right, I understand that."

I picked up the bag with the beer and chips.

"Bear, why do we have that paper sack?"

"I don't know what we'll find around the block. I'm carrying the bag so we'll look like a couple of guys coming from the local 7-11. Like we live down the street, and we're walking home after picking up a six-pack of beer."

He nodded. "I have it now. Two buddies are going

home to drink some beer. Of course, had you asked, I would have chosen wine to drink, but—"

"For God sakes, shut up and follow my lead."

We rounded the corner and Bedrosian's place was the fifth house down on the opposite side of Peachland Way.

"Pinky."

"Yes."

"No matter what happens, or what you see, we have to keep walking and talking, like we belong in the neighborhood. We'll talk about baseball, or something stupid like that."

We started to walk down Bedrosian's block.

"Bear, if we discover your plan is not working, my strategy includes a detailed study of the—"

All of a sudden, Pinky did the one thing I told him not to do. He stopped talking, put his hands on his hips, and stared at something. Out of the corner of my eye I could tell he was looking in the direction of the Bedrosian house.

"Bear, there's a man washing a car in the Bedrosian driveway. He's smoking a cigar, wearing a pair of swimming trunks, a tee shirt, and sandals. Do you think that's the man we are seeking?"

I doubled back, grabbed Pinky's elbow, and just like before, when we were in the motel parking lot, I carried his worthless butt down the row of houses and around the block.

Once we cleared the corner, I set him down. "Pinky, are you nuts? I told you to keep walking and talking no matter what happened."

"Oh, I forgot."

I peeked around the corner and Bedrosian was still soaping up his car. "It looks like we got lucky. I don't think he noticed you stopped and stared at him."

Pinky's face lit up like a dog that just found his favorite fire hydrant. "So far your plan seems to be working. We know where Bedrosian lives, and that he smokes cigars. What's the next step?"

"Quiet down. I'm trying to remember the license plate number on the car he's washing."

"Pardon me?"

"4HGF5, but I can't remember the last two numbers."

"I could walk back and check out the plate."

"No!" This guy needed a keeper. "If you did that, he'd know something was up. Look, we're pretty sure that guy washing the car is Bedrosian, and if that's him, killing people like you and me comes as easy as flipping off a light switch. Pinky, Bedrosian's more dangerous than the Hell's Angel guy back at the motel. That motorcycle dude might pull out all your teeth with a pair of pliers, but at least you'd still be alive. Bedrosian would pump a bullet through your brain so fast you wouldn't have time to tell me adios."

"Bear, don't talk to me like I am a child. Remember, it was your plan that placed us in this dangerous situation. Now, do you have a way to extricate us from this precarious state?"

I got us into this pickle? For a second, I thought about punching him one, but I knew that Willow would never forgive me, and I didn't want the District Attorney on my ass for the rest of my life. "We'll walk back to your car and drive by the house. This time, I'll duck down so we won't look like the same two guys that walked down the street. No matter what happens, don't stare directly at Bedrosian or the car. Look straight ahead and try to pick up the last two numbers off the plate. If you can't, don't worry. I think we can trace the car with what we got. How many blue Buicks with the partial plate number 4HGF5 could there be in Fresno?"

We got back in Pinky's Jag. I ducked down, and as we passed what I guessed was Bedrosian's house, I watched Pinky's eyes get real wide. I wasn't sure if it was my weird angle, or what, but I knew we were in deep shit when I saw his lower lip quiver a whole bunch.

Pinky gulped. "You can sit up now. We're way past the house."

"What did you see, Pinky? What scared you?"

"As I drove past the Buick, I spotted a female inside the car. She was sitting on the front seat and washing the inside of the windshield. Bear, that woman was Lottie Evans."

FORTY-FOUR

Bear—Fresno, California

Now it was my turn to suck air. I tried to talk, but my tongue was so dry that it stuck to the roof of my mouth. Pinky and me had just driven by a hired killer who was washing his car, and in the front seat sat the only woman in the world who could blow the whistle on us.

She must not have seen us when we walked by because that Bedrosian guy would have killed us both before we got to the end of the block. My stomach sloshed around like it was full of ice water. How could I be sure that Lottie hadn't recognized Pinky, or his Jag? I turned and stared out the back window.

Pinky said, "What's wrong? What are you looking at?"

I didn't see Bedrosian's Buick, but I kept looking just in case. "I screwed up. We should have driven my pickup truck instead of your Jag to Fresno. Do you think there's any chance that Lottie nailed you?"

"I don't think so. She was scrubbing the inside of the window. Then she turned to talk with Bedrosian. That's when I caught her profile in my side view mirror."

Walking down the street had been a good idea because Pinky and me looked like a million other guys. Likewise, there must have been a thousand Jags driving around the streets of Fresno. But the combination of sticking Pinky behind the wheel of his Jag and rolling past Bedrosian's house was pushing it, the kind of screw-up that could cost a guy his life. I tried to convince myself that everything was cool, but in my gut, I knew I might have made one slip too many. All the way back to the motel I kept my eyes open for a clean blue Buick.

As Pinky pulled into the motel parking lot he said, "Bear, the last two numbers on the plate are 79."

"Damn it, Pinky, you're good. You remembered to get

the missing numbers even after you saw Lottie's face."

I held my hand up offering Pinky a high-five. It took him a couple of seconds to catch on to what I was doing, and then our hands came together with a slap.

I said, "Good job, boss."

"The same to you, Bear. Now what do we do next?"

"Come up to my room."

I unlocked the door, grabbed the phone, and called Willow. "Hi, this is Bear."

"Where's Pinky? He's not hurt is he?"

For someone who spent most of her time telling Pinky she didn't care if he was breathing, Willow sure sounded concerned.

I said, "He's fine. In fact, he's standing next to me. I'll let you talk to him after I ask you a question."

"Fire away."

I didn't laugh at Willow's dumb joke and glanced out the window to the parking lot below just to be sure Bedrosian wasn't driving in. "We need you to do what ever you have to do to find out the name and address for a California license plate, number 4HGF579."

"Got it. Why?"

"We think the car belongs to Bedrosian. I want to be sure before we do anything bad to the wrong guy."

"I'm on it, but Bear, remember, any evidence, and that includes DNA evidence, gathered illegally by an officer of the court is inadmissible. Now let me speak to Pinky."

I handed Pinky the phone and figured he'd want a little privacy, so I walked outside, sat down on the stairway, and tried to come up with a way to get a DNA sample from Bedrosian. I remembered what Willow had said, and I was pretty sure that I wasn't an officer of the court. Working alone was a lot easier than following Willow's chicken-shit rules. If I was by myself, I'd wait until Bedrosian and Lottie left the house. Then I'd slip in the back door, and steal a couple of hairs off of Bedrosian's comb, or cop a pair of his dirty underwear. But Pinky might make me get the DNA using Willow's rules and that was going to make things a lot tougher.

I gave up and headed to the pool. Flo was there, lying on her stomach in the warm sun. The top of her bathing suit was unhooked, and she was not so quietly sawing logs.

Around her was a circle of eight horny guys who had moved about as close as they could, praying they'd catch a peek at her bare boobs when she woke up.

Hey, all guys play the same game. Lots of warm summer days I'd cruise over to one of the nicer motels in Carson City, walk around the pool until I found a looker with her top unsnapped. Then I'd join the group of guys lying real close, hoping that when the broad woke up, she'd forget all about her top, and we'd be in for a few seconds of summer delight.

I tiptoed my way through the sea of guys and lay down on the warm concrete next to Flo. I leaned real close, and said, "If you sat up right now, you'd cause five or six heart attacks."

Flo snorted. "Heart attacks? What are you talking about?"

"There's a herd of turned-on sea elephants lying around you, just hoping somebody will yell fire, on the chance that you'll jump up."

Eyes still closed, she smiled. "Bear, you're cute when you joke with me like that. How was your day? Did you come up with anything?"

"Sort of." I laid back and closed my eyes. The sun felt good, and I was about to join Flo in sleepy–land when I heard a sharp metal click—the same sound I'd heard when I opened the gate to the pool area. It's really weird how you can pick up a noise like that with Flo's snoring, and all the heavy breathing coming from the horny guys. I opened one eye a crack and watched Bedrosian walk through the pool gate. He glanced around, saw me and Flo lying on the deck, and headed toward us. He was wearing his car-washing trunks so he fit right in with the rest of the pool crowd. And he was holding a towel, but the towel was wrapped around his right hand. I was pretty sure what he was hiding underneath that towel. I put my right hand on the concrete to get ready to jump away from Flo. I knew I couldn't outrun

258

Bedrosian's bullet, but if I got away from Flo, maybe he wouldn't take her out with me. Then I noticed that Bedrosian wasn't looking at me, or where he was walking. His eyes were locked on Flo's bare back.

Flo had gone back to sleep and was snoring softly. I remembered that as tough as she was, she didn't like bugs in general, but spiders really spooked her.

I waited until Bedrosian's feet were stuck between the bodies of the testosterone-charged men that circled Flo. Then I whispered in her ear, "Sweetheart, there's a giant, hairy spider on the edge of your towel, and he's about to crawl up your . . ."

Flo let out a scream, popped straight up like a jack-in-the-box, and stood there waving her arms and banging her hands all over, like she was trying to smash a hairy spider.

Every guy lying on the deck, including Bedrosian, was stunned at the sight of Flo in all her glory, and they all leaned closer for a better view. The fattest one of the bunch, a guy who was lying not six feet away, lunged to his knees, and his bowling-ball-sized head crashed into Bedrosian's crotch. Bedrosian's eyes and mouth bulged and his face turned bright red. He looked like he was in so much pain that I think he forgot why he was there. His right hand jerked, the towel fell away, and a large gun hit the concrete deck. The pistol bounced once, glanced off the edge of the pool, and made a loud splash as the blue metal hit the water.

Flo stopped waving. Her arms dropped to her sides, and she glared at me, like she'd just figured out there wasn't any spider.

The bowling-ball head guy, his eyes still locked onto Flo's classic set, finally staggered to his feet. Bedrosian, still thinking about the condition of his manhood, didn't stand a chance. The fat guy fell backward in a weird, sort of Sumo-style move. Bedrosian, trying to keep his balance, spun his arms around like a pair of sideways helicopters, but the fat guy and gravity won, and Bedrosian ended up like a slab of meat, sandwiched between three hundred pounds of blubber and the concrete. Everyone heard the loud crack as the back of Bedrosian's head smacked concrete deck.

For a second, it was like time stopped. Then a breeze tickled Flo's naked chest. She let out a loud scream and covered her assets.

Once the free show was over, most of the guys got up and moved away, but a couple of them came to Bedrosian's side. A third guy jumped into the pool and grabbed the gun off the pool drain where it had settled under ten feet of water.

Finally, the fat guy rolled off the nearly squashed hired gun and waddled away.

I ran to the side of the pool, and when the guy with the gun came up for air, I grabbed the pistol out of his hand and wrapped it in my towel.

By this time, Bedrosian was moaning and groaning. He opened one eye and looked up at me.

Actually, he didn't look like a bad guy. I nodded.

He nodded back and slowly sat up.

Then he saw the spot of blood where his head had hit. He looked around for his towel, like he was going to wipe it up.

I unwrapped his pistol, aimed the barrel at the center of his forehead and said, "I don't think that's a good idea."

Once he figured out where his gun was pointed, he shrugged and gave me a little smile, like I had just caught him stealing candy from the corner drug store. We both knew that once he was fingered, his only way to keep breathing was to rub me out. He had tried and missed. Now Bedrosian's hours in Fresno were numbered, and the clock was ticking fast.

I waved his gun toward the gate to say bye-bye.

Acting a little dizzy, Bedrosian stumbled away.

I rewrapped the towel around the gun, tucked the package under my arm and clapped my hands. "Okay, everybody, the show's over. By the power vested in me, I declare this an official crime scene. That means everybody has to get away from the small spot of blood where that dumb shit's head hit the deck. Any person still in the pool area sixty seconds from now will have to give me an official statement explaining why you were screwing around the pool when you should have been out selling cars or something."

That did the trick. Except for Flo and me, the pool area emptied faster than a pint of beer on a hot summer afternoon.

I walked over to the nickel-sized spot of blood. "Flo, I'm going to stand guard over this spot. Run up to our room and bring back some cotton swabs and those special envelopes Willow gave us at Pinky's. I think that dumb bastard just handed us the DNA sample we were looking for."

FORTY-FIVE

Pinky—Fresno, California

Once I concluded my call with Willow, I crawled onto one of the beds in Bear's room. A couple of seconds later, I heard the phone ring in my room next door. On the third ring I lifted my head, but by then the ringing stopped.

Jet lagged from the long flight, and the lack of sleep last night, I must have drifted off again, because the next thing I knew, the door crashed open and Flo stormed in.

I jumped off the bed. "I apologize, Flo. I know this isn't my room, but after Bear left, the urge to close my eyes just overwhelmed—"

"Shut up, Pinky! I don't give a damn what you do. Bear sent me up here to get that crap Willow gave us."

"Why?"

"Don't ask me. Sometimes I think that ungrateful bastard keeps me around so he has someone to do all his dirty work."

My mind was fuzzy from sleep. Had Flo just said something about the DNA kit? "But why does Bear require those unusual items at this precise moment?"

"I told you, I don't have a clue. I was just soaking up those rays, working to get a nice tan, and the next thing I know, some guy falls down and then Bear struts around like he's the new cock of the roost."

I glanced out the window. My heart stopped and I grabbed onto the windowsill as I watched Bedrosian's blue Buick pull out of the parking lot. "Flo, was the guy who fell down driving a blue Buick?"

"Pinky, you're as bad as Bear. How in the hell would I know what the guy was driving? I told you, I was laying by the pool and the next thing I knew, a guy fell down."

Flo dug through her suitcase and said, "Here it is," and she marched out of the room.

262

I followed her down the stairs, but instead of going to the pool, I ran to the office.

The man behind the counter said, "May I help you?"

I clutched both of my hands tightly because I couldn't stop them from trembling. "Yes. I'm Mr. Delmont in room 202, and I was hoping to meet up with an old friend who lives in Fresno. I was out by the pool and when I returned to my room, I saw the red light flashing on my phone. I believe that indicates I missed a phone call. Was my friend just here by any chance?"

The man eyed me suspiciously, as if someone pulled that exact line of bull on him every day. He checked a panel of lights in front of him, and then nodded. "Yes, Mr. Delmont. A few minutes ago, a man walked into the office and asked for you by name, but he told me you were in town for a family reunion. I tried your room, but received no answer. He said that he'd look for you at the pool. The man didn't leave his name. I did notice that he was driving a blue Buick. Nice car don't you think? I'm sorry, but I'm afraid you just missed him."

It took all of my reserve of calm to return his smile. "Don't worry, I'm sure he'll call back soon."

I ran to my room, threw my shaving kit back into my suitcase, and closed the top.

Then, suitcase in hand, I ran out of my room and pounded on Bear's door.

No answer.

I sprinted down the stairs to my car, tossed my suitcase into the trunk, and ran to the pool. There was Bear, on his hands and knees, and it looked like the big lunkhead was praying, or playing marbles, or something. Flo, arms folded and her face displaying her usual angry expression, paced back and forth.

I rushed to Bear. My heart pounded so hard that I had trouble catching my breath. "Bear . . . I hate to tell you this . . . but . . . Bedrosian was here."

"I know that, and he was nice enough to leave us this little spot of blood."

I looked over Bear's shoulder just in time to watch him

drag the end of a cotton swab through the center of a small red spot.

"Bear, is that what I think it is?"

"Yup, it's Bedrosian's blood."

I yelled, "Stop!"

Bear's hand jerked back. Flo squealed. The two looked at me as if I had just lost my mind.

I took a deep breath. "From what Willow told me concerning blood evidence, you get a better DNA sample with dried blood. I'm packed and my suitcase is in the trunk. I'll stay here, and by the time you've placed your suitcases into my car, perhaps the edge of the blood will have dried sufficiently. That should give us a wet and a dry sample, and we'll be on the road before that murderer returns."

Bear jumped up, handed me a swab and a second envelope. He said, "Good idea, but don't wait too long. We need to get our butts out of this town fast."

Bear grabbed Flo's arm.

She pushed him away, and said, "Don't forget. Someone has to pay for the motel rooms."

Bear and I looked at each other. Damn, the witch was right, and that little detail had slipped both of our minds. We had checked in, and we owed the man behind the counter for two rooms, beds slept in or not.

I grabbed my wallet and pulled out three hundred dollars. "Flo, while Bear packs up, you pay for the rooms."

She shook her head. "I will not. You pay for the rooms. What would that man in the office think of me? I check into a motel room, in the middle of the afternoon with two men, and a few hours later, I check out and pay him in cash. He would think I was some kind of—"

Bear shoved the cotton swabs at me and said, "Flo, if we aren't leaving this joint inside of three minutes, that man sitting in the office will be attending our funerals."

Flo said, "I don't understand why we're in such a hurry, I'm getting hungry and—"

Bear grabbed her arm and growled, "Flo, go pay the man."

I watched in sheer wonder as Flo stopped arguing and

did what Bear told her to do.

Alone, I straddled the blood spot and counted to one hundred and fifty, although under oath, I would have to admit that my final thirty counts were cursory to say the least. I then scraped the driest edge of the blood, dropped the swab into an unused envelope, and ran to my car.

Bear and I reached the Jag together. He threw the bags in the trunk, I started the engine and backed into an empty parking slot next to the office as Flo exited through the door. Bear reached back and opened the back seat door. Flo got in and before she had time to reach for her seat belt, I hit the accelerator and the Jag shot out the motel driveway. A half-mile northwest I spotted the freeway on-ramp. Throwing caution to the winds, I ran through the red light at the base of the on-ramp, and in a few seconds, we were heading north on Highway 99. I set the cruise control at 78 mph, and said, "So far, so good. I don't think we can go much faster, or the Highway Patrol will stop us."

After a moment of silence, I said, "How in the hell did that guy find us so fast?"

Bear said, "Like I told you before, Lottie must have fingered your Jag. Once they knew we were in town, all they had to do was grab the yellow pages and start calling motels."

Rows of grape vines flew past our speeding car. A minute of deathly quiet passed before Flo said, "Pinky, the next time you don't give me time to get my seat belt on, I'm going to give you a knuckle sandwich on the top of your pea-sized head."

I said, "I apologize for my ungentlemanly behavior, but the unusual circumstances dictated a prompt departure."

Flo snapped, "Unusual circumstances? Prompt departure? Would someone tell me what the hell is going on?"

FORTY-SIX

Bear—On the road to Carson City, Nevada

While I explained to Flo about our close call with Bedrosian, every couple of seconds, I'd scan the mirror on my side to make sure that there wasn't a blue Buick following us.

She said, "Come on. Are you trying to tell me that guy at the pool, the one that fell down, was the same guy that shot Bill Page in the head?"

"Yup."

"But if that's true, why didn't he shoot me while I was catching a few rays?"

I knew if I told her how close she'd come, she'd freak out. "Babe, that's why I told you there was a spider crawling on your towel."

Flo hit my shoulder. "Damn it, that was a chicken thing to do to me. You know how I hate spiders." Then she said, "Promise me that you'll never do that again."

I nodded. "I promise."

Flo said, "Is that why you keep looking in that mirror, to see if that man's following us?"

I nodded again. "Yup, but if I was that poor bastard, I'd hit a few ATM's, grab as much cash as I could and head for Mexico. Once his boss finds out he's been fingered for the Page murder, they'll hand out a new contract on him, and maybe the contract will include Lottie, or whatever her real name is. Those guys at the top of the mob didn't get there by leaving loose ends lying around. If the police ever got hold of Bedrosian and Lottie, they'd give up the Pope to escape the needle."

Flo thought for a minute. "Are you trying to tell me that my life was in real danger back there?"

I nodded.

She said, "Bear, living with you is really exciting. See

266

there, Pinky? There's another example of how Bear and I work together. If it hadn't been for me laying by the pool, we wouldn't have a sample of the murderer's blood."

Flo patted my shoulder, sat back and slept through most of the drive back home.

Finally, we drove through the south end of Lake Tahoe, and as we started down the mountain toward Carson City, Pinky's cell phone rang.

He handed it to me. "Bear, there are too many curves in this road to talk and drive."

"Hello?"

"Bear? This is Willow. Where's Pinky?"

"He's driving."

"How are things going in Fresno?"

"We've finished that job."

"You're kidding me?"

"Nope."

"Where are you now?"

"About ten minutes west of Carson City."

"But you couldn't have . . . is Flo with you?"

"Yup."

"Tell her I have some good news. Her analysis of the Page printouts was correct. According to my white-collar crime experts, Page was skimming money. They also dug into Page's past and discovered that before he moved to Eureka, Nevada, he was a CPA in Bakersfield, California."

"That makes sense because Bakersfield was where his Pop died."

"But there's more. My investigators also found that he was charged with a few ethical violations while he worked in Bakersfield. This all happened a long time ago, so the details concerning what he did are gone, but we do know that Page was suspended for six months. To gain reinstatement, he had to pass the AICPA's comprehensive ethics course."

I said, "Did he make it?"

"Yes, with a score of 91%."

I said, "Then Bill Page moved to Eureka, Nevada, where he skimmed off the top until Bedrosian iced him. It's weird how he had half the money from his brother and he still skimmed from the mob. What did he do with all that cash?"

Willow said, "You've got me. Gambling—drugs—poor investments, some people find a way to live beyond their means no matter how much they have."

"I guess you're right. Willow, I just thought of something funny."

"What's that?"

"Bill Page would still be breathing if he had failed that fancy ethics class."

She laughed. "Bear, you have a rather convoluted, but interesting way of viewing ethical matters. And speaking of ethics, Sheriff Durham called to tell me that someone broke into the Page ranch house through a jimmied back door. That someone also opened the safe and stole the computer that used to reside in the office. Bear, I'm an officer of the court—I hope that wasn't some of your handiwork."

"Willow, you know me better than that. I'm as clean as a new born baby."

"Would that be before or after the baby's diaper was changed?"

"Ah . . . . didn't you say you wanted to talk to Pinky?"

"I'll get to him in a minute. Tell me what you came up with in Fresno?'

"Everything you'll need to let Richard Page out of jail."

"Are you kidding me?"

"Nope. We found Bedrosian, and that broad who was pretending to be Pinky's secretary, Lottie Evans. We saw both of them washing Bedrosian's Buick."

"And the license plate you asked me to run was on Bedrosian's car?"

"Yup."

"You two are either very lucky or very good."

"How about a little of both."

"I'll buy that. So what are you bringing me that's so good?"

"Blood samples from Bedrosian."

"Oh my God. Bear, you didn't shoot him did you?"

"Nah. It's a long story, but he sort of accidentally fell down and hit his head."

"I'll bet. Hold on, that guy was a hired gun. Didn't that interesting fact slow you down a little?"

"Nah. I figured that once we got the sample of his blood, and the mob found out, Bedrosian was in more trouble than we were."

"I guess you're right. He's probably boarding a plane to Tahiti as we speak. Let me talk to Pinky now."

"Okay."

Before I handed Pinky the cell phone, I checked out Flo. She was asleep. That broad could be a real pain at times, but with a body like hers, I could learn to live with her faults.

I glanced at Pinky, a world-class bastard, but he was my new full-time boss.

A good woman and a cool job! What more could the son of a Basque sheepherder from northeast Nevada hope for?

FORTY-SEVEN

Pinky—Carson City, Nevada

Bear handed me my cell phone, and Willow said, "Bear just told me you did a great job in Fresno."

"He's right."

"I'll be at a fund raising cocktail party until nine. Were you planning on going straight home?"

My hand gripped the wheel tightly. Did I detect a hint of reconciliation in her tone? "Yes, after I drop off the wicked witch of the south and Bear at his apartment, I'm going home. Why the sudden interest concerning my whereabouts later?"

"Pinky, you shouldn't call Flo the wicked witch of the south. She's a good influence on Bear. God knows he could use one, and he obviously fills her needs. Pardon me, that didn't come out right. What I meant to say was Bear and Flo were made for each other. Concerning your whereabouts, don't read anything more into my question than what it is. While you were gone, I did a lot of thinking, and I discovered that apart from my work, you are the most important thing in my life. But before you say anything, we both know that I can't live with you."

I gripped the steering wheel as my heart started to beat wildly. "And I can't live without you."

There was a long pause. "Exactly. That's why I'll be at your house later tonight."

I drove to Bear's place. Flo exited without acknowledging my stellar driving, but that was no more than I had expected from her.

After Bear grabbed their luggage out of the trunk, he said, "I'll stop by your office tomorrow to pick up my next assignment. This investigating job is a lot more cool than tending bar."

"I'm not sure that I'd classify coming that close to be-

270

ing shot by a hired killer as fun, but you're right about one thing, we accomplished a lot in a very short time. However, I have two nagging problems. First, if you're not behind the bar at the Globe, who'll make me the perfect gin and tonic?"

"You mean give you a triple shot and charge you for a single? Maybe it's time to call in some of those favors you told me John owed you. Shit, he owns the Globe. What's your other problem?"

"In the future, we need to spend more time going over our plans before we act. I'm not positive, but I think my strategy would have come up with similar results."

Bear lowered his giant head. "Just what was your plan?"

Flo called from the apartment door, "If you two are going to stand out there and talk all night, I'm going to pour me a glass of wine."

Bear pulled back. "Whoops, I'd better go. I'll stop by your office tomorrow morning and settle up my expense account. Afterwards, you can tell me about your plan."

"I'll do that, and Bear, thanks for stopping me from doing something stupid with that Hell's Angels gang back at the motel."

"No problem. Now I gotta head upstairs before Flo downs more than her share of vino."

As I drove across town, I pulled out my cell phone and called Willow.

I said, "Would you consider canceling your appearance at the cocktail party and meeting me in thirty minutes?"

"Are you asking me to cancel a fund raiser?"

"Yes."

"What the hell, they've all seen me before. I'll be at your place in half an hour."

The following morning, after breakfast of coffee, juice and rolls, I followed Willow's car north into town. Two blocks past Highway 50, she pulled into the county complex parking lot. I gave her a wave and completed the short journey to my office.

When I rolled into my parking lot, I noticed the lights inside the office were on. I guessed that I had forgotten to turn them off the night I returned from Rome. When I reached for the door, I saw it was ajar. My mouth went dry, and my stomach tightened. Was Bedrosian inside? I fought the urge to run, crept closer and listened. Whoever was inside was humming that damned melody from <u>Evita</u>. That was strange because the only person I knew who liked that insipid tune was Mabel.

I quietly pushed the door open and there sat Mabel, behind her desk, as if she had never left.

My stomach untwisted a bit, and I entered my office. "Mabel Sullivan, you are a sight for sore eyes."

"Hi, Pinky. I hope you don't hate me."

"Hate you? My good woman, I want to hug you."

"Pinky, I'm sorry that I was so chicken and ran away, but that note said if I stayed here, someone would throw my Puffy into a pot of boiling canola oil. I didn't care about myself, but my cat is totally dependent on me. I'm responsible for her well-being. I hope you understand why I had—"

"I understand completely, but what gave you the courage to return today?"

"I realized that I could leave Puffy with a lady friend in Reno. I don't know why I didn't think of that before. I'm glad I came back. When I opened up an hour ago, every phone in the office was ringing. I've done nothing but answer calls since I sat down. Pinky, I know you're the boss, but I feel it's my duty to tell you that your law practice is too busy to leave this place without someone to answer the phones. You should have hired a temp to take care of things while I was gone."

I nodded. "I did, but the woman I hired turned out to be a modern-day Mata Hari."

Mabel shook her head. "I've worked with you for many years, and there have been occasions when you were prone to exaggeration. Might this be one of those moments?"

"No!" I snapped. "Lottie Evans was truly an evil woman. She monitored every move I made, and recorded every word I had with a client who was accused of murder."

"And why would she do that?"

"The woman was associated with the real murderer. I

don't know if she was his girlfriend, his wife, or what, but she nearly caused my client to be convicted of a murder he didn't commit. And if I was a betting man, I would place a substantial wager that she and her boyfriend were the ones who threatened your cat with death via a deep fat fryer."

Mabel's round face paled. "Thank God you discovered the duplicity and those two are now sitting in jail. Anyone who would threaten a defenseless cat should . . . ."

"I'm sorry to be the bearer of bad tidings, but to the best of my knowledge, they have not been incarcerated."

Mabel reached down and pulled out her purse from the lower right drawer of her desk. "Pinky, until that happens, you can reach me at my sister's phone in Montana."

"Mabel, relax. I'm positive that Lottie and her boyfriend have left the country."

Mabel dropped her purse and closed the drawer. "Are you sure?"

"Yes. To quote Bear, they had to leave the country or wake up dead. Lottie's boyfriend was a hired gun, and you know what happens to hired guns once the police find out who they are."

"Good riddance, but just in case, you might find it prudent to change the lock on the front door."

"An excellent idea. And while we are at it, we need to change the password that allows you access to all my files."

Mabel said, "And how about the pin number for the law office bank account?"

"We'll need to change that too."

"Pinky, this Lottie, was she good at her job?"

"She was . . ." I nearly said she was light years faster than you, Mabel, but I managed to hold my tongue before that truth tumbled out. "She was nowhere as experienced as you are. During those dark days, when you were gone, I came to realize how much I depend on you. In fact, effective today, I am raising your monthly remuneration twenty-five percent."

Mabel's face lit up brighter than the neon sign that hangs over the Old Globe Saloon. "Thank you, Pinky, that's most generous of you. Someday, after I catch up the office backlog, you'll have to tell me the whole story."

"I'll do that when I find the time, and I'll include all the gory details. Now what about those phone calls? Were any of them for me?"

She handed me three pink messages all marked urgent. The first came from Willow. I smiled and tucked that note into my pocket.

The second was from Sheriff Durham. I frowned, crushed the note into a tight, pink ball, and tossed it into the trashcan.

The third message came from a Mr. Endrezzi representing the Oildale Bank and Trust Company. Neither the company nor the phone number was familiar to me. For a moment, I considered giving Mr. Endrezzi's note the same fate as Sheriff Durham's. However, one never knows, so I carried the message into my private office. Mabel followed close behind with a cup of coffee.

"Thanks for the coffee. Now let's talk about my schedule for the next few days. Tomorrow I'll require at least thirty minutes at eleven for a final meeting with Richard Page."

"Isn't he that client who paid your retainer with a nearly new car?"

"Yes, but while you were away, because of the diligent efforts of moi, Richard Page will soon be a free man."

"Do you want me to make up Mr. Page's final bill before your meeting with him?"

"Yes. In addition to the billable hours you can pick up off my log, I'll need to show additional expenses for Bear Zabarte. He is to receive a stipend of $150, no make that $200 per day, plus all of his expenses."

Mabel's mouth pinched in, the same action most people make when they get a whiff of a rotten egg. "Is he the same Bear Zabarte you defended a few years ago?"

"Yes, and Mabel, in the future, Bear will be doing investigative work for me. You don't have to like the man. Just make sure he's paid promptly so the witch he lives with won't have an excuse to stop by my office." I reached into my top desk drawer and pulled out the expense log from my trip to Italy. "Also, these expenses need to be included with the Richard Page bill."

"My, my, you were a busy boy while I was away. Need more coffee?"

"No thank you."

Without further ado, Mabel turned and left me alone. Until that moment, I had never understood how much I appreciated her ability to comprehend when it was time to talk, and when it was time to go to work.

I pulled out a fresh legal pad and titled the page:

Final meeting—Richard Page

    1.   Inform Richard about his father's Italian wife, Maria Gotelli, and the fact that he has a half-brother.

    2.   Inform Richard that his father left Maria, and his half brother, in an untenable financial situation.

I buzzed Mabel.

She walked into my office with her steno pad in hand.

"More coffee?"

"No, I'm fine. I need a—"

My phone rang.

Mabel reached for it, but I waved her off.

"Law office, J. Pinkus Delmont speaking."

Mabel started to leave, but I gestured for her to remain.

A man's voice said, "Mr. Delmont, I understand you are the attorney of record for Mr. Richard Milhous Nixon Page. Is that correct?"

My ears perked up and I paused. Once I had stepped on the plane for Italy, I had removed myself as Richard's attorney, but now I was back in Carson City, and had resumed control. "You are correct. What can I do for you?"

"My name is Albert Endrezzi. I am the first vice-president with The Oildale Bank and Trust. A few weeks ago, I was contacted by a deputy District Attorney from Carson City. Mister Vaca informed me his office was holding, as evidence, a substantial check from my trust department made out to Theodore Roosevelt Page. It seems that the check was found in the wallet of Richard Page who's been accused of murdering his uncle, William Page."

"Mr. Endrezzi, I'm with you so far, but I don't understand the reason for your call."

"I have some good news for you and your client, but first I need to explain the complete situation. Mr. Delmont, some years ago, my trust department made an error, and that error has caused great embarrassment to me and my department. After I received the call from Mr. Vaca, we did some research and discovered that the instructions of Theodore Roosevelt Page were being circumvented."

I turned on my phone recorder and said, "Mr. Endrezzi, I just turned on a voice recorder to be sure there will be no confusion concerning what was discussed from this point on."

"Oh dear."

"Nothing to worry about. Now explain what you meant when you told me that the instructions of Theodore Roosevelt Page were circumvented."

"Oh dear."

"Mr. Endrezzi, I am a busy man so get on with it, or I will have to say good bye."

He sighed. "Many years ago, Theodore Roosevelt Page set up a trust fund through our trust department so that upon his death, all proceeds of his estate would be distributed to his grandson, your client, Richard Page."

I sat up in my chair. I had hit the mother lode. "And?"

"As I said, we just discovered that Theodore Roosevelt Page has died. In fact, he died seven years ago. Mr. Delmont, the error was not actually ours. We were never informed of Theodore Roosevelt Page's death. And because we lacked that knowledge, we continued to send his semi-annual distribution checks to an address supplied to us by Theodore Roosevelt Page's son, Herbert Clark Hoover Page."

"Mr. Endrezzi, would you please cut to the bottom line!"

"I'm afraid that after Theodore Roosevelt Page's death, fourteen semi-annual distributions of the trust were sent to the wrong recipient."

"I assume all the distributions were made by check?"

"You are correct."

"And I assume that each of the fourteen checks was properly endorsed by Theodore Roosevelt Page, as required by law?"

The long pause informed me I had the banker by the short hairs. We both knew that Theodore Roosevelt Page had not endorsed the checks because he had died long before the checks were issued.

I said, "Are you telling me that over a seven year period, your bank accepted fourteen forgeries?"

"Ah—"

"Mr. Endrezzi, I fear your misfeasance has caused irreparable harm to my client, Richard Page."

"Mr. Delmont, my bank agrees that due to an unavoidable error, your client missed fourteen semi-annual payments."

I took a large sip of my lukewarm coffee. As caffeine-laced liquid trickled down my throat, I couldn't stop a smile from spreading across my face. "Mr. Endrezzi, just how much money did your unavoidable error, as you defined it, cost my client?"

"The exact amount is, $6,894,106.34."

I held my hand over the transmitter. "Mabel, please get me the Richard Page file."

Returning my attention to Mr. Endrezzi, I said, "I think we can both agree that nearly $7,000,000 is an impressive figure."

Mabel handed me the Page file. I pulled out the first legal pad, and flipped back through my old notes. "And do you have my client's current address where you will send his payments in the future, Mr. Endrezzi?"

"No, I do not."

Ah-ha, there it was. "Richard Page's current address is 1268 Sunset Avenue, Arcata, California, 95518."

He repeated the address back to me, and said, "Mr. Delmont, thank you for that information. You need to know that we at The Oildale Bank and Trust realize that your client could file a suit against our firm to—"

"Mr. Endrezzi, I'm pleased that you've been up front with me, so I will offer you the same courtesy. A few weeks ago, I had an investigator in Bakersfield. It took him less than a day to discover that your client, Theodore Roosevelt Page, had died seven years ago. I believe that any court of law, even a California court, will question why the discovery of Theodore Roosevelt Page's death took your bank seven years.

"It's time we shift gears and discuss a settlement above and beyond the $7,000,000 you owe my client. The incompetence exhibited by your bank forced my client to live in abject poverty for seven years. To compensate for the deprivation and humiliation my client suffered because of your grievous error, first thing tomorrow morning I will file a suit against your bank demanding $35,000,000. When I prevail, and Mr. Endrezzi, I will prevail, I believe the court will eventually settle on an amount in the neighborhood of $20,000,000.

"I am now going to make you an offer, and I will make this offer only one time. If you turn my proposal down, the next time we talk will be in court. If you agree to pay my client $12,000,000 in a one-time cash settlement, I will advise my client to drop further action caused by your bank's appalling blunder. My offer will save your bank at least $8,000,000, plus all the exorbitant legal expenses of going to court. And do not forget the endless negative publicity this story will generate concerning your bank's incompetence. I am positive that the details of how you defrauded a young man out of his rightful birthright, a legacy worth millions, will make bold headlines in the Bakersfield newspaper. I should also mention that my press people will be giving the story to CNN, along with all the major television networks.

"Mr. Endrezzi, prior to you initiated this phone call, I am positive that the officers of your bank, and your board of directors, gave you the authority to come up with a settlement that both sides could agree upon. You have my proposal. Now it is time for you to make a decision."

I sat back and eavesdropped to a muffled, but heated discussion on the other end of our phone conversation. After a few moments had passed, Mr. Endrezzi came back and said, "We accept your settlement proposal. I'll wire transfer the agreed upon amount to your bank in an hour."

I gave him my banker's telephone number, and said, "Thank you, Mr. Endrezzi. If I'm ever in Bakersfield, I'll stop by and buy you a glass of wine to celebrate."

Without so much as a thank you for my generous invitation, Mr. Endrezzi hung up.

"Mabel, add to the Richard Page bill, $4,000,000 with the note that that charge is 33.3% of the Oildale Bank and Trust settlement of $12,000,000."

She nodded. "Are you ready for more coffee?"

"No thank you."

Mabel said, "I'll have Mr. Page's bill ready for your perusal in ten minutes."

"Thank you. It's good to have you back."

I picked up the note pad with my agenda for tomorrow's meeting with Richard and added a few final items:

3. Explain to my client that he is the legal heir to his grandfather's trust fund. From this day forward, compliments of Theodore Roosevelt Page, every six months Richard will receive a check from the Oildale Bank and Trust for approximately $500,000.

4. Advise Richard to accept Oildale's proposed settlement of $12,000,000

5. Offer to sell Richard his old BMW back at fair market value. If he wants the vehicle, have Mabel adjust the final bill.

6. Inform Richard his father's estate owes Florence Sonderlund $11,500 to payback a series of personal loans.

7. Present Richard with his final bill.

I reviewed the last four items, leaned back and smiled. God I love the law!

Ken lives with his lovely wife Arlene in a picturesque town in northern California where he spends most of his waking hours locked in a tiny home-office pounding a computer keyboard.

On a few rare occasions, he has been known to escape his self-imposed incarceration to seek out new locations for future Pinky And The Bear sagas.

The above picture was taken at the Plitvice Lakes National Park in Croatia. It didn't take Ken very long to figure out that the country of Croatia would be a perfect spot for Pinky to visit. The bikini-clad beauties along the Dalmatian coast—the awesome splendor of Plitvice Lakes—the cosmopolitan city of Zagreb—the world-class wines . . . everything Pinky Delmont seeks to satisfy his insatiable desire for more.

But where would Bear and Flo go—what miserable hellhole would they be required to inhabit while Pinky wandered through Croatia indulging in *la dolce vita*?

Finding the ideal vacation spots of the world is a relatively easy process because those are the places everyone wants to go. But discovering the undesirable areas, those locations that most travelers consciously avoid, is not as easy a job as you might think.

If you have a suggestion for a future nightmarish location for Bear and Flo, send your idea to Ken, via ken@kendalton.com.

If your disagreeable spot is selected, Ken will send you a signed copy of the novel (wow!), a Pinky And The Bear tee shirt (a double wow!), and recognize your contribution on the Acknowledgements page of the book, giving you a shot at immortality—a really cool prize that's even better than a tee shirt.

For more information than you'd ever want to know concerning the fictitious world of Pinky And The Bear, or the author, please check out the web site at www.kendalton.com